SLEEP NO MORE

Affair

Mischief

Mystique

Mistress

Deception

Desire

Dangerous

Reckless

Ravished

Rendezvous

Scandal

Surrender

Seduction

TITLES BY JAYNE ANN KRENTZ WRITING AS JAYNE CASTLE

Sweetwater and the Witch

Guild Boss

Illusion Town

Siren's Call

The Hot Zone

Deception Cove

The Lost Night

Canyons of Night

Midnight Crystal

Obsidian Prey

Dark Light

Silver Master

Ghost Hunter

After Glow

Harmony

After Dark

Amaryllis

Zinnia

Orchid

THE GUINEVERE JONES SERIES

Desperate and Deceptive

THE GUINEVERE JONES COLLECTION, VOLUME I

The Desperate Game

The Chilling Deception

Sinister and Fatal

THE GUINEVERE JONES COLLECTION, VOLUME 2

The Sinister Touch

The Fatal Fortune

SPECIALS

The Scargill Cove Case Files

Bridal Jitters

(WRITING AS JAYNE CASTLE)

ANTHOLOGIES

Charmed

(WITH JULIE BEARD, LORI FOSTER, AND EILEEN WILKS)

TITLES WRITTEN BY JAYNE ANN KRENTZ AND JAYNE CASTLE

No Going Back

JAYNE ANN KRENTZ

SLEEP NO MORE

BERKLEY

New York

BERKLEY
An imprint of Penguin Random House LLC
penguinrandomhouse.com

LIBRARY OF CONGRESS CATALOGING-IN-PUBLICATION DATA

Names: Krentz, Jayne Ann, author.
Title: Sleep no more / Jayne Ann Krentz.
Description: First edition. | New York: Berkley, 2023. | Series: The lost night files ; 1
Identifiers: LCCN 2022026629 (print) | LCCN 2022026630 (ebook) |
ISBN 9780593337820 (hardcover) | ISBN 9780593337851 (ebook)
Subjects: LCGFT: Novels. Classification: LCC PS3561.R44 S544 2023 (print) |
LCC PS3561.R44 (ebook) | DDC 813/.54—dc23/eng/20220609
LC record available at https://lccn.loc.gov/2022026629
LC ebook record available at https://lccn.loc.gov/2022026630

Printed in the United States of America
1st Printing

For Frank,
with love

SLEEP NO MORE

CHAPTER ONE

Carnelian, California . . .

BLOOD DRIPPED FROM the bottom of the laundry cart.

Ambrose Drake flattened one hand against the wall to keep himself on his feet. He was back in the underwater world. That meant he was dreaming again. He struggled to focus on the glary aura of the figure pushing the cart toward the swinging doors at the far end of the corridor. Was that what a ghost looked like?

"What's going on?" he said.

The words came out in a slurred, raspy jumble that he knew probably made no sense, assuming he had managed to say them aloud. It was hard to talk underwater. He thought he had been getting better at navigating the strange atmosphere down here below the surface, but either he had been fooling himself or he had regressed, because tonight he was having trouble just staying upright.

And what the hell was he doing on his feet? He was supposed to be in bed.

Shit. Was he sleepwalking again? That was not good. It meant the nightmares and hallucinations were getting worse. But did you know if you were sleepwalking? That didn't sound logical. If you were aware that you were walking in your sleep it meant you were awake. Didn't it?

Or did it mean you had slipped over the edge of sanity and fallen into the abyss? Maybe his worst nightmare had finally become his new reality.

The rattle of rubber wheels on the tiled floor distracted him. The glowing figure propelling the cart was leaning into the task now, picking up speed. Seconds later cart and ghost vanished through the swinging doors.

That seemed to indicate the figure had heard the question and had reacted by leaving the scene as quickly as possible—which led to another disturbing conclusion. Maybe the ghost with the laundry cart leaving a trail of blood drops on the floor was real. You could never be sure when you were in this deep.

"Am I awake or asleep?" he mumbled. "Only one way to find out."

He took his hand off the wall, pushed aside the hallucinations, and managed another couple of steps forward. His progress was complicated by the fact that the corridor was drenched in under-water shadows. He finally realized what was wrong. The window in his mind was open. That explained why he had seen a glowing ghost pushing a laundry cart.

"I really do not need this."

It took some doing, but he succeeded in shutting down his aura-reading vision. He was back in his normal senses now. The eerie, murky shadows disappeared. The hallway was abruptly illuminated in the light of the overhead fixtures.

Okay, he was not dreaming and the window was closed, but something was very wrong. He did not have overhead fixtures in his bedroom.

A whisper of horror sent a jolt of panic across his senses. He had walked out the front door of his house and into an unknown building. The damned sleepwalking was going to get him killed. Another terrible thought struck—was he in his underwear? *Please don't let me be strolling through some strange place in my underwear.*

He made himself look down and was overwhelmingly relieved to discover he had on a pair of pajama bottoms. Or was he still dreaming?

"Shit. Wake up. Wake up."

This time he was sure he had spoken aloud. The sound of his own voice was reassuring. It drew him back toward the surface. He rubbed his eyes and tried to make sense of the white walls of the hallway and the cold white tiles underfoot.

Sleep clinic.

A murky memory swept back, bringing in the tide of semi-reassuring reality. He was spending the night in the Carnelian Sleep Institute in an effort to get control of the nightmares. He should be in a bed. There ought to be a lot of wires attached to him. What the hell was he doing out here in the hallway?

The scream.

He had heard a woman scream. That's why he was standing barefoot in the hall. The answer to the mystery was in the laundry cart. He had to find it and look inside.

He lurched forward a few more steps and nearly lost his balance. The problem with staying upright was a new one. He had always taken his fast reflexes and excellent coordination for granted. After the spell of amnesia eight months ago, both had actually improved. His sleeping habits had gone to hell, but he was faster and quicker than he had ever been. Tonight, though, it was all he could do to keep his feet under him.

He steadied himself, but the sudden change of position caused him to look down again. This time he saw a crimson rivulet trickling under the closed door of a patient room. Maybe he was still dreaming. Still sleepwalking.

To test the theory, he leaned down to take a closer look at the blood.

"Mr. Drake, what are you doing out of bed?"

The stern masculine voice was familiar. Dr. Conrad Fenner, the director of the Institute. He sounded seriously agitated. Alarmed. Furious.

Startled, Ambrose lost his balance altogether and pitched forward. He would have fallen flat on his face if his reflexes hadn't finally kicked in. About time.

He landed on one palm and a knee and instinctively started to get back on his feet. His fingers skidded through the little river of blood.

"Get up, Mr. Drake," Fenner ordered. "You should not be out here. We must get you back to your room."

"Something's wrong," Ambrose said, his voice little more than a hoarse whisper. "I heard a woman scream."

"No, you did not," Fenner said. "You are dreaming. Sleepwalking. Here, let me assist you."

Ambrose started to tell him about the blood on the floor but was interrupted by a sharp stinging sensation in the curve of his shoulder.

"What?" he mumbled.

He wanted to ask another question, but he was going back down into the depths, and this time there were no shadows. No light at all. A great weakness was overtaking his senses. He was vaguely aware of Fenner urging him to his feet and steering him back to his own room.

"Hurry," Fenner snapped. "I can't carry you."

The next thing Ambrose knew he was slumped in a chair. Fenner was leaning over him, working swiftly to clean his hand, the one that had slipped into the crimson stream.

"Blood on the floor," Ambrose said. He stared at his fingers but he could no longer see the red stain.

"There was no blood," Fenner said. His authoritative tone was infused with anger and anxiety. "It was just a dream, Mr. Drake. Trust me, you won't remember it in the morning."

When he was finished, he helped Ambrose get out of the chair and stumble onto the bed.

The darkness was closing in fast, but Ambrose managed to open the window in his mind one more time. Fenner's aura pulsed in a way that indicated he was telling the truth. He was certain that Ambrose would not remember what had happened tonight.

"A woman screamed," Ambrose said, not because he believed he could convince Fenner of that fact but because he hoped repetition would anchor the memory in his brain. "A woman screamed. A woman screamed."

"It was just a dream," Fenner insisted. "You experienced a brief sleepwalking episode. Nothing more. You won't remember a woman screaming."

The last thing Ambrose saw before he fell into the oceanic trench was the small indicator light on the camera that was aimed at the bed. It glowed bloodred. That was good, he thought. In the morning the video recording would tell him the truth.

If he woke up.

CHAPTER TWO

Carnelian, California. Six weeks later . . .

THE SNAKES SPILLED down the old staircase, coiling, unfurling, seeking prey. Pallas Llewellyn's fingers flew across the page of her sketchbook. She had to work quickly. She could not risk remaining in the trance too long. It was like dropping into a dream— in this case, a nightmare—an interesting place to visit, but you would not want to live there. Her greatest fear these days was that she would slip into her other vision and get trapped.

And yet there were too many times now when she could not resist the temptation to slide into her enhanced vision. She needed to see the images concealed in the small storms of energy that she frequently stumbled into.

She had gotten much better at controlling the automatic drawing trances; at least, she told herself she had more control. She saw things when she was in this other vision, sometimes terrifying things— snakes falling down a staircase, for example. But there were answers to be found here, too. It was the promise of discovering the secrets concealed in the visions that was irresistible.

The snakes were closer now, reaching for her. If she had any sense she would get out while the getting was good. Her intuition was shrieking at her.

As if detecting her presence, two of the snakes stretched out to grasp her and draw her deeper into the trance. She could have sworn she heard them hissing. That was new. In the past the visions had never had an audio component.

"Okay, okay, I'm gone," she gasped.

With an effort of will she came out of the trance, riding a senses-disorienting wave of panic charged with a giddy thrill. She had done it. She had once again leaped into the abyss and made it safely back to the surface.

The triumphant elation receded swiftly but the panic did not. It was growing stronger. She realized she was too close to the scene. She needed to put some distance between herself and the now-invisible snakes spilling down the staircase.

She snapped the sketchbook shut and tossed it and the pencil into the well-worn messenger bag. Later there would be time to try to interpret whatever the episode of automatic drawing had revealed. The answers might elude her, though. They often did. Her intuition told her there were truths to be found in the pictures she created while she was in her other vision, but she was still learning how to see those truths. She had discovered she needed context in order to figure out what she was looking at.

Her pulse was still beating too rapidly. She cradled the messenger bag in both hands, holding it as if it were a shield, and headed for the front door of the abandoned asylum. Her instinct was to run, not walk, to the nearest exit, but running was not a good idea. There were too many obstacles in her path, and she had never been the most coordinated person on the planet.

She had always been easily startled. For as long as she could remember, the tiniest flicker of light or the slightest sense of movement at the edge of her vision had been enough to make her flinch and send her veering off-balance. The unfortunate tendency to overreact to the slightest surprise had gotten markedly worse after the amnesia episode seven months ago. She had learned to compensate by moving slowly and deliberately whenever she was in unfamiliar surroundings. The ruins of the old asylum definitely qualified as unfamiliar. The hidden storms of bad energy were scattered everywhere.

The bones of the Carnelian Psychiatric Hospital for the Insane still stood, surrounding her on all sides. The four-story structure had been constructed of stone and stout timber, but the interior, now sunk in an eternal gloom, had been slowly crumbling for decades. She was forced to scramble through a minefield of broken chairs, rusted bedsprings, sagging doors, shards of broken glass, and the discarded medical equipment of another era.

The scene came straight out of her nightmares. At least this time the place wasn't on fire. She probably ought to see another therapist about her little obsession with scary old buildings, but she craved answers, and she had concluded no therapist could provide them. She also knew she would not be able to let go of her morbid fascination until she got the answers she needed.

She was halfway through the rubble of the hospital lobby when a figure detached itself from the shadows and came toward her, blocking the path to the door.

Focused on escape, her senses still in an adrenaline overload, she yelped in alarm, swerved to the side, and tried to change course. Her intention was to steer a path around the stranger, but the sudden move caused her to stumble into a three-legged table. It toppled under her weight. Of course it did. Sometimes she wondered if every stick of furniture in the world was out to get her.

She knew she was going down. She thought about the jagged chunks of glass that littered the floor. This was going to be a bad fall. She could only hope the messenger bag would protect her from the worst-case scenario.

The man who had been in her path was suddenly at her side. A strong hand gripped her forearm, steadying her.

She was shocked by the speed with which he had moved. It was as if he had *known* she was going to change course and run into the table.

"It's all right," he said. "I've got you."

The physical contact sent an electrifying jolt of intense, intimate awareness across her senses. Maybe she was still in the automatic drawing trance. Maybe this time she really had stayed under too long.

"Let me go," she screamed.

She was amazed and reassured when the earsplitting cry escaped her throat and echoed through the ruins. In her dreams she was always voiceless.

"*Shit.*" The stranger released her, clamped his hands over his ears, and took several steps back. "I'm not going to hurt you. I just want to talk."

Freed, she headed for the front door again. She reached into the messenger bag, groping for the Taser she had carried religiously since Lucent Springs.

She managed to grab the electroshock weapon, but in her frenzy she dropped it. The stranger scooped up the device. Simultaneously he used his free hand to keep her from tripping over a door that had come off its hinges and was now on the floor.

Another flash of breathtaking intimacy rattled her nerves. She had never experienced anything like it. She froze, frantically trying to figure out what was happening. Before she could recover from the shock, the stranger released her and stepped back.

"We're getting off on the wrong foot here," he said. He held the Taser just out of reach. "If you'll give me a minute, I can explain."

He was still between her and the door. She launched herself at him, hoping the head-on attack would catch him by surprise.

He didn't appear surprised, but he moved out of the way.

"Don't touch me again," she said. "You'll be sorry."

Clutching the messenger bag, she rushed past him. Miraculously, she did not stumble this time.

"I'm the reason you're here," he called after her. "Ambrose Drake. I sent the email about the asylum to *The Lost Night Files*."

She shot through the doorway, out of the ruins, and into the foggy daylight of the rugged Northern California coast. His words began to sink in. They did not register fully until she was a few feet away from her car.

The mention of the podcast made her scramble to a halt. She recognized his name, too. She was here today because of a listener named Ambrose Drake.

She realized there was one other vehicle parked in front of the asylum. Drake's car, no doubt. She should have heard him arrive. The asylum stood on an isolated cliff above a cove, connected to the main road by a long, narrow, graveled lane.

Yes, she ought to have heard his car, but she had been so deep into the trance that she had been oblivious to the warning sounds of gravel under tires and footsteps on the creaking, groaning floorboards of the asylum.

The realization of just how vulnerable she had been while in her other vision was unnerving. In the old days—before Lucent Springs—she had never gone so deeply into the drawing trance.

She retreated a few more steps and flattened a hand on the side of her car to steady herself. Drake was on the front steps now. He had the Taser in his hand but made no attempt to pursue her.

He didn't need to chase her to make her nervous. His slick, fast reaction ability aside, he looked like he had barely survived a shipwreck, followed by a long stretch of time lost at sea on a life raft. He still had some muscle on him—the line of his shoulders beneath the windbreaker was strong and sleek—but it was obvious he had lost too much weight in the recent past. The fierce planes and angles of a face that at one time had probably qualified as interesting, even intriguing, could only be described as haggard now. He had the eyes of a man who was haunted by ghosts.

"You're Ambrose Drake?" she said, trying to process the swiftly moving events.

"Yes. I didn't mean to scare you. I apologize. I'm the one who suggested this old hospital would make a good series for the *Lost Night Files* podcast."

She opened the car door and positioned herself behind it, prepared to leap into the driver's seat and lock herself inside the vehicle. Logic told her she ought to drive straight back to the hotel, pack her bag, and leave town. Ambrose Drake might look like he was down-and-out, but that didn't mean he wasn't dangerous. She hated the idea of leaving her Taser behind but it wasn't worth the risk of trying to get it back. She could buy another one.

Still, she was a woman who was looking for answers, and these days there was no knowing where they would come from. She had to stay open to all possibilities.

"What is this about?" she asked. "Why did you sneak up on me?"

His jaw tightened. "I didn't sneak up on you. If I had wanted to do that I would have waited until . . . never mind." He stopped. "You saw something inside the asylum, didn't you? That's why you came running out in a panic. I need to know what you sensed in there. Please."

It was the grim desperation in his words that stopped her. She paused, one foot inside the car. "What do you mean?"

"You and those other two women who do the *Lost Night Files* podcast claim you investigate cold cases and mysterious disappearances that have a paranormal angle."

"So?"

Ambrose glanced briefly back into the shadows of the hospital. "I think someone was murdered in there about two weeks ago. I need help proving it."

She froze, remembering the snakes on the staircase. "What makes you believe there was a murder inside the asylum?"

"I was supposed to meet someone here. He never showed. At first I assumed he had changed his mind. But I found something near the stairs that I think indicates he was murdered."

She tightened her grip on the car door. "What is it?"

"Meet me tonight for a real conversation and I'll show you."

"If you think you can dangle that kind of bait and get away with it—"

"Not bait," Ambrose said. "Bribery. Here's my problem: I don't know who I can trust, so until I'm sure you're going to get involved in a serious investigation, I can't take the risk of giving you any more information than necessary."

Once again the memory of the vision of snakes uncoiling down the stairs sent a chill across her nerves. She grabbed a small straw of common sense that was floating past and reminded herself that the podcast attracted its share of card-carrying members of the Tin Foil Helmet crowd.

"You've got to admit your story is pretty bizarre," she said.

"You picked up some bad vibes in there, didn't you? On my way here I told myself you were probably a fraud like all the others, but now I think you just might be the real deal."

"Were you *testing* me?" Outrage crackled through her, flushing out a lot of her fear and unease. "Is that what this is all about?"

"Can you blame me? Most people who claim to be able to investigate psychic phenomena are either frauds or flat-out delusional."

"Yes, I blame you," she shot back. "What you did is worse than an insult. It's an invasion of my privacy. Or something. I don't appreciate being set up. My friends and I run into this sort of nonsense a lot, and we don't like it."

"Are you talking about what happened in Saltwood?"

She stared at him. "You know about Saltwood?"

"Sure. I'm a dedicated subscriber to your podcast," he said. "A psycho lured you and your friends to Saltwood to investigate a missing persons case that appeared to have paranormal elements. Turned out the psycho was the killer and he wanted to play a game with you."

"He thought he could prove we were frauds."

"But you found the body. You tried to convince the police that they had a homicide on their hands. They blew off your evidence, so you kept digging. The psycho was furious. He grabbed you. He was about to slit your throat when he had some sort of seizure and collapsed."

"Right." Pallas cleared her throat. "A seizure."

"We're in this together until we get answers."

The easy way he recited the *Lost Night Files* signature introduction and sign-off threw her for a beat. She recovered quickly. "Well, as far as I'm concerned, the stunt you just pulled is reason enough for *The Lost Night Files* to reject your so-called investigation. Go find yourself a genuine fraud."

"A genuine fraud?"

"You know what I mean."

"Well, no, not exactly," he said. "But I think I get the underlying subtext. You're pissed."

"Very."

"Look, I understand why you resent being tested. I apologize. Again. But I need your help. I'm out of options."

"That is not an acceptable excuse."

"Just tell me what you saw inside the asylum." Ambrose paused, evidently forced to grope for the next words. "I've got to get some answers."

This was getting weirder by the minute. It was tantalizing to think he really did have reason to believe someone had been murdered on the asylum staircase and wanted her to help him prove it. His certainty went a long way toward validating her vision. She needed the reassurance, because every time she went into a trance she wondered if she was hallucinating.

There was, however, another, extremely chilling possibility. Perhaps this was a version of the Saltwood disaster. Maybe Ambrose Drake knew someone had died on the asylum staircase because he was the one who had committed the murder.

Ice touched the back of her neck. She started to get into the front seat.

"No," Ambrose said, sounding exhausted. "I didn't kill the man who died on those stairs."

It was as if he had read her thoughts.

"Are you sure it was a man who was murdered in there?" she asked.

"As sure as I can be without proof."

"If you're so certain, why not go to the police?" she said.

He gave her a cold smile. "For the same reason you won't be going straight to the cops. You don't have any evidence to back up your story. You know as well as I do the authorities will assume you're out to get some free publicity for *The Lost Night Files*, just like they did in Saltwood."

"You seem to know a lot about me and the podcast."

"I've been listening to the program for a while now," he said. "Downloaded the archives. I even went to the cold case crime scenes you investigated. I wanted to be as sure as possible that you and the others were legit before I sent that email suggesting you come here."

"You mean before you ran your annoying little experiment on me."

"Do you have any idea how many fakes, frauds, and cons I had to sort through to get to you?" he said.

She gave him a steely smile. "Trust me, I know exactly how you feel."

"You do?"

"Ever since we fired up the podcast, my colleagues and I have had to deal with the same crowd of fakes, frauds, and cons, to say nothing of the truly delusional people who contact us. So, yes, I've got a pretty good idea how many people are running around claiming to solve paranormal mysteries. But we've discovered that the real problem is the other group."

Ambrose frowned. "What group is that?"

"The dangerously obsessed gang. It includes those who think psychics, by definition, dabble in the occult and that we can talk to the dead."

"Oh, right." Ambrose inclined his head in a knowing way. "I've run into my share of that type, too. I admit I'm focused on getting answers, but I don't think I'm in the *dangerously* obsessed category, at least not yet. Got to admit there are days when I wonder, though."

"That's not particularly reassuring. What, exactly, do you expect me to do for you, Ambrose Drake?"

"Help me prove that six weeks ago a woman was murdered at the Carnelian Sleep Institute."

"Hold on, we're talking about a second murder?"

"That's where it started," Ambrose said.

She stared at him, aware that she was officially going down the rabbit hole but unable to stop the fall. "There's a sleep clinic here in Carnelian?"

"Right. It specializes in dream disorders."

"What makes you believe a woman was murdered at the clinic?" she asked. She told herself she was just gathering context and data before she made the executive decision to get the heck out of Dodge.

"I think I was a witness," Ambrose said.

She watched him, saying nothing.

"Not to the actual murder," he said quickly. "But I'm almost certain I heard the victim scream. I think I saw the body being taken away in a laundry cart."

"But you're not sure."

"No," Ambrose admitted.

"Why the doubt?"

"Because I've been told I was sleepwalking at the time. There's a possibility I dreamed the whole thing. If that turns out to be true, I'm in worse shape than I thought—and I need to check myself into a psychiatric hospital."

CHAPTER THREE

A RE YOU SURE it's a good idea to meet with Drake again?" Talia March asked. Technically it was a question, but her cool, firm tone was infused with disapproval. It was clear she was against the idea. "You know as well as I do that the podcast attracts its share of weirdos."

"Get real," Pallas said. She put the phone on speaker and reminded herself that Talia was inclined to be a bit of a control freak. She did not handle change well—unless the change was her idea. It was a perfectly understandable side effect of her strange new talent. "We both know that these days the distinction between weird and normal can get extremely murky."

Talia fell silent for a moment. Pallas could almost hear the synapses firing on the other end of the connection. Talia had trained as a librarian, but her talent for finding that which had been lost—people, things, history—had attracted the attention of a series of employers, all of whom had, in turn, let her go in short order. Her last job had been with a consulting agency that did contract work for various corporations and the occasional clandestine government intelligence client. As usual, she had not lasted long. Two months into her position as an analyst she had been fired and escorted off the premises by security.

Talia's version of the tale was somewhat vague. She claimed she had found the work interesting but had soon discovered she did not take orders well. Pallas and the third member of the podcast team, Amelia Rivers, suspected there was more to the story, specifically that a man might have been involved, but Talia had not volunteered any details.

She had been in the process of establishing her own one-woman research agency when her life had been derailed by the events at the Lucent Springs Hotel.

"You're right," she said. "The line between weird and normal is not exactly crystal clear these days. Nevertheless, this Ambrose Drake person appears to be rather sketchy. You said he's a writer?"

"Apparently," Pallas said. "Only two books so far, though."

She carried the phone across the hotel room and stopped in front of the window. In the end, Ambrose Drake had been the first to drive away from the abandoned asylum. She had waited in her car, the doors locked, until he was gone before collecting the Taser that Ambrose had left at the entrance.

She had taken a moment to duck back inside the ruins for one last look at the creepy staircase. The shock of violent death still seethed on the steps. She knew that if she heightened her talent she would see the snakes again. That was when she had decided she would keep the appointment with Drake that evening. He wasn't the only one who wanted answers.

"I did some research on Drake after I got back to the hotel," she continued. "He really is an author. He writes twisty, creepy stuff. *Thrillers infused with an element of modern Gothic horror,*' according to some of the reviews. He's not one of the big names. He didn't hit the top of the bestseller lists with his first two books, but he did hit some lists."

"I'm at his website now," Talia said. "It's very well done, by the way."

"The website?"

"Yes. Excellent design. Easy to navigate. Good branding. The links all work."

Pallas cleared her throat. "We're not having this conversation to discuss his online marketing skills. Try to focus."

"I *am* focused." Talia sounded offended. "Doesn't mean I can't multi-task. Our podcast website is competent but not exactly inspired. It needs an upgrade. Also, our social media efforts suck."

"Because the three of us are competent but not exactly inspired when it comes to navigating the online world."

"We need more reach," Talia said. "Got to build our brand."

She sounded thoughtful now. That was dangerous. If you lost Talia to her newly enhanced imagination, it could take a while to get her attention again.

"Forget the social media crap, Talia." Pallas sharpened her voice. "We're discussing Ambrose Drake and the possibility of two murders."

"Right. Okay, I see that he has two titles out, *A Fall of Shadows* and *A Snare of Dreams*. He's writing a series featuring an investigator named Jake Crane."

"So?"

"I've never heard of either of those novels," Talia said, as if that explained something very important.

"Exactly how many authors of twisty, creepy thrillers infused with an element of modern Gothic horror can you name?" Pallas asked.

"Not many," Talia admitted. "None, now that I think of it. I was never a fan of scary books and haven't read any at all in that genre since Lucent Springs. They make me nervous."

"Me, too. Look, his name recognition and online branding are not critical factors here. What is important is that he is who he claims to be—Ambrose Drake, author. I found some video interviews and photos of him online. The man I met today is definitely the same person."

Strictly speaking, that was only partially true. Yes, the photos and videos had captured Drake's intriguing features. But it was clear they had all been recorded before the exhaustion and weight loss had struck. None of them had done justice to his haunted and haunting eyes.

Astonishingly, the images had managed to convey some sense of the tempered steel will and the self-control that, in person, charged the atmosphere around him. Somehow you just knew that if you were wounded and left behind on the battlefield, this was the man who would come back for you or die trying.

No, she could not be sure of that, she told herself. There was no way to predict how he would act in a crisis. She knew almost nothing about Ambrose Drake except that he was inexplicably fascinating. And exhausted. And determined to find answers. And he needed a good meal. And a good night's sleep.

She closed her eyes very tightly for a few seconds and gave herself a silent lecture on the risks of allowing her imagination to get the better of her common sense. Yes, there was something about Drake that suggested he would be relentless when it came to pursuing an objective, but that quality could easily be adapted to revenge or building a criminal empire. Determination was a superpower, but like any power, it could be used for bad ends.

"All right, so Ambrose Drake is the writer he claims to be," Talia said. "That just tells us he's got a day job. A lot of serial killers and scammers are gainfully employed."

Pallas opened her eyes and braced one hand against the window frame. It was a little after five o'clock in the afternoon. Four floors below, the bustling main street of Carnelian was lightly crowded with a mix of shopkeepers closing up for the day, office workers heading home or into their favorite after-work hangouts, and students drifting into coffeehouses and fast-food restaurants.

There were a *lot* of students. Carnelian College was a small, private institution, but it occupied a large chunk of real estate in the center of town, and it appeared to be the primary economic engine of the community.

"You've made your point," Pallas said. "I do think he's convinced his story is true, but he might be just another deluded conspiracy theorist."

"Why so quick to believe him?" Talia asked. "That's not like you. What happened to the *trust no one* motto?"

"Something bad went down in that asylum," Pallas said.

"It was a hospital for the insane. I'm sure a lot of terrible things happened there."

"I told you, what I sensed was recent. The energy was still very disturbed. According to Drake, whatever happened on that staircase is connected to another possible murder at the local sleep clinic."

"That he *thinks* he witnessed," Talia said.

"Well, he admits he did not see the actual act, but he's convinced a woman was killed there." Pallas paused a beat. "I did a drawing of the asylum stairs."

"Excellent," Talia said, doing one of her disconcerting about-faces. She was now enthusiastic. "What did you see in the picture?"

"Not much." Pallas turned away from the window and moved to the small table. Her sketchbook was open to the drawing that had sent her running for the exit in the asylum. "I need more context.

Another reason for meeting Drake this evening. He claims to have an object that he found at the scene. He thinks it's evidence of murder. He promised to show it to me."

"He's using whatever it is as bait to get you to come to the meeting."

"He said it was more like bribery, but yes, it's bait, and it's working."

Talia said quietly, "You're sure that what you sensed on the staircase happened recently?"

"It's not last-night hot, but the energy was definitely laid down within the past few weeks. I think. I'm getting better at being able to calculate the age of the storms, but it's a steep learning curve."

"I understand," Talia said. There was some sympathy in her tone this time. "Amelia and I struggling, too."

"I know."

"The thing is, you must not lose sight of the possibility that Ambrose Drake knows about the death because he was the killer."

"If that's the case, why try to get us to investigate?"

"Because he's a sociopath who likes to play games? Don't forget what happened in Saltwood."

"Trust me, I remember," Pallas said. "But I don't think Drake was playing games today. He was testing me, running an experiment to see if I picked up the vibe on the stairs. It was annoying, but I must admit I understand why he did it. In his shoes, I'd want some proof, too."

Talia sighed. "As we know and continue to prove, psychic-land is populated with frauds, fakes, cons, and the sadly deluded."

"Yes."

There was a long silence before Talia spoke again. "Are you going to the police with what you sensed in that asylum?"

"No, of course not." Pallas suppressed a shudder. "Not yet, at any rate. We tried that in Saltwood. It did not end well. The bottom line here is that I know something happened in the asylum, and the man I'm supposed to meet with in an hour wants to talk about it and what he thinks he witnessed in the sleep clinic. There's something in this, Talia. Something important."

"I agree," Talia said finally. "We can't ignore the sleep clinic angle, but there may be a perfectly logical explanation for what Drake thinks happened during that sleep study. Maybe they gave him some medication. People who take sleep meds often report short-term amnesia. Others have bizarre dreams. Some hallucinate. I assume you've done some initial fact-checking?"

"Yes, but it wasn't helpful."

"You mean Drake's story doesn't hold up to close scrutiny?"

"Not as well as I would have liked," Pallas admitted. "On the way back from the asylum I stopped at the public library and went through the files of the *Carnelian Gazette* for the past couple of months. I found no record of a suspicious death at the asylum or the Carnelian Sleep Institute, and no one seems to have gone missing during that time. No bodies were discovered."

"If two people had died by violence it would have been in the news," Talia said. "Carnelian is a relatively small town."

"A small *college* town," Pallas said quickly. "That means a highly transient student population. Visiting lecturers. Prospective students and their parents probably come here year-round to check out the campus. Strangers disappearing might not have been noticed."

"I don't know," Talia said. "Feels like a rabbit hole. I wish Amelia was available. I'd like her perspective."

"Is she still in Lucent Springs?"

"Yes. She left yesterday. There's no cell coverage out there in the desert. She'll be back in a couple of days."

"I wish she wouldn't get these sudden urges to go back to that damned hotel on her own. I know there's no one around and it's boarded up, but it's so isolated out there in the desert. Just thinking about that horrible place gives me nightmares."

"Lucent Springs gives all of us nightmares," Talia said. "But you know how it is for Amelia. This isn't the first time she's awakened in the middle of the night and announced that she has to go back to the hotel and take some more photos."

"She's so sure that one of these days she'll look through the lens of her camera and see something important. Something that will tell us who is responsible for what happened to us. She's obsessed, Talia."

"Who among us isn't? Amelia will be all right. It's not her first trip to Lucent Springs alone. Right now we need to make a decision about the Carnelian situation."

Pallas did not take her eyes off the drawing in the sketchbook. Why snakes? There was always a reason for the imagery her intuition dictated when she was in the trance. The fact that it was a picture of snakes cascading down the stairs instead of something else—a waterfall or flames or tentacles—was important.

She needed context.

"Maybe this is a rabbit hole of a case," she said, "but it warrants some preliminary investigation. I've got a feeling this story is real, and it fits the podcast brand."

"How?"

"I told you, there's a lost night involved. Okay, it all happened at a sleep clinic, so technically it's not entirely lost. There will be some records. What matters is that Drake is convinced a woman was murdered at the Institute and that he saw some evidence of it but his memories are jumbled and blurred."

"Like ours were after Lucent Springs," Talia said quietly.

"Yes."

Talia went silent for a moment. "All right. You're the one on the scene. It's your call. How do you plan to investigate?"

"The usual way—one step at a time. I'll start by conducting a full interview with Drake. I want to see whatever it is he found in the asylum that makes him think someone was murdered. After that, assuming I believe him, I'll get some more information. I need to verify that he really did spend a night in the sleep clinic and if there was another patient there on the same night."

"That last bit might not be so easy," Talia warned. "There are a bunch of laws that protect patient confidentiality. You can't just walk into the clinic and ask if Drake was undergoing a sleep study on the night in question, let alone if there was another patient on the same night."

"I'll figure it out."

"Okay, you've made the decision to interview Drake. Please tell me you'll take precautions."

"Of course. We agreed to meet on neutral ground, a tavern at the end of the main street. I can see it from my window. It's only a few blocks away from the campus. It will be crowded."

"Be careful. Don't let him talk you into going someplace where you'll be alone with him."

"I've already been alone with him, Talia. If he wanted to murder me he could have done it this afternoon at the asylum. He's very . . . fast."

"Fast?"

"Excellent reflexes."

"Oh, I see," Talia said. "The athletic type."

"Not exactly. More like a big cat. A really big, very hungry, and exhausted cat."

"Never mind. The thing is, you can't make any assumptions about his intentions. Text or call when you're back in your hotel room. I want a full report. Meanwhile, don't do anything dumb."

"Hey, thanks for the terrific advice," Pallas said. "I never would have thought of that on my own. *Don't do anything dumb.* Yep, words to live by, all right. I'll write them down as soon as we hang up so I don't forget."

"I'm serious, Pallas. We aren't playing games here."

"I know. I'll be careful."

"So, how's the hotel room?" Talia asked. "Are you okay?"

"Yes, it's fine." Pallas looked around the room. "Just the usual. It's not like anyone died in this room, at least not recently."

"No major redecorating required?"

Pallas smiled at the tiny container of succulents sitting on the windowsill. "Nothing my travel plants can't handle."

"Good," Talia said. "I'll say goodbye for now, then. Just be careful with that writer—and remember, we're in this together."

"Until we get answers."

CHAPTER FOUR

ALLAS PUT HER phone on the table. *We're in this together until we get answers* was more than a signature for the podcast as far as she and Talia and Amelia were concerned. For the three of them the words had become a way of renewing the vow they had made to each other in the days following their lost night at the Lucent Springs Hotel.

They had promised to stick together until they got answers because they had quickly discovered they were on their own. Some people, including law enforcement, had concluded they had spent the lost hours doing heavy drugs. Those who believed they were telling the truth assumed the amnesia had been caused by the trauma of the earthquake and fire and assured them their memories would return in time.

Back at the start, they hadn't known what to believe themselves. Amnesia left a huge psychic black hole. But it had soon become apparent that whatever had happened to them in the ruins of the Lucent Springs Hotel had changed them in ways they were still trying to understand. They would not be able to rest until they got answers.

They had been strangers before Lucent Springs. They did not even live in the same town. Pallas's home was currently a cozy little apartment in Keeley Point, a boutique community on the coast a few miles south of Los Angeles. Talia was located in Seattle. Amelia lived near San Diego.

Night was falling fast. Pallas turned on a lamp and took another look at the drawing. Why snakes? To anyone else the image would appear fantastical or surreal, perhaps the product of a fevered brain. She knew there was meaning in the picture, but it wasn't obvious what that meaning was. It was up to her to decode the message her other senses had sent her.

She had been a child when she had discovered it was easy to slide into a daydreamlike state and draw for hours on end. The ability had been as natural to her as breathing, and for a time she had assumed she was destined for a career as a serious artist. Her parents had discouraged her, and so had every art teacher she had met along the way. Something about being good but not good enough. The word *competent* had been used a lot. For her, everyone said, drawing would make a nice hobby but not a career.

In the tradition of countless generations of undiscovered and unacknowledged artists, she had forged ahead with her dreams right up until that day when she was seventeen and began to realize what she was attempting to do when she went into a drawing trance. She wasn't compelled to create something new and insightful. She wasn't looking to give others a fresh perspective or see the world in a different light. She wasn't trying to enlighten anyone. She had no message to convey. She was attempting to fix something that she could not see but that she knew intuitively was wrong in a space. She was struggling to rebalance the feel of a room.

For some reason she was motivated to adjust whatever it was in the atmosphere that disturbed her sense of harmony on a visceral level. Unfortunately, there was a great deal that was wrong, off-balance, and disturbing in the world, and she had a tendency to stumble into the hot spots. The experience always sent an unpleasant frisson across her nerves.

By the time she was in college it had become apparent that she was dealing with a low-level case of generalized anxiety that promised to make her life miserable. She had sought counseling. After a number of false starts, she had gotten lucky when, on a whim in her junior year, she had volunteered to participate in a psychological research study. When the results came back she had been advised to consult a professional career counselor named Gabriella Jones.

"Drawing the bad stuff won't help much," Gabriella Jones said. She tossed aside the folder that contained the results of the study and clasped her hands on her desk. "You'll have to find a way to fix the underlying lack of harmony in a space, at least some of the time. If you don't, the anxiety will only get worse. It could become crippling."

"I don't understand," Pallas said, baffled. "How do I do fix bad energy?"

"I suggest a career in interior design."

"You mean like be a decorator? I don't think my parents would approve of that. Everyone in my family becomes a research scientist or a doctor or a professor."

"You asked for my advice," Gabriella Jones said. "I'm giving it to you. Go out and rebalance some of the negative energy in the places where people live, work, and play. Pretty sure that's your calling. You will find it very satisfying."

"I thought I was supposed to blunder around until I figured out what I wanted to do with my life. Everyone says at this age I should be on a voyage of self-discovery."

"Blundering around works for some people, and there certainly is a long-standing tradition of doing that," Gabriella Jones said. "But why waste your time with gap years, false starts, and dead-end jobs when you've got a genuine calling?"

"I'm not sure interior design qualifies as a calling."

"It does in this case."

"How do you know that?" Pallas asked, still uneasy about the prospect of such a career path. "The only experience I've had with decorating was when I painted my bedroom orange. Mom was horrified. I did buy some bookshelves and a couple of ferns for my dorm room, but I don't think that counts."

Gabriella Jones peered at her across the desk, evidently seeing something other than what Pallas saw when she looked in a mirror.

"You know that thing you're trying to do when you get the urge to draw after you stumble into a bad space?" Gabriella Jones said. "That's what I do when I figure out what sort of career someone should pursue."

"Yeah?" Pallas was intrigued. "Does everyone take your advice?"

"Nope. And not everyone will want your designs. Don't worry, you'll get over it."

"Okay," Pallas said, wondering how she was going to explain a career path focused on balancing energy to her parents, who were pushing her to get serious about grad school. "Well, thanks. I guess."

She got to her feet and reached down for the backpack she had left on the floor. A shadow flickered at the edge of her vision, startling her.

She yelped and turned much too quickly. The back of her knee hit the edge of the chair and she lost her balance. She grabbed the corner of Jones's desk to steady herself.

"Sorry," she mumbled, flushing.

"My fault," Gabriella Jones said. "I apologize. Are you all right?"

"Yes, I'm fine." Pallas straightened and hitched her pack over one shoulder. She started toward the door, stopped, and turned back. "Why did you say it was your fault?"

"I should have told you about Dr. Metcalf."

"Who is Dr. Metcalf?"

"My predecessor. The poor man suffered a heart attack while working late one night. In the morning they found his body on the floor right where you lost your balance. You obviously picked up traces of the energy he left in the space during his final moments."

Horrified, Pallas stared at Gabriella Jones. "Is that the kind of stuff I'm sensing when I see the little flickering shadows?"

"I think so, yes. Strong energy of any kind leaves a stain or, in your case, a shadow. But sometimes you'll be able to rebalance the bad stuff."

"No offense, but that sounds pretty woo-wooish."

"I know. Please don't tell anyone, okay? My boss doesn't believe in psychic talents. She would fire me if she found out that I use them to counsel students. You will probably want to keep your own talent to yourself, too."

"Wow. Just wow. Don't worry, I won't tell anyone. Especially not my parents."

Gabriella Jones regarded the floor where Metcalf had died with a considering expression, and then she looked at Pallas.

"Do you have any suggestions?" she said.

Pallas stared at her. "What?"

"Can you think of a way to rearrange this room to rebalance the energy flow?"

"Oh." Pallas blinked. "Are you serious?"

"Yes. That spot on the floor bothers me a bit, too."

"Huh. Well. Okay. I guess I could try."

Pallas set her backpack on the floor, pulled out a sketchbook and a pencil, and took a breath. Cautiously she slipped into the drawing trance.

As usual, she lost track of time, but when she emerged from the trance she saw that only a few minutes had passed. She looked down at what she had drawn.

"You need to bring in some greenery," she said. "A couple of plants, I think. And water."

"Water?" Gabriella Jones said.

"Maybe a bowl of goldfish or one of those little fountains you see in the home-and-garden catalogs," Pallas said.

"Got it." Gabriella Jones jotted down a note. "Anything else?"

Pallas looked at the framed photo of a stern, humorless man on the wall. "You should take that down and store it somewhere."

Gabriella Jones regarded the photo. "That's Dr. Metcalf."

"I think he was a very unhappy man," Pallas said.

"I agree. I'll get rid of the photo immediately. Tomorrow I'll bring in a plant and perhaps see about getting some goldfish." Gabriella Jones smiled. "There you go—your first satisfied client."

The Llewellyn family had not been thrilled when Pallas announced her decision to pursue a career in interior design, but Gabriella Jones had been right—she had a talent for the work. She had discovered an intuitive sense of how to use color, texture, proportion, greenery, and, in tough cases, a water feature to achieve balance in most rooms.

The creative aspect of design work was exhilarating, for the most part. But some of the things she had discovered early on were that she could not fix the bad energy in every space and that in some cases that she considered successes, the clients did not care for the results. She wasn't going to save the world by rebalancing all the bad energy in it, but she could change the way people felt when they walked into a house or a theater or a store or an office or a hospital. She had the ability to make people feel a little happier, more peaceful, more positive, or more optimistic, at least for a while. That was a calling.

She did not necessarily seek tranquility and serenity in a room. There were interiors and clients that demanded drama, excitement, or sensory stimulation. But regardless of the emotional response she aimed for, she used her underlying sense of balance and harmony to achieve her vision.

Unfortunately, the business side of interior design had proven to be more complicated. In hindsight, it had been a serious mistake to get involved with the firm of Theodore Collier, Architecture & Design. Nevertheless, she had been in the process of extricating herself from the situation when the real disaster had struck.

Her career had fallen off a cliff after Lucent Springs. Most of her semi-normal life had followed her work and her art into the darkness. Her talent for sensing unbalanced energy in a space and finding ways to adjust it had metamorphosed into a curse.

Before Lucent Springs her inner vision had allowed her to glimpse the distortions in the energy of an interior space and adjust them. Now her other sight was far more acute; more disturbing. These days when she picked up a pencil, opened her sketchbook, and prepared to slide into a trance, she experienced a serious vibe of anxiety. What if she saw something she could not handle? What if she did not come out of the trance?

In the weeks after Lucent Springs her drawings had become increasingly ominous, bleak, and grim. In the beginning they had frightened her. She had not dared to show them to anyone except Talia and Amelia, both of whom understood because they were going through similar experiences.

The only upside was that she was getting better at interpreting her pictures. Prior to the lost night in Lucent Springs, the trances had produced vague impressions of wild, chaotic storms, churning seas, and dystopian landscapes. Now the images were sharper and more detailed—like the picture of snakes.

She studied the drawing again. It showed a portion of the lobby and the lower section of the main staircase of the asylum. There was not a lot of detail in the handrails, balusters, and newels, but the focal point was the spill of snakes. The creatures tumbled down the last few steps and disappeared into the shadows behind the staircase.

It didn't take a degree in psychology to conclude that snakes were not a good sign. She was very certain that the death on the staircase could not be attributed to natural causes.

She closed the sketchbook and went back across the room, automatically pushing aside the tingle of awareness that lifted the hair on the back of her neck. The creepy sensation of being watched was so omnipresent these days that she had been forced to learn how to ignore it. She knew that if she let the vibe take hold, it would turn her into a nervous wreck. It was amazing what the human mind could block, at least partially. Probably a survival skill of some kind.

When she glanced up she caught sight of herself in the mirror. For a few seconds she wondered, as she often did these days, how she could still look the same. Lucent Springs had changed her. It was hard to believe those changes did not show in the mirror. Only Talia and Amelia were aware of what she had become. She did not dare tell her family. She would never be able to confide in a lover.

Lucent Springs had done more than enhance her talent for perceiving the disturbing energy laid down by strong emotions. Whatever had happened in the ruins of the old hotel out in the desert had turned her into something very scary.

Memories of the final blowout quarrel with Theo sent a chill through her. Yes, their relationship would have ended sooner or later even if he hadn't cheated and even if their business partnership hadn't disintegrated. But it was the look in Theo's eyes on that last day when she had walked out the door of the offices of Theodore Collier, Architecture & Design that haunted her.

Theo would never admit it, but she knew the truth. She had terrified him.

She had frightened herself as well. That was the day she had begun to realize exactly what she could do with her enhanced psychic senses.

It wasn't until Saltwood, however, that her fears had been confirmed. She could use her new talent to kill.

CHAPTER FIVE

PALLAS LLEWELLYN WALKED into the tavern just as Ambrose convinced himself she would not show up.

She wore the black jeans, gray sweater, and sneakers she'd had on earlier. The strap of the big messenger bag was slung over her shoulder. Her shoulder-length, whiskey-brown hair had been in a chaotic tangle when she had fled through the ruins of the asylum, but now it was neatly brushed and parted slightly to one side. The style framed her strong, interesting face and sorceress eyes.

She was here.

His first reaction was to wonder if he was hallucinating again. These days he was afraid to trust his normal senses as well as his other vision. San Diego had changed everything, and the very bad night in the Carnelian Sleep Institute had made the situation even worse. At the rate his life was deteriorating he would likely end up on the street or in a locked ward.

Just inside the tavern Pallas paused, searching for him in the loud, bustling, dimly lit space. He got to his feet and started to raise a hand to signal her but she saw him immediately. She slipped the messenger bag off her shoulder and held it in front of her with both hands in a gesture that struck him as protective. She had gripped the bag the same way that afternoon when she had fled the asylum.

She started toward him, weaving a slow, cautious path through the crowd.

He opened his inner window. The room shifted into the underwater shadow zone. Glowing, ghostly figures lounged against the bar, occupied booths, and served drinks. Each individual radiated a perceptible energy field.

He had been aware of human auras since his early teens, but after the amnesia episode in San Diego he had begun perceiving them with disturbing clarity. He was still learning how to handle his upgraded vision. He had always sensed on some level that each human aura was unique, just as human faces and eyes were unique, but before San Diego the differences had been subtle.

He had realized, too, that he responded in various ways to other people's energy fields. Some auras felt frail and weak, as if the individual was ill or depressed. Others came across as anxious or fearful. A disturbingly high percentage appeared dangerous—too hot or too cold. Some were alarmingly unstable.

For most of his life he had told himself that what he perceived in auras was just a step beyond what he could read in a person's body language, if he paid attention. No big deal. Nevertheless, after some guarded conversations about his ability with his family and a few close friends, he had learned to keep his mouth shut.

That tactic had worked well right up until San Diego. But the amnesia episode had changed everything. Whatever had happened there had given him the equivalent of twenty-twenty vision for auras.

It turned out that, for the most part, he really did not want to know too much about other people—not even family and friends, let alone strangers or lovers. Especially not lovers.

But Pallas Llewellyn was different.

Over the years his reactions to other people's auras mirrored his reactions to their personalities. Some people gave off a good vibe. Some did not. But this was the first time he had been fascinated and compelled by someone's energy field. Pallas Llewellyn's aura *thrilled* him. There was no other word for it.

Her energy field was sharp and strong and there was an exciting vitality in the radiance around her that made him want to get closer. He reminded himself he had been living a monastic existence since Maureen had announced that their relationship was over. Under the circumstances, he probably shouldn't read too much into his reaction to Pallas's aura.

Maybe the attraction was nothing more than relief at the knowledge that she appeared to be the real deal, an investigator with at least some genuine extrasensory perception. Okay, an amateur investigator with some ESP, but still.

He desperately wanted to believe that she had detected murder on the staircase in the asylum. He needed a little hope. But what he was feeling as he watched Pallas come toward him was a lot more complicated than a sudden infusion of optimism. It had been a while since he had felt the energy of sexual attraction, but it wasn't the kind of thing a man ever forgot.

Shit. This was not a good time to discover that he was once again interested in sex. He had other priorities. Saving his sanity was currently at the top of the list.

Pallas was no longer in panic mode. There was a lot of tension and some anxiety in the wavelengths of her aura, but she was calm and back in control. Her energy burned in a way that made every other aura in the tavern appear pale in comparison. Or maybe that was just his imagination.

He closed his inner window. She was here. That was the only thing that mattered. A moment ago he had been convinced she would not show and he'd have no one to blame but himself because he had screwed up that afternoon at the asylum, but here she was.

Sure, he'd had his reasons for running the test. He'd needed some evidence that she was not a fraud. There was too much at stake. Losing Maureen had been depressing, but in a way, it had also been a relief. The relationship had been going nowhere fast. Having his family stage an intervention had been a jarring shock. You knew the situation was not good when you discovered that the people who cared about you the most were deeply concerned for your mental health. The realization that his career as a writer was in mortal jeopardy because he could not focus on it long enough to complete a single scene was traumatic. Cataclysmic. But what really scared him was the possibility that he might be losing his mind.

It dawned on him that Pallas was picking an odd path to the booth. He knew she had spotted him immediately after arriving. That was hardly a surprise. Even if he hadn't stood and raised a hand to get her attention, she would have noticed him. He was too old and too off-trend and looked too beaten up and wrung out to pass for a student. After weeks of nightmares and enforced insomnia, no one was likely to mistake him for a member of the faculty, either.

The woman making her way toward him didn't belong in this crowd any more than he did. She wasn't here to postpone the process of becoming an adult, and she wasn't climbing the notoriously slippery academic ladder. He did not have to view her aura to read her bone-deep wariness of her surroundings and everyone in the vicinity. He already knew she did not trust him, but now he got the impression she didn't trust others in general. He could respect that. These days he didn't trust anyone, either.

Something in common, he thought. The realization ignited a tiny flicker of ridiculous optimism. As Rick had speculated in the last scene of *Casablanca*, maybe this was the beginning of a beautiful friendship. He'd settle for a useful temporary alliance, though.

The path she followed across the tavern made him curious. Yes, she was in a room full of strangers, and she was naturally doing her best to avoid brushing up against them, but something about her aura and her body language told him another factor dictated her erratic course.

When she walked past a table where two women sat drinking margaritas, she visibly flinched for no obvious reason. He watched her clutch the messenger bag a little more securely and sidestep a nonexistent object on the floor.

She looked like she was dodging ghosts that only she could see.

There was no time to analyze the observation. She was suddenly there, standing in front of him, watching him with her hypnotic eyes.

"Thanks for giving me another chance to explain," he said.

"Let's just say I'm interested in your story," Pallas said.

Right. His story. He reminded himself that he wasn't the only one with an agenda. She was after material for *The Lost Night Files*.

She angled herself into the booth and positioned the messenger bag within easy reach. He remembered the Taser. He didn't need his psychic talent to warn him she was making it clear she would leave in an instant if she did not like what he had to say. He sat down across from her and motioned toward the beer he had ordered for himself.

"What would you like to drink?" he asked.

The question evidently surprised her. She was in a tavern, but her mind was not on ordering a drink.

"A glass of the house red, whatever it is," she said. She hesitated. "Thanks."

She rummaged around in her large bag, took out a phone, and set it on the table.

Should have seen that coming, he thought. Of course she intended to record whatever he told her. She was here in Carnelian because she wanted content.

He would work on that problem later. First things first. He caught the eye of a server and requested the wine. When the woman disappeared into the crowd, he turned back to Pallas and reminded himself that he needed to sound rational. Logical. Above all, he had to appear mentally stable. He had already frightened her enough for one day.

"I apologize for scaring you this afternoon," he said.

She waved that aside and picked up the phone. "Tell me your story."

He eyed the phone. "Do you mind if we talk for a while before you start recording?"

"Why?"

She was no longer running from the hounds of hell. She was in control, focused, on a mission.

In that moment he was certain he was looking at a woman who was walking a tightrope over an abyss. *Like me.* For some reason he found that reassuring. They both had secrets but neither of them was going to play games. They didn't have the time.

"I'd rather you didn't record me at this point because I'm not sure I'll sound coherent," he said. "I haven't had a lot of sleep lately."

"Yes, I can see that."

He winced. "Do I look that bad?"

"You don't look great. Try meds?"

"They make the dreams and the sleepwalking worse."

"You sleepwalk?"

"Sometimes. If I'm not careful."

Pallas watched him with a speculative look, not speaking. Then she glanced at the bar food menu.

The server returned and set the glass of wine on the table. Pallas smiled at her.

"One order of the buffalo cauliflower and tahini dip, please," she said.

"Sure," the server said. She dove back into the crowd.

Ambrose wondered if he should have ordered something to eat, too. It occurred to him he was hungry.

Pallas looked at him across the table. "All right."

He blinked, wondering if he wasn't tracking. Maybe he was in worse shape than he realized.

"All right?" he repeated.

"I won't start recording until you convince me to move forward with the podcast."

He relaxed a little. "Thanks."

"Talk to me."

He drank some of the beer and set the bottle down with great care.

"I've had what my family and my teachers called an 'overactive imagination' for as long as I can remember," he said. "So when I started seeing auras in high school, everyone assumed I was either imagining them or trying to fool people."

Pallas went very still. He knew then that whatever she had expected him to say, what he had just told her wasn't it. But she did not grab the messenger bag and leave. He took that as a good sign.

"You see auras?" she asked, wary but curious now.

"Up until a few months ago all I saw were shifting waves of radiance around other people. That had some practical uses. It was a lot like being able to read body language. It gave me a real edge when I played sports in high school. As I got older I realized I could sometimes tell when someone was lying or running a con, but not always. It complicated the hell out of my dating life."

"I can imagine."

"But when I realized no one believed me, I quit talking about it." He swallowed some beer and wished he'd ordered a hamburger or a sandwich. "Didn't want anyone thinking I was hallucinating."

"Okay."

"The aura reading thing was a real asset when I got my first good job," he continued.

Pallas tipped her head a bit. At least she was paying attention.

"What was the job?" she asked.

"After floundering around for a few years I got hired as an analyst at a private security firm. Failure Analysis."

"That's what you did? Failure analysis? Isn't that engineering work?"

"It's the name of the company," he explained. "They investigate security failures for their clients."

"I see."

The server arrived with the platter of buffalo-style cauliflower and dip. Pallas smiled at her again. "Two forks, please."

"You bet." The server produced the forks and two small plates. "Will there be anything else?"

"Not now, thanks," Pallas said. When the server left she nudged the platter to the center of the table. "Help yourself."

The cauliflower looked good—better than anything he had eaten in a very long time.

"Thanks," he said. He picked up a fork.

"Go on," Pallas said.

"Where was I?" he said around a mouthful of hot, spicy cauliflower. "Oh, right. Failure Analysis. It was a great job, but somewhere along the line I got the writing bug. The aura reading thing gave me the inspiration for the protagonist, Jake Crane. I wrote nights and weekends. Finished the book, got very, very lucky and found a publisher. Wrote another book in the series. Got an agent. Quit my day job at Failure Analysis and figured my life was damned swell."

"And then?"

He wolfed down another chunk of cauliflower. He wasn't just hungry, he realized. He was ravenous.

"And then shit happened," he said.

She sipped some wine and looked at him over the rim of the glass. "Is this where you tell me how you wound up at the sleep clinic here in Carnelian?"

"I'll get to that in a few minutes. Unfortunately there's a prologue. You see, the night at the Institute isn't the first night I've lost."

She watched him with a new intensity. "Do you suffer from blackouts?"

He tightened his grip on the beer bottle. "No. But eight months ago I went to San Diego. I lost one night and most of my memories of the day before and the morning after that night. When I woke up, my aura reading talent had changed."

Pallas did not even blink. She stared at him as if he had just revealed the date the world would end.

"Explain," she said.

"Up until that night in San Diego, I could detect only very strong emotions in auras. Fear. Anger. Excitement. Violence. Anxiety. Not a lot more than what most people can see if they pay attention to body language."

He stopped and waited for her reaction.

"Tell me about San Diego," she said.

Her voice was utterly neutral now. He didn't have to open his inner window to know that she was waiting for another shoe to drop, but there was no way to know what that meant. Maybe she was trying to decide if he was delusional. This was not going well, but he had to try to hold on to her. He didn't have any other options.

"A writers' organization in San Diego invited me to give a talk," he said. "The event was held at a hotel. I was told I would be picked up at the airport. I remember getting into the back of the car, and that's the last thing I remember until the following day when I woke up on a beach."

Pallas watched him as if he were one of the ghosts she tried to avoid brushing up against when she walked through a crowd. Her eyes, until now cool and wary, flashed with comprehension. He did not have to slide into his other vision to know that her aura was flaring. He could feel the heat.

He had her full attention.

Pallas appeared to recover quickly from her moment of stunned shock. Now she was riveted.

"Did you go to a doctor?" she said.

She was no longer asking questions. She was conducting an interrogation. *Be careful what you wish for, Drake.*

"I headed for the nearest emergency room," he said. "I was given a thorough workup, but there was no sign of trauma. They did come up with a diagnosis—according to the doctor I had apparently experienced an atypically extended version of transient global amnesia."

The fact that she did not request a definition of the term told him she was familiar with it. Of course, given the themes of *The Lost Night Files*, that shouldn't come as a surprise. He, on the other hand, had been startled to discover transient global amnesia was not a particularly rare phenomenon. What was unusual in his case was how long the episode had lasted.

"What about the writers' conference?" Pallas asked. "Did the organizers contact the police?"

"No. When I called to try to explain, I found out the organizers had been told that I had fallen suddenly ill and had canceled."

Pallas reached into her messenger bag and took out a small notebook and a pen. "Have you been able to recover any memories of what happened during those missing hours?" she asked.

He watched uneasily as she flipped open the notebook. "Maybe."

She glanced up, frowning. "What do you mean?"

He realized the platter of buffalo cauliflower was empty. He sat back and picked up his beer.

"Sometimes, before I checked into the Institute here in Carnelian, I thought I'd catch snapshots of that lost night in my dreams. Nightmares, really. But the scenes made no sense. A portion of a room. Someone in a mask leaning over me. A hot aura. A sense of dread. Nothing concrete. But it was the sleepwalking that scared the hell out of me. You could say I deliberately developed insomnia as a defense mechanism."

Pallas nodded. "You were so anxious about the sleepwalking that you started resisting sleep."

"My ex called it quits. I became a recluse. I tried to avoid my family and friends, because I knew they would realize I was falling apart. I had trouble writing. Finally, my parents and my brother and sister concluded that I was having a nervous breakdown. They staged an intervention. Insisted I get help and gave me the number of the Carnelian Sleep Institute."

"Wow," Pallas said. Her tone was not without empathy now. "An intervention. That's serious."

"Yes, it is. Made me realize I had to take action, though. That's how I wound up checking into the Institute for an overnight sleep study."

"And now?" Pallas said, her voice gentling.

He tried to smile but he knew it probably looked twisted. It certainly felt twisted. "The short version is that things got bad and then things got worse. Since the sleep study the nightmares have become intolerable and the sleepwalking has become a nightly event unless I take precautions."

"The enforced insomnia?"

"Right. If I let myself slide too far into a dream I'll find myself in the front room, opening the door. My biggest fear is that one of these nights I won't wake up until I'm outside the house, walking to some unknown destination. Maybe into traffic."

"That is . . . terrifying," Pallas said. "No wonder you've developed insomnia."

"It wasn't easy. I had to work hard to become an insomniac."

"Are you telling me you don't sleep at all? That's impossible." Pallas tapped the pen on the table. "I think."

"I've gotten very good at limiting myself to catnaps," he said. "As far as I can tell, the sleepwalking only happens if I fall into a deep, sound sleep and slide into a nightmare. I think the riskiest time is around two o'clock in the morning, so I make sure I'm awake then."

"No wonder you look like you just washed up on a beach."

"Thanks. You know how to make a guy feel like a winner."

She ignored that. "Let's go back to San Diego. You mentioned the nightmares. Tell me how your aura-reading talent changed."

This was getting tricky. He wondered how much to tell her. He had already given her a lot of information. She seemed inclined to believe him but maybe he wasn't interpreting her energy field correctly. The aura reading talent was far from foolproof, especially these days, when it was complicated by sleep deprivation and stress.

A server carrying a tray stacked high with dirty dishes and glasses that he had just picked up at a neighboring table made to walk past the booth. At that moment a young man who had been arguing with a woman at a nearby table leaped to his feet, enraged.

"Get over it, you stupid bitch," he said through his teeth. "It was just a hookup. We don't have a fucking relationship."

He swung around, intending to head for the front door, but his trajectory carried him straight into the path of the server. Ambrose knew the impending collision would send the tray full of dishes showering down onto the table where he was sitting with Pallas. He did not need that kind of distraction. Priorities.

He got to his feet, reached out, and took the tray in both hands just as the furious young man slammed into the server. There was a thud and a couple of grunts as the two collided. The server reeled to one side but managed to catch himself by grabbing a divider that separated two booths. Angry Guy pitched up against someone who looked like he probably played football.

There were a lot of muttered comments along the lines of "What the fuck?," "Get off me," and "Hey, it was an accident, okay?" before, with a final "Fuck this," Angry Guy headed for the door.

The server finally realized his hands were empty. He looked around and saw Ambrose holding the tray. The dishes and glassware were still neatly stacked. He grinned in relief.

"Nice work, man," he said. "Thanks."

"No problem," Ambrose said.

With a nod of thanks the server took the heavy tray and went toward the kitchen. Ambrose closed the window in his head. Time went back to normal. He sat down.

But Pallas got to her feet and went to the table Angry Guy had just vacated. The young woman was still there, trying not to cry as she gathered up her things. She looked startled when Pallas lightly touched her arm and spoke quietly. It was impossible to hear what she said, but the woman's mood shifted from hurt and humiliated to resolute and scornful.

She grabbed a napkin and used it to wipe away the last of her tears. She got to her feet, collected her jacket and her backpack, and gave Pallas a steely smile.

"You're right," the woman said. "He's a dickhead. Used me to do all the work on those papers he had to turn in for his history and English classes. I'll make sure every woman on campus gets the news."

She turned and strode toward the door, chin high, shoulders back. Ambrose opened the window and took a quick look at the departing woman. Her aura had undergone a transformation. A moment ago it had been pale with humiliation and hurt. Now it was stronger, determined.

Pallas sat down. He closed the window. He didn't need it to see that her amazing eyes were a little brighter than they had been a moment ago and her aura was quite . . . fierce. He could not think of another word to describe it. The energy in the atmosphere around her was already lessening rapidly, sinking back to what he thought of as normal for her.

"Do you mind if I ask what just happened?" he said.

She gave him a cool smile. "I did a little quick redecorating. You'd be amazed what you can do with a fresh coat of paint."

"Excuse me?"

"Never mind. Your reflexes are rather extraordinary, aren't they? It was as if you knew that tray was going to fall before dickhead crashed into the server."

Translated, he wasn't going to get an answer to his own question. Fair enough. He was the one asking for help. That made him the one who was supposed to produce explanations.

"You wanted to know how my aura reading changed," he said. "The answer is that my ability got stronger. Sharper. In the past I viewed energy fields through a fogged-up window. Since San Diego I've been able to open the window."

"What, exactly, do you see when you read auras?"

"The future."

CHAPTER SIX

ER FIRST REACTION was acute disappointment. It was a ridiculous response, given her recent experience. She and Talia and Amelia had spent the past few months interviewing people who claimed to have paranormal talents. As far as they could tell they had encountered only frauds, fakes, and the sadly deluded. But she had allowed herself to believe this time was different.

"I should have known better." Pallas picked up her phone and dropped it into her messenger bag. "This was a complete waste of time. Thanks for the wine. You can pay for the bar food, too, since you ate most of it. I'm going back to my room to pack. Long drive back to Keeley Point. Now that I think about how much this trip cost me, I ought to make you pick up the hotel bill and gas as well."

He didn't look surprised by her abrupt decision to exit the scene. He regarded her with weary resignation.

"Will you give me a couple of minutes to explain?" he asked quietly.

"What is there to explain?" She ought to be sliding out of the booth, but for some reason she hesitated. "You think you can see the future. *The Lost Night Files* does not do shows featuring fortune-tellers, palm readers, and storefront psychics. I don't know what sort of scam you're trying to run here, but I don't have time for it."

"I'm not claiming that I can tell you what will happen tomorrow or in ten days. I can't even tell you what's going to happen in ten minutes. But when I focus on someone's aura I can usually figure out what they are going to do a split second from now. It's all there in the energy field."

She tightened her grip on the strap of the messenger bag, but she did not get to her feet. "I don't understand."

"There is a flash of intent before the action takes place. There's nothing paranormal about it, at least not in the way most people define the paranormal. It's the biophysics of the human nervous system. Neurons, synapses, and electrical and chemical signals. After San Diego I began to realize that I'm picking up some of the energy of those signals in an individual's aura. Most of the data goes by too fast, lightning fast, and it's too complicated for me to interpret, but I'm learning to read the hot stuff."

She would give him a few more minutes, she decided. It wasn't like she had anything better to do tonight. She did not want to drive the twisty highway out of town this evening. The forecast was calling for fog.

"What do you call 'the hot stuff'?" she asked.

He moved one hand in a small, dismissing gesture. "Big physical actions are fairly straightforward, especially if they are driven by strong emotions. Dickhead's aura told me he was furious and frustrated and a little panicky. I knew he was going to leap out of that chair a split second before he did, and I could tell that his trajectory was going to send him crashing into the server."

"You're saying you developed this enhanced ability after you woke up on that beach in San Diego?"

"Everything about my aura reading was more powerful after I woke up," he said. "Something happened to me during those hours that I can't remember. Whatever it was also triggered the nightmares and sleepwalking."

"Those are the problems that eventually caused you to book the sleep study here in Carnelian."

"During which I'm almost positive I witnessed the body of a dead woman being taken away in a laundry cart," he concluded.

"Have you noticed any changes in your aura reading talent since the night of the sleep study?" she asked.

"No." He looked at her with his ghost-ridden eyes. "But like I said, the nightmares and the sleepwalking have gotten worse."

Pallas tapped one finger against the surface of the table and took a moment to process what Ambrose was telling her. She told herself she needed to think it through and make a logical decision. But deep down she knew she would not be able to walk away. Not now. The first part of Ambrose Drake's story had too many parallels with what had happened to Amelia, Talia, and herself at the Lucent Springs Hotel. Part two—the story of his night at the sleep clinic, during which he had experienced partial amnesia—raised the frightening prospect that she and her friends might be in danger of a similar repeat episode. They all needed answers.

She could not leave now.

"Judging by the incident with the falling tray a short time ago," she said, "your ability seems useful. You can literally see trouble coming."

"Sometimes," he said. "Aura reading has its uses. But if the nightmares and the constant possibility of sleepwalking are the price I have to pay for that talent, I can't afford it."

She contemplated him for a long, thoughtful moment, and then she understood. A chill snapped across her senses. "You're afraid the talent will drive you mad, aren't you?"

"Or get me killed," he said. "One of these days I'm going to lose control of the catnaps and sleep too long and too deeply. If that happens I might sleepwalk off a cliff."

"Did you lure me here to solve two murders or to find out what happened to you in the Institute?"

His eyes heated. "I think that solving the murders will go a long way toward telling me why I'm sleepwalking and having nightmares."

She made an executive decision. "You've got my attention. I want to hear the whole story of your night in the Institute, but first you need a proper meal. I'm hungry, too. It's getting too crowded in here. Let's go find a restaurant."

"All right," Ambrose said. He paid the bill and reached for his windbreaker. "Thanks. I appreciate this."

"Don't thank me yet." She started to slide out of the booth. "Where are you staying?"

"Same place you are," he said.

That news pinged her intuition. She frowned. "You just happen to be staying at the Carnelian Hotel?"

He sighed. "Yes. And before you ask, no, I did not choose it because I knew you had booked a room there. I picked it because it's the only full-service hotel in downtown Carnelian."

"You wanted access to room service and a bar?"

"I can do without room service and a bar," Ambrose said evenly. "What I'm paying for is a front desk that is staffed twenty-four hours a day. When I'm at home I can barricade the doors and double lock the windows. I've got alarms set up in case I try to get out of the house, and I've put a couple of other security measures in place, but traveling complicates things."

She stared at him, appalled. "You're afraid you'll sleepwalk out of the hotel?"

"This is going to be my first night in an unfamiliar environment since the sleep study," Ambrose said. "What's more, I'm back in the town where the nightmares and sleepwalking took a turn for the worse. I figure if I do end up going for a walk at two in the morning and if I manage not to break my neck on the stairs, the front desk staff will probably stop me in the lobby. At least that's my backup plan."

She took a deep breath. "And I thought I had problems." She started to get to her feet again and found herself pausing. Again.

"What other security measures?" she asked.

Ambrose was on his feet, shrugging into the windbreaker. He frowned. "What?"

"You said you have a couple of other security measures in place to ensure you don't walk out of the house. I wondered what they are."

"Just a couple of alarms. Nothing fancy. Let's go find dinner."

She gave up, cradled the messenger bag in front of her as she always did when she was in an unfamiliar place, and headed toward the door. The big bag would not keep her from stumbling into a hot spot, but it had the potential to help cushion a fall if she went down hard.

She concentrated on forging a path through the crowd, but Ambrose was suddenly there beside her. He wrapped one hand lightly but firmly around her arm. She got the same intense frisson of awareness that his touch had given her earlier at the asylum. She glanced at him.

What aren't you telling me, Ambrose Drake? she wondered.

"What did you find in the asylum that made you so sure someone was murdered on the staircase?" she asked.

"A used hypodermic needle."

"That doesn't seem unusual. Addicts frequently use abandoned buildings as injection sites."

"In places that are routinely used as injection sites, there are always a lot of old needles lying around. I found only one."

"Not much to go on," she warned.

"I know," he said.

CHAPTER SEVEN

I T WAS CLOSE to midnight when Ambrose let himself into his hotel room. He was startled to realize that for absolutely no logical reason he was feeling calmer, more centered. Maybe it was just the result of eating a substantial meal in the company of a woman who understood what he was trying to tell her, a woman who showed no signs of wanting to see him locked up in a psych ward.

In a weird way the evening had given him what felt like a dose of normal, or at least a taste of a new normal. He had been greatly in need of a reminder that there was such a thing as normal, new or otherwise.

He opened his duffel bag and took out the hotel security devices he had brought with him—a motion detector, a door alarm, and portable door and window locks. The goal was not to keep intruders out—it was to keep himself a prisoner.

He moved methodically through the room, positioning the various pieces of hardware. When he was finished he looked around for a large item of furniture to block the door. He settled on the heavy reading chair. After shoving it into position he went into the bathroom to brush his teeth. On the way out he stripped off his shirt. He did not bother to undress. These days he always wore his pants to bed. If he found himself walking down a sidewalk at two in the morning, at least he would not be wearing only his underwear.

He sat down on the side of the bed, reached back into the duffel bag, and took out the length of coiled chain. He looped the chain around one of the bed legs and fastened the manacle on his ankle. He secured the manacle with a combination padlock. His theory was that he would have to be awake in order to spin the dials. It didn't seem like a task he could accomplish while in a sleepwalking state. But who knew?

When he was finished he picked up his phone and checked his messages and email. These days he sorted his correspondence according to his personal triage guidelines. Desperate pleas and warnings from his agent and editor were filed under POTENTIAL CAREER DISASTERS. Anxious inquiries and not-so-veiled threats from members of his family were labeled POTENTIAL INVOLUNTARY COMMITMENT. The third category, THINGS CAN ALWAYS GET WORSE, was reserved for bulletins from Iona Bryant, his virtual assistant.

He checked the subject headings in the emails under POTENTIAL CAREER DISASTERS first, even though he knew what to expect from his agent and his editor. As usual, there were no surprises.

Marketing needs first three chapters of the next Jake Crane novel was from his editor. He recognized a plea for reassurance when he saw one and whipped off the traditional response from a writer who was late on a book. Doing final polish on first three chapters. Will send soon.

The chatty note from his agent was equally transparent: How's it going out there in sunny California? Your editor called again today. She's getting nervous about the next Jake Crane book. I know you're still polishing but could you please send

SLEEP NO MORE

her the first three chapters? We don't want to delay the pub-
lication date of your third book. That would not be good at
this stage of your career. Don't forget, we're up for contract renewal as soon as your next manuscript is accepted.

He copied the response he had used for the email from the editor.
No sense wasting time reinventing the wheel. Doing final polish
on first three chapters. Will send soon.

Most of the communications from his family came in the form of
text messages. There were several of them.

From his sister, Hannah: Better call Mom. She's getting anxious. Says she hasn't heard from you in a week.

He sent the standard excuse, the one that had been refined by
writers over the centuries. Remind Mom I'm on deadline. Will call
as soon as I get this book finished. Next contract depends
on completing it in a timely manner.

The message from his brother, Ethan, was succinct. Everything
okay on your end? Dad's worried. He responded with a reply that
was only a partial lie. All good. Holed up in a hotel on the
coast. Working twenty-four-seven to finish this book.

When he was finished he braced himself and opened category
three, THINGS CAN ALWAYS GET WORSE. Most of the items under
that heading had already been handled by his virtual assistant. He
had been able to dump most of the routine chores of life on her capable virtual shoulders, buying himself time to try to write and deal
with the fallout from San Diego. But there were always things that
needed his personal attention. He glanced at the list of queries and
updates.

Request for a virtual chat from a writers'
organization. I told the organizer you would not be

available for any speaking engagements in person or
online until you finish your current manuscript.

Your housekeeper reported that your kitchen
faucet was leaking. I scheduled a plumber.
Housekeeper will meet him at the door and let him in
with her key.

Request for a podcast interview. Looks like a small
platform. Very few subscribers. Probably why they
contacted me instead of your publicist at the
publishing house. I forwarded it to her for
consideration.

Updated all of your social media platforms with
creatives reminding readers that the paperback
edition of *A Fall of Shadows* is out and available
everywhere.

The last email was more personal. I hope the writing is going
well. Let me know if you need anything. Meanwhile, don't
worry. Everything on this end is under control.
His two favorite words in the English language. *Under control.* If
only.
He dashed off a quick email.

Thanks, Iona. Don't know what I'd do without you. All
is well here. Polishing first three chapters for the
editor. How is the beta testing going on that new
game?

Iona's response zinged back a moment later.

So glad the writing is going well. The new game is
amazing. Performance testing now. With the right
marketing rollout this one could be huge.

They should give you a piece of the financial action if
that happens, Ambrose responded. After all, you and the other
beta testers are essentially providing the developer with
free consulting.

I know, but it's fun.

Ambrose set the thirty-minute alarm on the phone and put the device on the bedside table. The chain attached to his ankle clanked as he stretched out on top of the bed. The sound brought to mind a nest of mechanical rattlesnakes.

That image produced another one. During dinner Pallas Llewellyn had shown him the drawing she had made while she was inside the asylum—a scene of snakes gliding down the old staircase and disappearing into the shadows.

By the end of dinner they had formulated a strategy. It started with an early-morning return to the ruins of the Carnelian Psychiatric Hospital for the Insane. Pallas had explained that she needed more context to interpret her drawing. He understood. The more context he had, the easier it was to read auras.

He stopped mulling over the plans for the morning and allowed himself to think about Pallas Llewellyn. Her energy whispered to his senses in a way he could not explain. All he knew was that it felt good to be near her. He was no longer alone in his quest. He had a partner.

CHAPTER EIGHT

T HE STRUGGLE DIDN'T last long," Pallas said. "Whatever went down here happened quickly. It was all very sudden and very violent."

Ambrose studied the staircase that connected the four floors of the Carnelian Psychiatric Hospital for the Insane. It was a little after eight o'clock and he had his second grande-sized cup of take-out coffee in one hand. These days he relied on large quantities of caffeine in the mornings in an effort to ward off the effects of limited and disrupted sleep. Pallas, he noticed, had stopped after one regular-sized serving.

The morning coastal fog was light and wispy, but it was enough to blot up most of the sunlight and drape the ruins in gloom. They had used his car to make the four-mile drive from Carnelian. There had been almost no traffic on the narrow road.

"In the real world that's how violence usually works," he said. "It's more likely to be impulsive and explosive than well-planned and carried out with control. Adrenaline always kicks in, regardless of whether or not there was some planning."

He watched Pallas as she stood at the foot of the staircase. The messenger bag was on the floor at her feet. Her arms were folded beneath her breasts in a gesture that struck him as protective. When she moved, she did so with exquisite caution. He did not need to view her aura to see the tension radiating from her in waves.

The knowledge that she was reacting to the dark vibes in the atmosphere was incredibly reassuring. She was for real.

"You know a lot about violence," she said. She did not take her eyes off the staircase.

"These days I can usually see it coming if I watch for it. You'd be amazed how many people are walking around with a lot of anger just beneath the surface. Makes you realize how thin the veneer of civilization and good manners really is."

"I know what you mean," she said. "I've always been easily startled, but these days I feel like I'm on a dark ride at an amusement park—one of those tunnels of terror. Every time I turn a corner I never know what's going to pop out at me. I'm getting better at learning how to keep my new vision under control, but it's been a steep learning curve."

"Same with me," he said.

"Ever get flashbacks?" she asked.

"I think so but I can't be certain. Memory is a tricky thing."

She frowned. "But you do remember details like the laundry cart."

"Any cop will tell you eyewitnesses are notoriously unreliable."

She took her attention off the staircase and gave him a speculative look. "You think that whatever happened here on this staircase and at the Institute is connected to that night you lost in San Diego, don't you?"

"The writer in me doesn't like coincidences, but logic tells me I have to allow for the element of random chance." He drank some coffee and lowered the cup. "I should also make room for the possibility that my family might be right. Maybe I'm having some version of a nervous breakdown."

Her brows rose. "Pretty sure that term is no longer used to describe psychological disorders."

"Semantics. You know what I mean."

"Yes, I do, and even by your out-of-date terminology it's safe to say your diagnosis is wrong."

He looked at her. "What makes you so sure?"

"I think it's clear that the common understanding of a so-called nervous breakdown is that when stress becomes so overwhelming an individual can no longer function well enough to deal with normal life. He can't work. Can't make plans. Can't focus. He retreats from the world."

"You just described my life. I'm late on a book and I haven't written a page since before the sleep study. I'm in danger of single-handedly destroying my career. I'm avoiding my family and my agent and my editor. And, oh, yeah, my ex dumped me."

"You have been forced to shift priorities," Pallas said. "That is a very different matter. You are trying to research the mysteries in your own past and, oh, by the way, you need to solve a couple of murders to achieve that goal. To that end you have developed a strategy, i.e., drag the *Lost Night Files* podcast crew into the investigation. You conducted a test of the investigator who showed up at the scene of the crime and concluded she was for real. Said investigator, despite being pissed off, has agreed to assist you. We are now moving forward with a coherent strategy. I'd say you've definitely got your act together. You are not falling apart."

He watched her for a long moment. "Hadn't thought about it in that light."

"Obviously. So here we are at the start of a new investigation for *The Lost Night Files*." Pallas cleared her throat. "You do realize we're a bunch of amateurs, right? I mean, you're not under the impression that my friends and I are trained journalists or licensed private investigators, are you?"

"Nope. I think I mentioned I used to be in the security business before I got the cool writing gig. I know how to run a basic background check. Frauds tend to leave a lot of red flags behind."

"So why come to us instead of hiring professionals?"

"Two reasons. The first is that I doubt a professional would believe my story. The second is that I have a reputation to protect. I can't afford to have my publisher and my agent conclude that I'm a whack job who believes in the paranormal."

"How will you explain contacting *The Lost Night Files?*"

Ambrose smiled. "That's easy. I'm doing research for a Jake Crane book."

Pallas narrowed her eyes. "I'm not sure how I feel about that."

"Don't worry, I'll mention *The Lost Night Files* in the acknowledgments."

"Gee, thanks." She turned her attention back to the staircase. "All right, you gave me an outline of what happened last night at dinner. Walk me through it again."

"A couple of weeks ago I got a message from a guy named Emery Geddings telling me he had information about what happened during my sleep study at the Institute. He reminded me that he had been on duty as Dr. Fenner's assistant that night. He promised to give me hard evidence of what was going on at the Institute. He wanted money. A lot of it. I agreed to pay him but I insisted on verifying the so-called evidence first. He set up the meeting here at the asylum."

"Did he say anything about a death at the Institute?" Pallas asked.

"No, but he indicated he had information regarding something that had happened to me. That was enough to get my attention."

"What time were you supposed to meet Geddings here?"

"He stipulated midmorning because there would probably be fog. Less chance of someone noticing my car. That was fine by me. I live in the Sonoma wine country. It's about a three-hour drive to Carnelian. I got here at eight thirty. When I arrived there was no other vehicle parked in front of the asylum. I figured Geddings was late. I came inside to wait. He never showed up. I assumed he had changed his mind. But something felt off."

"Such as?"

He gestured toward the staircase. "There was an undisturbed layer of dust on the upper steps, but the bottom steps were smeared. I could make out what looked like a boot print on the bottom and a handprint on the railing. It's harder to see now, because it's been a couple of weeks and there's a fresh coating of grime."

"Show me where you found the used hypodermic needle."

He pointed toward the rusted bedsprings a few feet away. "Under that old bed. My theory of the crime is that someone used a powerful sedative to subdue or murder Geddings. Maybe there was a short struggle before the drug took effect. Whatever—the killer dropped the needle and either didn't bother to search for it later or didn't think it would be a problem."

"Because even if it was found, it would look like an addict had used it and discarded it," Pallas concluded.

"Right."

She waited a beat.

"Go on," she said when he didn't continue his tale.

He drank some more coffee while he contemplated the staircase. "The use of a drug as a murder weapon points toward the Institute, but I admit it's a very thin piece of evidence."

Her eyes widened. "You think the director of the clinic, that doctor you mentioned—"

"Fenner. Conrad Fenner."

"Do you think he murdered Geddings?"

"If he found out that Geddings was going to sell me information about what happened at the clinic that night, he had motive."

"Was Geddings a big man?" Pallas asked.

"Over six feet and solid."

"What about Dr. Fenner?" she asked.

"Shorter and much softer. You're wondering what happened to the body, aren't you?"

"Yes," Pallas said. "That, combined with the fact that no one seems to have reported Geddings's disappearance, raises a few questions. It's not that easy to dispose of a body."

"I'm aware of that." He finished the last of the coffee. "I write thrillers for a living, remember? Or at least I used to."

"Any idea why Geddings wanted to meet you here at the asylum?"

"I assume it's because of the remote location and the limited access. Just the one narrow road. You can see a vehicle coming long before it gets here."

Pallas gave him a very bright smile. "Assuming you don't happen to be in a trance."

Ambrose raised his empty cup in a faint salute, silently acknowledging the accusation that he had taken her by surprise. "When you think about it, this makes a logical rendezvous point. Everyone's got a camera these days. The one thing you can be sure of out here on the cliffs is that no one is hiding in the bushes. There aren't any."

Pallas shuddered and looked up the staircase. "This place is horrible. I don't even want to think about what it must have been like to be locked up in one of those little rooms."

"Given your claim that you can draw the energy left at the scene of a death and my claim to being able to see human auras, there's a damn good chance that, a few decades ago, both of us would have wound up in a place like this."

"I know." Pallas turned away from the staircase and picked up her messenger bag. "I've seen enough. Let's get out of here."

"Good idea."

Without another word he wrapped his fingers around her arm and steered her gently through the rubble. She did not attempt to pull away.

She did not ask any more questions until they were in the car, driving down the narrow, badly rutted lane that would take them back to the main road.

"Tell me again what you recall about the night in the Institute," she said.

"I checked in shortly after ten," he said. "I was in bed and hooked up to the monitors before eleven. That's early for me. I'm a late-night person these days, but the clinic has rules. I planned to read for a while before I tried to sleep."

"Before you *tried* to sleep?"

"Dr. Fenner assured me that many people are surprised to discover that they sleep surprisingly well in a sleep study. He suggested it's because they register it as a safe place. He had a point. I knew that if I did have nightmares or try to sleepwalk, the staff would awaken me. He was right about one thing—I went to sleep as soon as I turned off the reading light."

"Even though you were in unfamiliar surroundings. Interesting."

"But not uncommon, according to Fenner. The next thing I knew, I heard a woman scream, or at least I thought I did. I woke up, but I was groggy and very disoriented. Hallucinating. At first I did not know where I was."

"Are you sure it was a woman who screamed?" Pallas asked.

"Good question. No, I can't be absolutely positive, but I think it was a woman. What's more, I think it was the woman who checked in ahead of me that night."

Pallas turned quickly in the seat. "The woman you think was murdered was also a patient?"

"All I can say for certain is that a woman checked in about the same time I did. She was escorted to the room next to mine, room B. There were no other patients that night. For some reason—maybe because I didn't see any other women around—I assumed she was the one who screamed."

"Did a receptionist handle the check-in process?"

"No. Fenner did. There was no receptionist on duty that night."

"What's the next thing you remember?"

"I was outside my room, viewing the world the way I do when I'm using my aura reading vision. I don't see physical details well, but I could make out what looked like a large laundry cart. Someone was pushing it down a hallway. I tried to ask what was going on. No one answered, but I know the figure pushing the laundry cart heard me, because he moved more quickly. He and the cart disappeared through the swinging doors."

"Any idea why you wanted to follow the cart?"

"There was blood dripping from the bottom."

Pallas drew a sharp, audible breath. "Okay. Good reason."

He paused to make sure she understood. "I *think* I saw blood dripping from the cart. I also remember seeing a stream of blood beneath the doorway of room B. I bent down to get a better look. Started to lose my balance. I put my hand on the floor to keep from falling. My fingers went into the pool. It was wet and sticky."

"That sounds like a real memory," Pallas said.

"Fenner shouted at me. I'm pretty sure I felt a needle in my shoulder."

"He sedated you?"

"I think so. I remember sitting in a chair while he wiped the blood off my hand. The next thing I knew I was in the bed and Fenner was reattaching the electrodes. Suddenly it was five o'clock in the morning."

"Did you awake refreshed, as if you'd had a normal sleep?"

"No, I was groggy, but otherwise I was okay. Fenner came into the room. Acted like nothing had happened. He removed all the sensors and wires. I tried to tell him what I thought I'd seen. He said I'd had a nightmare and had experienced an episode of sleepwalking. I got dressed. He took me to his office. I was supposed to get the results of the sleep study. Fenner handed me a summary and assured me that aside from the nightmare and sleepwalking event, my NREM and REM patterns were normal and undisturbed."

"Non–rapid eye movement and rapid eye movement cycles?"

"Right. In addition, there were no indications of oxygenation, heart rate, or blood pressure issues. No signs of sleep apnea. In short, my sleep patterns were stone-cold normal, with the exception of the sleepwalking. He suggested I consult a psychiatrist."

"What do you know about Fenner?" Pallas asked.

"At the time I didn't do a lot of research. My brother had already vetted Fenner. I did take a quick look online. Fenner has all the appropriate degrees and licenses, he specializes in dream disorders, and the Institute is affiliated with Carnelian College. That seemed enough to go on. It was just a simple sleep study. I booked the appointment."

"You said you didn't do a lot of research on Fenner at the time," Pallas noted. "But I'm guessing you know more about him now?"

"When I started getting flashbacks that I thought were linked to my night in the Institute, I took a more in-depth look at Fenner. The only obvious red flag was his career path. He started out as a star in his field. Worked as a lead researcher at a major pharmaceutical company. But his career trended downward after he left the firm. I asked a friend, Calvin, who is a magician when it comes to researching in the online world, to take a deeper look."

"And?" Pallas said.

"And that's when I discovered that Fenner was forced out of his position at the pharmaceutical firm for violating research protocols."

"That doesn't sound good," Pallas said.

"It gets worse. He was terminated from his next position after being accused of falsifying the results of his research. I know, I should have done a better background check on Fenner. In my own defense and in defense of my brother, all I can tell you is that neither of those two scandals is easy to find online. Both pharmaceutical companies buried the records as deeply as possible because the truth would have embarrassed the firms and affected stock prices."

"You said Fenner suggested you consult a psychiatrist. Did you?"

"I made an appointment with one after the flashbacks started, but I canceled it."

"Why?"

"Take a guess," Ambrose said.

She nodded. "You were afraid of the diagnosis."

"I'm either having flashbacks or I'm hallucinating," Ambrose said. "Neither lends itself to a diagnosis of sound mental health."

"Have you talked to anyone else about your experience at the Institute?"

"No. The only person I might have tried to discuss it with is Maureen, but she had already ended things by then."

"Maureen?"

"My ex. She gave up on me a few weeks after San Diego." He stopped at the junction of the lane and the main road and then turned toward Carnelian. "She assured me it was me, not her."

"I've heard that one a couple of times myself," Pallas said. "It never gets better."

"No, and in my case it was true."

"Did you see the other patient the next morning?" Pallas asked.

"No. I asked about her. They told me she had checked out ahead of me. I didn't know what to believe at that point. I couldn't think clearly. But later when I was in the car I noticed some reddish-brown stuff under my fingernails."

"Blood?"

"I'm sure of it."

Pallas watched him for a long moment.

"What are you thinking?" he said.

"That it's time to go to step two of our strategy," Pallas said. "Lucky for us, Carnelian has a very handy local legend."

"The Carnelian ghosts? I saw something about it in the guide-book in my room. The last descendant of the town's founder went mad. Thought he was being haunted by the ghost of his wife, who died in the asylum."

"Yep, that's the legend," Pallas said. "Our cover story is simple and straightforward. The *Lost Night Files* crew is in town to answer the burning question 'Was Xavier Carnelian murdered by the ghost of his dead bride, Catherine?'"

"Do you really think this is going to work?"

"Trust me," Pallas said. "Everyone wants to be on a podcast."

CHAPTER NINE

S MALL BELLS TINKLED merrily when Pallas and Ambrose walked into **Prism: Your destination for all things metaphysical.** Pallas stopped just inside the door and gave herself a moment to absorb the good energy that flooded the little shop.

She had occasionally visited stores featuring crystals, candles, chimes, and other assorted products promoted as having the potential to elevate good energy in a space, but this was the first time she had encountered the real deal. Prism was awash in balanced and harmonious vibes.

"Wow," she said. She looked around in wonder. "Just wow."

Ambrose raised his brows in silent inquiry.

The woman behind the counter was unpacking a carton filled with various colored crystals swathed in a lot of bubble wrap. She smiled a warm smile.

"I'll be right with you," she said.

She spoke in a gentle, sparkling voice that made Pallas think of musical instruments. It was a voice that suited the scent of incense in the atmosphere. The rest of her went with the ethereal voice. She appeared to be in her late twenties, but she could have been a few years older. She had the delicate features and good bones that ensured she would always look younger than her real age.

"I'm Pallas Llewellyn and this is Ambrose Drake," Pallas said. "Are you Serenity?"

"Yes," Serenity said. "Welcome to Carnelian and to Prism."

"Nice to meet you," Ambrose said. "Sorry, I didn't catch your last name."

"I stopped using it a few years ago," Serenity said. "It was one of the ways I severed my connection to some bad energy in my past."

"I see." Ambrose went forward a few steps to examine a large metal gong that stood atop a pedestal. "Interesting shop you've got here."

"Thanks," Serenity said. "Prism has been a legacy institution in Carnelian for decades. Years ago it was founded by a meditation master who searched the entire coast of California to find the right place for the shop. She said Carnelian had the positive energy she needed. Each successive owner has taken care to make sure the shop passes into the hands of someone who understands that Prism has a mission."

"What is the mission?" Ambrose asked.

Serenity rewarded his brusque question with a gracious smile. "We like to think that we are selling products that are infused with the good energy in this area."

"Right," Ambrose said, not bothering to conceal his skepticism. He moved to examine a row of crystal pyramids.

Pallas shot him what she intended as a quelling look. They had agreed that she would conduct the interview. He was supposed to play the part of scriptwriter and assistant. He caught her eye and shrugged.

She turned back to Serenity. "Don't mind my assistant. He gets paid to be skeptical. The podcast attracts a lot of fakes and frauds."

"Of course," Serenity said. She chuckled. "I understand. You'd be surprised how many fakes and frauds there are in my business. Mr. Drake has every reason to be skeptical. When I walk into other shops that cater to the same market Prism does I'm inclined to be skeptical, too. But generally speaking, it isn't difficult to decide if others share the vision of Prism."

Pallas took another look around the shop. "You are trying to help your customers find harmony and balance."

Serenity almost glowed. "Exactly. I'm so pleased you understand." She glanced at Ambrose. "Not everyone does."

"We got your message," Pallas said. She tightened her grip on the messenger bag and moved toward the counter. She was not as concerned with stumbling over bad energy as she was with maneuvering her messenger bag through the rows of glass shelving filled with delicate crystals, chimes, incense burners, and dainty teacups. "Thank you for offering to speak to us about the Carnelian ghosts."

"You are very welcome, but I'm sure you're being inundated with offers from people who want to talk about the local legend. Everyone in town will be thrilled to know that our ghosts will be featured on your podcast. I'm sure you know the story?"

"I think so," Pallas said. She made it to the front counter without incident and set her big bag on the floor. She took out a notebook. "From what we've been able to tell, it's a classic ghost story. *The Lost Night Files* doesn't usually do that kind of thing, but the asylum connection in this case makes it potentially interesting."

Ambrose spoke from the other side of the shop. "We understand there is a history of disappearances associated with the old hospital for the insane."

"Sadly, yes," Serenity said. "They say the patients who were committed there walked through the front doors and were never seen again. To be honest, that was probably true of most old asylums."

"Families had their mentally ill relatives committed as a way of making them disappear from society," Ambrose said. "Wouldn't want rumors of insanity in the bloodline to get around."

"It was also a convenient technique for getting rid of 'troublesome' women or those who were standing in the path of a lot of money," Pallas said.

"That's certainly what happened to poor Catherine Carnelian," Serenity said. She glanced at Ambrose and then looked down at the large messenger bag beside Pallas. "Aren't you going to record me?"

"We're just gathering background at this stage," Pallas said smoothly. "We haven't decided if we're going to do the story."

"Oh." Disappointment flashed briefly in Serenity's eyes, but she brightened immediately.

Pallas flipped open her notebook. "What do you know about the history of the Carnelian Psychiatric Hospital for the Insane?"

"What everyone here in town knows," Serenity said. She smiled. "It's haunted, of course. What abandoned asylum isn't?"

"What's the story of the haunting?" Pallas asked.

"There are a lot of stories," Serenity said, "because many of the patients died there, including Catherine Carnelian. But the most well-known haunting didn't take place in the asylum. According to the legend, Xavier Carnelian, the last descendant of the town's founder, ran through the fortune he inherited from his lumber baron father and married Catherine for her money. As far as anyone knew, she was alone in the world. The assumption is that he planned to get rid of her after the wedding, but he found out that her trust fund paid out only as long as she was alive. That meant he had a problem."

"He couldn't arrange for a convenient lethal accident," Ambrose said. "The money would have stopped."

"Exactly," Serenity continued. "So he did the next best thing. Two months after the marriage he got poor Catherine declared incurably insane and had her committed to the local asylum. But much to his horror she died a year later. Carnelian tried to keep her death a secret. He paid the hospital authorities to pretend Catherine was still alive. But this was a very small town, and several of the locals worked at the hospital. The rumors of Catherine's death soon began to circulate, but they didn't reach the bankers in New York."

"Because the hospital agreed to keep the death a secret?" Pallas said.

"Right," Serenity said. "At the time, Xavier Carnelian owned this town, and that meant he controlled everything, including the hospital, which, as it turns out, was raking in a lot of cash from people who were happy to pay whatever it cost to keep difficult relatives out of sight."

Ambrose picked up a glass candleholder and checked the price on the bottom. "When you think about it, Carnelian had every reason to think he could keep his wife's death a secret indefinitely. If someone had come around demanding proof that Catherine was alive, it would have been easy enough to pass off one of the other lost souls in the asylum as the real Catherine."

Serenity raised her delicate brows, clearly impressed by his logic. "Exactly. The plan should have worked. But then, of course, Xavier Carnelian became convinced that Catherine was haunting him. He went mad and fell to his death. Now his ghost haunts the old Carnelian mansion."

Pallas looked up from her notes. "One of the clerks at the hotel front desk told us that Carnelian was afraid to go to sleep at night because he feared he would be awakened by Catherine's ghost looming over the bed with a butcher's knife in her hand."

"That's the story," Serenity said. "They say he walked the floors of his mansion all night long. One morning, the housekeeper found him dead at the foot of the stairs. He had fallen and broken his neck."

Pallas smiled. "And not long afterward, Catherine's long-lost twin sister, Eugenia, turned up to claim the inheritance."

Serenity chuckled. "The rest, as they say, is local history. The twins had been separated at birth. Eugenia had ended up in an orphanage. She didn't learn the truth about her family until she saw the news of Xavier Carnelian's death in the papers. That was when she discovered that the sister she had never known had been married to Xavier and that there was a large inheritance. It was Eugenia who founded the college and built the library and the hospital in town. She also made certain that the director of the asylum was replaced with a proper, modern-thinking doctor. Eventually, of course, the asylum was closed altogether."

"And to this day, the ghost of Xavier Carnelian haunts his old mansion and his dead wife haunts the ruins of the asylum," Pallas concluded. She tapped her pen against the page of her notebook. "It's an interesting story, but there's no real mystery to investigate."

"What about the mystery of Xavier Carnelian's death?" Serenity asked. "Did he fall down those stairs by accident or was he pushed by the ghost of his wife?"

"Pretty sure he was pushed," Ambrose said. "Probably by the long-lost sister who decided to avenge Catherine's death and claim the fortune."

Pallas and Serenity both looked at him.

"I haven't heard that twist on the legend," Serenity said.

"What makes you think that's what really happened?" Pallas asked.

Ambrose set the candleholder on the shelf. "Speaking as a writer, I can tell you that you can never go wrong using revenge as a motive."

Serenity's eyes widened. "You're a writer?"

Ambrose gave her a polite smile. "Yes. *The Lost Night Files* has been kind enough to let me accompany Pallas on this case. I'm doing research."

"I've been thinking about writing a book," Serenity said.

"Is that so?" Ambrose said.

"I'm going to call it *The Crystal Path: Ten Steps to Finding Your Power.*"

"That's great," Ambrose said. "Good luck with your writing."

"Thanks," Serenity said. "What kind of books do you write?"

"Thrillers," Ambrose said.

"What name do you write under?"

"My own."

"I've never heard of you."

"I get that a lot," Ambrose said.

Pallas cleared her throat. "I think we're finished here. Thank you for your help, Serenity. Really appreciate the background on the ghost story."

"You're welcome," Serenity said. "But I hope I haven't discouraged you from investigating the mystery of Xavier Carnelian's death. People here in town will be very disappointed if you decide not to do a podcast on our local legend."

Pallas leaned down to pick up her messenger bag. "An investigation of Carnelian's fall down the stairs is looking less and less likely, but we did hear a rumor of a recent disappearance out at the old asylum that sounds promising."

"Really?" Serenity stared at her, bewildered. "Who told you that?"

"We can't discuss our sources," Pallas said. "Not at this stage. We're still trying to verify the facts. You'd be surprised how often people plant a fake story to get our attention. Everyone wants to be on a podcast these days."

Serenity's expression cleared. "I suppose it's the new version of fifteen minutes of fame. Trust me, if someone had disappeared out there in the ruins, it would have been front-page news here in Carnelian."

"Not if there was no evidence and no missing person report," Ambrose said.

"I don't understand," Serenity said. "If there is no evidence and no report of a missing person, what makes you think someone disappeared?"

"Bad vibes," Pallas said, going for an ominous tone.

Serenity's elfin queen face tightened, first with disappointment and then with gentle disapproval. "Is your podcast fiction? If so, you really ought to make that clear."

"Oh, our programs are based on real cases," Pallas said. "That's why we do a lot of fact-checking first. Thanks, again, for your help."

"Anytime," Serenity said. She no longer sounded as warm and enthusiastic as she had a short time earlier. "Who else will you be talking to?"

Ambrose took a small spiral notebook out of the pocket of his jacket and flipped it open. "The reference librarian at the public library recommended that we interview the caretaker out at the cemetery, Ron Quinn."

"That makes sense," Serenity said. "No one knows local history as well as someone who tends the graves at the cemetery."

Pallas hitched the strap of the messenger bag over one shoulder and turned to make her way back through the maze of glass shelves. But she paused to take one last look around at the assortment of chimes, crystals, candles, books, and herbal teas.

"I do have one more question," she said. "Do you really believe there is such a thing as paranormal energy?"

Serenity laughed—a light, lilting laugh. "Of course I do." She waved a graceful hand at the array of metaphysical paraphernalia that filled the shelves and display cabinets. "I'm in the business of selling paranormal energy."

CHAPTER TEN

THE BELLS OVER the door chimed again when Pallas and Ambrose exited the shop. They started walking the two blocks to the Carnelian Hotel.

"I can tell you one thing about Serenity No-Last-Name," Pallas said. "If she hadn't found her calling with Prism she could have made a very nice living as an interior designer."

"Good energy back there?"

"Yes. Didn't you notice it?"

Ambrose squinted a little. "Eh, maybe. I wasn't paying attention to that aspect of things."

"Most people aren't aware of a harmonious interior on a conscious level. They take it as natural and right. We are all more inclined to register a negative vibe and say things like, *I don't like that color* or *What an ugly carpet*. I don't know whether Serenity is consciously or unconsciously arranging those crystals and chimes to achieve a balanced vibe, but regardless, it works."

"I'll take your word for it."

"One of these days I'm going to have to look into using crystals in my work," Pallas mused. "I've always relied on water features, greenery, and color, but there's no reason I can't expand my tool kit."

Ambrose cleared his throat. "About our investigation."

"Right." She pulled her attention back to the problem at hand. "That makes three places we've dropped the rumor this morning: the front desk of the hotel, the library, and the local crystals-and-candles shop. Let's give it a couple of hours. Word will spread quickly in a town this size. Later today we will hit the Institute. The staff will stonewall us, of course, on grounds of patient confidentiality, if nothing else. But someone may be encouraged to come to us later to talk."

"Think so?" Ambrose asked.

"In my experience, people are fascinated by true crime, especially if it's got a paranormal vibe."

Ambrose glanced at her. "You're right. For what it's worth, I'm pretty sure Serenity No-Last-Name was being truthful when she said she wasn't aware of a recent disappearance out at the asylum."

"I'm not surprised."

"She was also telling us the truth when she said she believes in the paranormal."

"Well, that's not surprising, either, is it?" Pallas said. "It explains her career path. She believes in her products and she's on a mission to put good energy out in the world. I used to be on a similar mission, back when I was able to devote myself to my work."

"I came across your website when I did some background checking on you. You're an interior designer. A successful one, from what I could tell."

"I was doing well," Pallas said. "Right up until Lucent Springs. Since then my career has been on a downward trajectory. I can't blame that entirely on Lucent Springs, however. It was my own fault. I made a bad business decision shortly before my amnesia episode."

"What kind of decision?" Ambrose asked.

She hesitated but then reminded herself that he had confided to her that his own career was in trouble because of writer's block.

"I was seeing someone at the time, an architect," she said. "We collaborated on a small boutique hotel project. The clients were pleased. I let Theo talk me into signing a contract with his firm. Unfortunately I didn't consult a lawyer. I thought I was going to become an equal partner. I found out too late I had a fancy title but no real power. I was assigned a project that I absolutely hated. And then Lucent Springs happened."

"What was the project?" Ambrose asked.

"Let's just say happy chickens, laughing pigs, and cheerful cows were involved."

"I don't follow."

She sighed. "I was supposed to design the interiors for a chain of fast-food restaurants. The company execs wanted the logo incorporated into everything—tables, walls, trays, even the restrooms. Do you have any idea how difficult it is to come up with a lot of ways to use images of chickens, pigs, and cows looking delighted by the prospect of winding up in burgers and breakfast patties?"

"You refused to do it."

"Theo was furious, because the client had seen my work and made it clear he wanted me on the project. But by then I was dealing with the fallout from Lucent Springs, so I was not at my best in terms of emotional balance. Theo and I had a terrible fight. He told me my energy-balancing theories were pure bullshit. Woo-woo nonsense. He suggested I might be delusional—well, he didn't suggest it. He stated it."

"You told him how you work?" Ambrose asked.

"Obviously that was a mistake. But up until then he pretended to

SLEEP NO MORE

take my claims seriously. In our last huge fight the truth came out. On top of everything else I discovered he was having an affair with one of the junior architects. That did it. I told him to tear up the contract or sue me. I didn't care. I was never going to do another project with him again."

That was not the whole story of the final confrontation with Theo. It didn't include the part where she had terrified him. But it was enough. She and Ambrose were working together, but that did not mean she had to share her secrets.

Ambrose looked intrigued. "You were heartbroken?"

"No. I was too pissed to be heartbroken. I was also embarrassed. Humiliated. Most of all I was horrified to find out I had been so incredibly naive. As I said, I was in bad shape because of Lucent Springs. Deep down I wondered if Theo was right. Maybe I was delusional. I mean, how does one know?"

"I think it's time you told me about Lucent Springs."

"I think you're right."

CHAPTER ELEVEN

A MELIA, TALIA, AND I lost most of a day and a night in the ruins of an old, abandoned hotel out in the Southern California desert," Pallas said. "Our story has several parallels with your very bad trip to San Diego."

"All three of you suffered an episode of amnesia?" Ambrose said around a bite of pizza. Sunlight sparked on his dark glasses. "On the same night?"

"That's what the emergency room doctor told us," Pallas said. "He had a little trouble explaining why the three of us had lost the same night, of course. I think he privately thought it was some form of group hysteria or that we had gotten very drunk and blacked out. But he was smart enough not to say that out loud."

They were sitting at a picnic table in a small park on the edge of the campus, two large coffees and a supersized pizza between them. Ambrose had ordered pepperoni on his half. Her side was topped with olives and a scattering of hot peppers.

Ambrose regarded her through his dark glasses. "Did the doctor tell you anything else?"

"No. Mostly we wanted to be assured that we hadn't been drugged and assaulted. We were told there were no signs of physical injury, and the drug tests came back negative."

"Drug tests can be inconclusive, especially if you don't know what to test for. He probably just went for the standard stuff. Any bruises indicating injection sites?"

"We didn't find any, and neither did the doctor." Pallas waved a half-eaten slice of pizza in a small arc, remembering the frustration of knowing something bad had happened but being unable to find any evidence of it. "There was absolutely nothing wrong with us except that we had lost several hours of our lives. One afternoon we walked into the lobby of the Lucent Springs Hotel. Early the next morning we woke up on gurneys in what looked like a vintage medical clinic. Everything in between is a blank."

Ambrose went still. "You woke up in a *clinic*? On *gurneys*?"

"An *old* clinic," she said. "It was housed in a section of the hotel that had been closed for decades. The walls were covered in dirty white tiles. The metal cabinets and fixtures were rusted out. I didn't have a lot of time to look around. There had just been an earthquake, and the hotel was on fire."

Ambrose looked stunned. "An earthquake and a fire?"

"The earthquake was small as such things go out here in California. The fire was pretty impressive, however. Anyhow, I remember thinking the interior reminded me of photos I've seen of 1930s-era tuberculosis sanatoriums. There were a lot of them built in the deserts of Arizona and California."

"Were you hooked up to any machines?"

"No, but we were groggy and dizzy. Our vision was blurred." Pallas hesitated. "For the next few days we thought we were seeing things."

"Hallucinating?"

"Yes. We were sure we had been drugged, but we couldn't prove it."

"You said you remember entering the hotel?" Ambrose pressed, very intent now.

"Yes, just as you recall getting into the car that met you in San Diego."

"Did you and your friends know each other before Lucent Springs?" Ambrose asked.

"No. But afterward we decided we had to stick together. We realized we were on our own."

"Because no one believed your story," Ambrose said. His jaw tightened. "I know the feeling."

A chill of understanding went through her. "It was different for you," she said. "Worse, because you were alone. At least I had Talia and Amelia for support. We could assure each other that we weren't going mad."

Ambrose looked as if he wasn't sure what to do with the sympathy. "What happened to the architect?" he said instead.

"As I told you, our personal relationship had begun to deteriorate before Lucent Springs. It fell apart altogether a few weeks afterward. But the business side of things is proving more complicated. He's been texting me lately, asking for a meeting. He doesn't see any reason why we can't work together even though we are no longer dating."

Ambrose nodded in understanding and finished the last of his side of the pizza. He looked at the remaining slice on her side.

"Are you going to eat that?" he asked.

"No, help yourself."

"Thanks." He picked up the slice and took a bite. "Did you and your friends go back to Lucent Springs to see if you could find any evidence?"

"Yes, a few times. Amelia is there now, as a matter of fact. So far we haven't found anything we can use. The fire that followed the earthquake did a lot of damage."

"What about your energy-sensing talent?"

"I've discovered that fire doesn't destroy the kind of energy I sense, but it does alter the vibe. That's the thing about energy, you see. You can't erase it but you can manipulate it. When I go back to Lucent Springs I can pick up some negative energy, but when I try to draw all I get are scenes of storms that I can't interpret, at least not in a meaningful way."

"Go back to the beginning," Ambrose said. "Why were you and your friends at the Lucent Springs Hotel in the first place?"

"It was supposed to be a job." She folded her arms on the table. "The hotel was architecturally interesting, an interpretation of the Frank Lloyd Wright style. But it was never very successful. According to the research Talia did, I was right. It started out as an expensive sanatorium for wealthy people who contracted tuberculosis. It didn't attract many patients, so the owners sold it to a developer, who converted it into a resort. That failed, too. From time to time new owners have come along, picked it up dirt cheap, and then wasted a lot of money trying to restore and reopen it. Nothing seems to have worked. Maybe its history as a sanatorium left too much bad energy around."

"Where is the hotel?"

"Outside the small town of Lucent Springs. About a hundred miles from San Diego. When it was first resurrected as a resort, it was pitched to attract the Hollywood crowd and East Coast vacationers, but it was never able to compete with Palm Springs and Phoenix."

"Location, location, location," Ambrose said. "Go on."

"About seven months ago a privately held corporation purchased the hotel with the intention of restoring it to its original glory days. The plan was to make it a destination spa resort. I was asked to submit a proposal for the interior design work. Talia said she had been contracted to research the history of the hotel. Amelia was supposed to document the project with before and after photographs."

She broke off because Ambrose had finished the pizza and was watching her with an unnerving intensity.

"I'm listening," he said when she fell silent.

"Right." She took a deep breath and regrouped. "Talia, Amelia, and I were instructed to meet at the site of the project. When we arrived we were greeted by a representative of the corporation. He said he would show us around. He opened the lobby door for us and explained that we would need flashlights because the windows were boarded up. We walked into the hotel, and that's the last thing we remember until the earthquake woke us at about four o'clock the next morning."

"That's when you found yourselves on gurneys inside an old clinic."

"We were dazed, trying to understand what was happening, when we realized the place was burning down around us. We barely made it out alive. By the time the first responders arrived most of the structure had been gutted."

"I'm betting the authorities didn't buy your story."

"No," Pallas said, pushing aside memories of the infuriating conversations she and Amelia and Talia had endured with the Lucent Springs police in the wake of the fire, "they did not. And we had no one to back up our version of events. The representative of the corporation who had met us at the hotel vanished. So did the corporation. The email addresses and phone numbers we had used disappeared without a trace."

"How did the fire start?" Ambrose asked.

"We don't know, but the local officials made it clear they thought we were responsible. They graciously allowed that it might have been an accident."

"What about the gurneys and the medical equipment?"

"There was some evidence left of the gurneys because they were made of metal. There was also a lot of old medical equipment from the hotel's days as a sanatorium. None of it proved our story. In the end everyone concluded that the three of us had lost a night either because of drugs and booze or because we were trying to perpetrate a scam in an attempt to get publicity and attention."

"Given that attitude, it naturally follows that you did not mention the fact that you came out of the wreckage of the hotel with an enhanced sensitivity to the paranormal," Ambrose said.

"Nope."

"Did your friends experience similar changes?"

"Each of us got a somewhat different version of sensitivity, but yes, we were all . . . changed by whatever happened that night."

Ambrose watched her. "Did you all possess some sensitivity before Lucent Springs?"

"Yes," she said. "Nothing major—at least, nothing that we thought was a big deal. But looking back, we realize we each possessed what could only be termed a psychic vibe. For the most part we took it for granted. Called it intuition."

It occurred to Pallas that it felt good to be able to talk openly about the lost night to someone who understood, a man who had gone through a similar experience. She and Amelia and Talia had been turning to each other for support and reassurance for months, but they had been forced to hide the truth from their families and friends. Now there was someone from outside their little group who believed that something very weird had happened in Lucent

Springs, someone who claimed to have gone through a similar experience. In spite of herself she smiled.

"What?" Ambrose asked.

"I'm just thinking that it's nice to be able to tell you about Lucent Springs," she said. "I expect this is how people who believe they have been abducted by aliens feel when they get together with others who are convinced they were abducted by aliens."

"I'm okay with that analogy so long as there are no anal probes involved. It's not a good look for an author."

Pallas was in the process of swallowing the last of her coffee. The deadpan comment caught her off guard. She choked on the laughter that welled up out of nowhere, sputtered, spewed, and grabbed a napkin. Ambrose watched, amused.

"I can't believe you made me laugh about Lucent Springs," she said when she finally recovered. "I've raged about it. Been depressed and frustrated about it. I've had nightmares about it and obsessed over it. But this is definitely the first time I've managed to laugh about it."

Ambrose surprised her with a quick grin. "Can't say I've done much laughing lately, either."

He collected the empty coffee cups and the pizza box and rose to dump them into a nearby recycle bin. By the time he returned to the picnic table and sat down, all traces of amusement had disappeared.

"It's the medical equipment connection that worries me the most," he said. "I have no solid memories of the night I lost in San Diego, but I know for certain there was medical equipment involved at the Institute here in Carnelian. I also know that my sensitivity to auras got a lot stronger after the San Diego episode. I started sleepwalking and having intense nightmares, and things got even worse after Carnelian."

Pallas held her breath, waiting for him to come to the same conclusion she and Talia and Amelia had reached, the conclusion that gave them all nightmares.

"Got a theory about what happened to all of us?" she asked.

"I think someone is running experiments with a drug that affects our sixth sense, our intuition, and for whatever reason chose you and your friends and me as research subjects."

Pallas shivered. "You do realize how weird that makes us sound."

"I do," Ambrose said. He got to his feet. "I think it's time to apply more pressure. Let's go interview Dr. Conrad Fenner, director of the Carnelian Sleep Institute. I'm sure he'll be excited to know that he's going to be featured on a *Lost Night Files* podcast."

"Of course," Pallas said. She jumped up and grabbed her messenger bag. "I keep telling you, everyone wants to be on a podcast."

CHAPTER TWELVE

T HE CARNELIAN SLEEP Institute was housed on the ground floor of an imposing but gloom-filled three-story mansion that had once been the private residence of Xavier Carnelian.

In Ambrose's opinion the building had more in common with a mausoleum than the stately home of a wealthy man. The windows were narrow and dark. The extensive gardens that surrounded it should have lightened the atmosphere, but somehow they managed to appear funereal. The upper floors were sealed off with a chain at the foot of the main staircase and a sign that read PRIVATE. The overall effect suited a structure said to be haunted by a man who had been driven mad by the ghost of his dead wife.

Fenner had agreed to see them immediately even though they had arrived without an appointment. That was not a surprise. The small waiting room was empty. It was obvious the Carnelian Sleep Institute was not attracting a lot of business. The middle-aged receptionist had been doing some online shopping when Ambrose and Pallas had walked through the door.

There appeared to be only one other member of the staff in the vicinity—a woman in her late twenties who was dressed in scrubs. She was on her phone. Ambrose did not recognize either of the two employees. He was certain he had not seen them on the night of his sleep study.

He had used the walk from the lobby to Fenner's office to take a look around. His scattered, snapshot memories of the night he had spent in the facility were blurred and distorted, but as far as he could tell they were fairly accurate.

"I'm afraid I don't understand, Mr. Drake." Conrad Fenner clasped his broad hands on top of his desk and peered through the lenses of his black-framed glasses. "May I ask why you are interested in a former employee of the Institute?"

Fenner was exactly as Ambrose remembered—brusque, rigid, and authoritarian. His lousy bedside manner probably explained the vacant waiting room. You had to be desperate to book a consultation with Conrad Fenner. Not surprisingly, he had refused Pallas's request to record the interview. With a cool smile she had taken a small spiral notebook and a pen out of her messenger bag. Fenner had not been happy about that, but his only choice at that point was to refuse to say another word. Instead he had pretended not to care about the notebook. It was clear he would not toss them out of his office until he discovered what was going on.

Ambrose glanced at Pallas. She quietly signaled him to take the lead.

He opened the window in his mind and studied Fenner's aura. There was a lot of hostility in the wavelengths, but there was something else as well—Fenner was nervous. Worried.

That was interesting.

Ambrose changed position ever so slightly in his chair, leaning forward just enough to project some don't-try-to-con-me attitude.

"A couple of weeks ago I was contacted by someone who identified himself as Emery Geddings," he said. "He reminded me that he had been the assistant working the night shift here when I checked in for the sleep study. He claimed to have some information about the results. He said I needed to see them. Geddings and I made an appointment to meet at the old asylum outside of town. He never showed up. He appears to have vanished. Ms. Llewellyn has agreed to help me investigate his disappearance."

Anger and alarm flared hot in Fenner's aura and in his eyes. It didn't require any psychic talent to know that he intended to give them as little information as possible.

Fenner glared at Pallas. "Are you a professional private investigator, Ms. Llewellyn?"

"No." Pallas smiled a smile that did not go below the surface. "Strictly an amateur. But I'm sure you're aware that cold case podcasts are very popular. My associates and I have had quite a bit of experience. Don't worry, I know what I'm doing."

"No, you do not," Fenner grated. "You are a cheap, muckraking promoter. If you were a real investigator you would know that there is no mystery here. Emery Geddings is no longer with the Institute. I have no idea where he is, and even if I did have a forwarding address I would not be able to give you the information. There are laws about that sort of thing."

"Did he quit or was he fired?" Ambrose asked.

Fenner shot him a fierce look. "Geddings left to explore other career opportunities."

"Right," Pallas said. She jotted down a note. "He was fired."

Fenner's jaw clenched but he did not confirm or deny the statement.

"Any idea why Geddings thought I would be interested in some data from my sleep study?" Ambrose asked.

"No," Fenner said. "You were given a printout of the results. You have all the information that was collected that night."

"Except for the video," Ambrose said.

"Because it doesn't exist," Fenner shot back. Anger splashed across his face in blotchy red patches. His pale eyes glittered. "The camera was not working properly. That was explained to you the morning you checked out. The equipment failure was noted in the file. I assure you none of the other information that was collected that night indicates that anything unusual occurred while you were asleep, with the exception of the sleepwalking incident. I recall suggesting that you consult a psychiatrist to deal with your nightmare issues."

"Yes, you did," Ambrose said.

Fenner abruptly pushed himself to his feet. "I'm afraid that is all the time I can spare to deal with this nonsense. I suggest you forget Emery Geddings and his connection with the Institute. There is no story here. Your so-called investigation is a waste of time. If you do or say anything that harms the reputation of the Institute, I assure you the college will sue. You will be made to appear mentally unstable. As for you, Ms. Llewellyn, your podcast will be ruined. Do I make myself clear?"

"Very clear." Pallas dropped her notebook into her messenger bag and stood. "Thank you for your time, Dr. Fenner." She looked at Ambrose. "I think we've learned as much as we can here."

"I agree," Ambrose said. He got to his feet and studied Fenner's wildly flaring aura. "One more question. Do you believe in paranormal energy and psychic talent, Dr. Fenner?"

Fenner's entire face twitched; whether it was in annoyance or anxiety was difficult to say. Both, Ambrose decided.

"Of course not," Fenner said. "You insult my intelligence. If you believe in such nonsense you are delusional. You really should follow my advice and get proper psychiatric care."

"I'll keep that in mind," Ambrose said.

He followed Pallas out the door. They went toward the lobby, but when they reached an intersecting corridor he abruptly turned the corner.

"This way," he said quietly.

He steered her along a white tiled hall marked with two closed doors.

"The lobby entrance is behind us," Pallas said in low tones.

"I know," he said. "These are the rooms where the sleep studies are done. By the way, Fenner was lying when he said he doesn't believe in paranormal energy and psychic talent."

"Really? Now, that is interesting."

"It is, isn't it?" He stopped in front of a door marked A. "This was my room."

He tried the knob. It turned easily. A quick glance inside revealed a pristine room that had been prepared for the next patient. With the exception of the camera and the black box with its array of wires and sensors, the space was furnished to look like a room in a budget motel.

"Sense anything that can tell us something useful?" he asked.

Pallas did not respond. He turned and saw that she had gone very still in the doorway. There was an otherworldly look in her eyes, as if she was looking into another dimension.

"Pallas?" he said.

He was starting to wonder if this was one of those situations that, when you looked back, had seemed like a good idea at the time but which you later regretted. The last thing he wanted to do was send her into another panic, the way he had at the asylum.

But she did not look panic-stricken now. She looked focused. Very, very focused. After a moment she walked deliberately around the room, lightly touching surfaces and objects—the chair, the reading lamp, the camera. When she put her fingertips on the bed she gasped and yanked her hand back as if she had touched a hot stove or a live electrical wire.

"Are you okay?" he asked.

She blinked and seemed to come out of the strange place where she had been seconds ago. "Yes. I've seen enough. I'll need to draw to make sense of the vision."

"There's no time for you to go into an automatic drawing trance here," he said. "Someone is going to come looking for us soon. I want to show you the other room before they throw us out."

"Ambrose, if this is another one of your tests, I don't think you understand how my talent works. I'm not an airport security dog. I don't sniff out guns and illegal drugs."

He touched a fingertip to her mouth. She stopped talking, but her eyes narrowed in an ominous way. Okay, she was pissed. He would deal with it later.

He looked over his shoulder to make sure no one had seen them and then he steered her down the hall to room B. The door opened easily enough, revealing a space that was furnished very much like room A. He moved inside and turned to see how Pallas was reacting.

She had once again gone still. He could tell by her eyes that she was back in that other dimension. He knew she had slipped into her other vision, but this time she looked as if she was viewing a nightmare. He had pushed the envelope a little too far.

"Shit," he whispered. "I didn't mean to drag you into hell. Let's get out of here."

He put his hand on her shoulder, intending to turn her around and guide her back out into the hall. She flinched, and stared at him as if he was a stranger. Hastily he raised his hand so that he was no longer touching her. For a moment she seemed bewildered. Then she closed her eyes.

"Do that again," she whispered.

He hesitated and then cautiously rested his hand on her shoulder. He felt the shiver that went through her, but she did not try to pull away. He was intensely aware of the energy burning in the atmosphere around her. The exhilarating rush of intimacy was heightened by the physical contact—at least that was how it affected him. He couldn't tell if she got the same jolt. She merely nodded once, evidently satisfied, and started to walk slowly around the room. Unsure of what to do, he maintained the connection and moved with her.

He opened his inner window and tried to analyze what he was seeing in her aura. The fire in some of the wavelengths told him that she was in her other vision, concentrating hard, but that was all it told him. He did not see any signs of incipient panic now. She was in control, working her talent.

She stopped twice, once to touch the bed and again to flatten a palm against the top of the bedside table. She flinched violently both times. He could feel frissons of nervy energy coursing through her, but she did not panic.

A moment later she gasped like a swimmer coming up for air. Her eyes burned.

"There's no lamp in this room," she said.

"Is that important?"

"Yes." She glanced at the bedside table and shuddered. "Yes, it's important. That's enough for now. I need to draw."

He took his hand off her shoulder. "Let's get out of here."

They moved out into the hall. He closed the door of the room.

A voice echoed down a corridor. "Mr. Drake? Ms. Llewellyn? Where are you?"

The woman in scrubs who had been on her phone earlier appeared from around the corner. Ambrose was still in his other vision. He could see that her aura was spiking wildly. Suspicion, probably. Or maybe anxiety. Or both.

"I'm afraid we took a wrong turn," Pallas said with a cool, faintly apologetic smile. "We were looking for the lobby."

"This way," the woman said. "I'll show you out."

"Appreciate it," Ambrose said.

He and Pallas walked toward the woman. When they got closer her name tag became legible. He glanced at it and made a mental note. J. LUCKHURST.

"Thank you, Ms. Luckhurst," he said.

"Call me Jodi. It's easy to get lost in this place."

The route back to the reception area took them past the chained staircase. Pallas abruptly stumbled.

"Damn," she muttered.

Ambrose caught her arm and steadied her.

Jodi looked back, frowning in concern. "Are you okay?"

"Yes, I'm fine," Pallas said.

Ambrose glanced up toward the darkness on the landing above. "Is this where Xavier Carnelian broke his neck?"

"Yes," Pallas said.

Ambrose glanced at her.

Jodi's eyes widened. "How did you know?"

"I read the story of the haunting of Carnelian House," Pallas said. "It's in my hotel room."

"Oh, right." Jodi processed that for a beat. "But there are a couple of staircases in this place. How did you know this was the one where Xavier Carnelian died?"

"It's obviously the main staircase in the mansion," Pallas said. "So I just assumed it was the right one."

"That makes sense, I guess," Jodi said. She looked disappointed. She glanced briefly at Ambrose and then turned to Pallas. "I heard you tell Dr. Fenner that you're looking for Emery."

"That's right," Pallas said. "Emery Geddings. Do you know where he is?"

"No, he just took off one day." They walked into the reception area. Jodi gestured at the front door. "There you go."

"Thanks," Pallas said.

The receptionist glared when Ambrose and Pallas walked by her desk.

Ambrose closed his inner window and pushed open the front door. Pallas went past him, her strong features set in resolute lines. He followed her onto the front steps, feeling a sense of relief now that they were out of the dark, claustrophobic confines of the clinic. They walked through the gardens toward the quiet street where his car was parked.

"Are you sure you're all right?" Ambrose asked.

She shot him a fierce glare. "I'm fine. But I need to draw. That's the only way I'll be able to interpret what I saw in those two sleeping rooms."

"What do you think you saw?"

"Bad stuff."

"That's not helpful. Can you be a little more specific?"

"No. I told you, I have to draw first. It's how my talent works, damn it."

"No pressure," Ambrose said.

She gave him a derisive, sidelong glance. "Right. No pressure."

He cleared his throat. "I told you Fenner was lying when he said he didn't believe in the paranormal. He was lying about almost everything else as well."

"Of course he was. He's trying to conceal whatever happened that night." Pallas paused. "You said he lied about almost everything else?"

"He wasn't lying about the camera. Apparently it wasn't working that night. But looking back, it occurs to me that the most interesting thing about that night is that I actually did sleep, and soundly, both before and after the sleepwalking incident."

Pallas gave him a curious look. "So?"

"I can't get past the fact that it is not normal for me to sleep so solidly, not these days. I haven't had a good night's sleep since before San Diego, yet at the Institute I went out like a light."

"Do you think you were drugged?"

"I'm almost positive Fenner gave me an injection to knock me out after the sleepwalking episode, but I know I wasn't medicated earlier when I went to sleep. I would have remembered an injection. I think."

"In fairness, Fenner did tell you that a lot of people who have sleep disorders do just fine during an overnight study," Pallas said.

"I know, but it seems odd in my case. What's more, my sleep issues got worse after the study."

"I don't know why you were able to drift off to sleep that night," Pallas said, "but I can tell that there was a lot of anxiety around your bed."

"Mine?"

"No, I don't think so. Fenner's, probably." Pallas hesitated. "I can also tell you that something terrible happened in room B."

He did not press her. He wasn't going to get anything more out of her until she had a chance to draw.

They got into the car. Ambrose pulled away from the curb. Instead of driving straight back to the hotel, he cruised slowly down the street and turned the corner. The side street allowed a view of the rear of the mansion. There was a small employee parking area. A short flight of steps and a ramp led up to the back door.

Another memory flickered. The sound of swinging doors opening. A draft of damp, chilled night air wafting down the hallway.

"What is it?" Pallas asked.

"The person pushing the laundry cart took it outside through that door," he said. "He must have loaded the body into the trunk of a car and driven it to wherever it was dumped."

"You have to be pretty cold-blooded to haul a dead woman away in a laundry cart and toss the body into the back of a car."

"Yes," he said. "Very cold-blooded."

Pallas fell silent.

He drove to the end of the block, turned another corner, and continued toward the center of town and the hotel.

"No more pop quizzes, okay?" Pallas said after a while.

He stopped at an intersection and glanced at her. "What are you talking about?"

"You deliberately took the wrong turn back there inside the clinic so that you could show me those two rooms. I'm okay with that. It was a reasonable thing to do under the circumstances. But you should have warned me."

"It was a spur-of-the-moment opportunity and I grabbed it. There wasn't time to explain."

"Bullshit. I swear, if you pull one more stunt like that without warning me I'm going to end this investigation and leave you here on your own."

She was sitting very still, staring straight ahead through the windshield. Her hands were in small fists on her lap.

"I'm sorry," he said. "I've been slogging through this mess on my own for a while now. I'm not used to working with a partner."

Pallas shot him a wry smile. "I noticed."

He tightened his hands on the steering wheel and drove slowly through the intersection. "I'm sorry," he said again.

"Forget it. Let's get back to the hotel. I need to draw."

"Do you mind if I ask you one more question?"

"You want to know if I was telling Jodi Luckhurst the truth when I said I guessed that the main staircase was the one on which Carnelian broke his neck."

Ambrose smiled a little. "It wasn't a guess, was it?"

"Nope. I don't need to draw to know that he died on that staircase. What's more, he had a little help going down."

"What makes you sure he was pushed?"

"Someone was there with him, and that someone was savoring the thrill of revenge."

CHAPTER THIRTEEN

A MBROSE DROVE INTO the hotel garage and parked. Pallas got out of the passenger seat. Together they walked to the elevator. She glanced at him, aware that he was having a hard time suppressing his anticipation. He wanted answers. So did she.

"Why do you need to go into a trance before you can draw what you saw back there in the clinic?" he asked.

"Beats me," Pallas said. "All I can tell you is that the trance is a form of automatic drawing but the pictures are not always easy to interpret. The more information I have, the easier it is to understand what my intuition is trying to tell me."

Ambrose considered that while he used the hotel room key card to summon the elevator. "Until I met you I'd never heard of automatic drawing. I was aware of automatic writing. Works like a Ouija board, I think. In the old days fake psychics used it to scam their clients."

Pallas looked amused. "Who says the psychics were all fakes?"

"Good point."

"All I can tell you is that I slide into a trance and start drawing," she said, slipping past him into the elevator. "I can feel the emotions that I'm translating onto the paper, but the pictures come out of a dreamscape."

He followed her through the doorway. "What emotions did you pick up back there in the other patient's room?"

"Rage and panic, mostly," Pallas said. She shivered at the memories. "Pain."

"That fits with my memories," Ambrose said, sounding gratified.

She started to warn him not to leap to conclusions, but she stopped when the elevator doors opened and revealed a large crowd milling around the hotel lobby.

"Uh-oh," she whispered.

"What the hell?" Ambrose said. He glanced past her into the lobby. "Never mind. I see the problem."

Pallas pretended not to see the man who had summoned the elevator. He was looking down at his cell phone and did not notice that the doors had opened. Hastily she punched the button to close the doors. The elevator continued on to the fourth floor.

"I told you there wouldn't be any trouble getting people to talk to us about the local haunted ruins," she said.

"We don't have time to waste listening to half the town tell us they've seen the Carnelian ghosts."

"I've been doing this for a while now," Pallas said. "Trust me, you never know where or how you'll get an important lead."

"Pretty sure it won't be coming from a lot of podcast groupies," Ambrose said.

She smiled. "Says the podcast groupie who dragged me here to investigate two mysterious disappearances."

"That's harsh," Ambrose said.

"But true."

"Well, yeah. But harsh."

CHAPTER FOURTEEN

S HE OPENED THE door of her room with a sense of relief. Ambrose followed her inside.

"This is going to take a while," she warned, setting the messenger bag on the floor beside the table. "Why don't you go downstairs and get a cup of coffee or something? I'll call you when I'm done."

"There's a coffee maker here in your room. I'll be fine."

She glared at him. "I do not want you hovering over me while I'm in a trance."

"Don't worry, I'll stay out of your way." He took his phone from his pocket and then shrugged out of the windbreaker. "I'll check my email. There are bound to be a few updates in the THINGS CAN ALWAYS GET WORSE file."

She couldn't tell if he was joking.

"That sounds ominous," she said.

"It is. Luckily I've got an assistant who can handle just about anything except for the actual writing of my book. I don't know how much longer she's going to be able to hold things together, though."

"*The Lost Night Files* is looking for an assistant who can act as our producer, but we haven't been able to justify the expense. Poor Talia is stuck dealing with all the tech issues."

"I'm not going to be able to justify an assistant, either, not for much longer," Ambrose said, his voice grim. "I need to get my life back."

"We all do." Pallas took her sketchbook and a pencil out of the messenger bag and sat down at the table. "I've never gone into a trance with someone watching me. It's going to feel weird. I might not be able to draw."

"If you can't do your thing with me in the room I'll leave," he promised.

"All right," she said. "But whatever you do, don't startle me or try to bring me out of the trance. Let me come out of it on my own. Is that clear?"

"Yep." He sank down into the large padded reading chair, phone in hand. "Take your time."

She hesitated a moment longer and then decided to give it a try. "I'll do the other patient's room, because I honestly don't think there is much to learn from yours that we don't already know. Lots of anxiety, but that's not helpful. Whatever was going on in room B was a lot more . . . volatile."

She opened the sketchbook, braced herself for the jolt, and slipped into her other vision.

CHAPTER FIFTEEN

I N THE TRANCE *she sees the interior of her hotel room in a ghostly, luminous glow, an eerie radiance that does not come from the visible portion of the light spectrum. It is the light of visions, hallucinations, and dreams. Just as luminol reveals hidden traces of blood at a crime scene, the vision light illuminates the murky layers of human energy that have been laid down over the years. The wispy stuff pools and swirls just above the floor and the bed like low-lying fog.*

There is other energy as well, the vital, compelling heat that is unique to Ambrose. She is getting used to it but she is still fascinated by the effect it has on her. The sense of intimacy is growing stronger with each hour they spend together. She can no longer pretend this is just simple physical attraction. Something else is going on here, something that should probably make her question her response to this man or, at the very least, make her more cautious.

She will worry about it later. Right now she has other priorities. She exerts some willpower and manages to ignore both Ambrose and the murky energy in the suite. She channels memories of what she saw in room B at the Institute and starts to draw . . .

. . . The monster rises from the surgeon's workbench, howling in rage and panic. The storm of chaos is closing in fast. The creature knows that it will bring madness and death. She also knows who did this to her. There is very little time. She will use the minutes she has left to exact revenge. She tries to throw herself at the man who has destroyed her, but the light winks out and there is nothing more . . .

Pallas came out of the trance on a tide of knowing. She did not realize she was crying until Ambrose thrust a couple of tissues into her hand. She blotted her eyes.

"Thank you," she whispered, her voice husky from the tears.

He pulled her up out of the chair and cradled her close. "I know I'm not supposed to interrupt you, but I have to ask, are you all right?"

"Yes. Sorry. Don't worry, I'm out of the trance."

"I thought so."

For a moment she allowed herself to press her face into his shirt. She wasn't accustomed to having someone comfort her when she came out of a particularly bad trance. She discovered she liked it— or, at least, she liked this version of it.

The temptation to sink into the warmth and scent of Ambrose's body was almost overwhelming. It took a lot of determination to pull herself free of his arms and step back. She dabbed at her eyes one last time, well aware that she was not one of those women who look good crying.

Ambrose watched her, eyes tight with concern. "You're sure you're okay?"

"Yes." She tossed the damp tissue into the trash container. "Usually I can keep my emotional distance but sometimes I get a little overwhelmed."

"You were crying."

"I felt so sorry for her."

"The patient in room B?"

"She was going mad, you see. She understood that. She was terrified and enraged, afraid she was turning into a monster. She wanted to kill him. She wanted revenge. No, she wanted justice before she drowned in the chaos, but she didn't get it. He killed her. I think he struck her with the reading lamp." Pallas clenched her fingers into a fist around the pencil. "Again and again. He panicked, you see."

"Who panicked?" Ambrose said. "Who killed the patient in room B?"

He spoke in a very neutral tone. She knew that he was trying not to pressure her for an explanation but that he needed one. She needed some clarification, too. Right now she was still fighting the tide of raw emotion. She struggled to suppress it.

"I can't say for certain," she said, "but you told me that you saw only Fenner and Geddings in the Institute that night. It must have been one of them."

"Unless there was someone else on the scene, someone I never saw," Ambrose said.

"Yes," Pallas said.

She turned back to the table and looked at her drawing. Ambrose moved closer to see the sketch. For a long moment he gazed at the picture with an intent expression. When he finally looked up she saw the sharp light of understanding in his eyes.

"This is Frankenstein's monster," he said.

"It's a cautionary tale. The takeaway of the story is that in the end—"

"The monster turns on the scientist who created him," Ambrose concluded.

"I think that is what happened in room B," Pallas said. "But the doctor killed her first."

Ambrose did not take his eyes off the drawing. "And Geddings helped clean up the scene. It's the only explanation that fits."

"I agree," Pallas said. "But all we've got is a theory."

"We need to identify the patient in room B," Ambrose said. "And then we have to figure out how they made her vanish without anyone noticing."

"First we have to deal with that crowd down in the lobby," Pallas said.

Ambrose groaned. "Are you sure?"

"If you want to retain our cover, we can't ignore all those people who are so eager to give us information."

CHAPTER SIXTEEN

I TOLD YOU TALKING to all those people would be a waste of time," Ambrose said.

"Stop grumbling." Pallas shoved her hands deeper into the pockets of her jacket. "We collected a lot of information. Some of it may prove useful."

Privately she had to admit it had been an incredibly long and boring afternoon, but she was not in the mood to give Ambrose the satisfaction. They had finished the last of the interviews an hour ago and were now walking to a restaurant that had been recommended by the front desk.

"I can't believe how many versions of 'I saw Catherine Carnelian's ghost one night when I drove past the old asylum' we had to listen to this afternoon," Ambrose said. "Not to mention all the sightings of mysterious lights on the upper floors of the mansion."

She smiled in spite of her mood. "You're not really a people person, are you?"

"I'm a writer," Ambrose said. "I can take people in small doses and for limited periods of time."

"Be sure to let me know if you find yourself unable to tolerate my company for an entire dinner tonight. We've already spent a lot of time together. I don't want to exhaust your limited supply of social skills."

"You're different," Ambrose said. He sounded annoyed.

"The only difference between me and those people who wanted to talk to us this afternoon is that, for now, at least, we are working together. Partners with a common objective."

Ambrose's jaw hardened. "Not exactly."

"Yes, exactly. Don't worry, I'm not offended."

"Yeah?"

"Not in the least," Pallas said, going for an airy, unconcerned vibe. "Our association is based on mutual usefulness and shared goals. That's a solid basis for a partnership."

"It sounds like the arrangement you had with that architect you told me about."

"Theo Collier?" Startled, she gave that a moment's thought. "Yes, it does, doesn't it? Feels different, though."

"Because we're not sleeping together?"

"*No*. That has nothing to do with it. Our association is just . . . different. That's all."

"Uh-huh."

She was amused by his bad mood. "Don't get me wrong. I'm not going out on a limb and announcing the beginning of a beautiful friendship, but I am getting the vibe that tells me we might be on the edge of a breakthrough. At the very least I think we're going to get a really good podcast out of this situation. Talia and Amelia will be pleased."

"I am shocked, *shocked* to find out that you are only interested in me because you need content."

Pallas stopped in front of the front door of the restaurant and looked at him. In the warm, welcoming light spilling from the interior of the restaurant, she caught a glint of wry amusement in his eyes.

"I thought it would make you feel useful," she said.

"Look at it this way." Ambrose pushed open the door. "If we can both quote *Casablanca* we must have a few things in common."

"Got news for you. Almost everyone who has seen a lot of movies can quote a few lines from *Casablanca*."

"I was trying to focus on the positive aspects of our relationship."

"Don't worry about it," she said. "You write thrillers infused with horror. You don't get paid to look for the positive."

"This is true." Ambrose was visibly cheered by that logic. "Let's eat. I'm hungry. Also I need a drink. Maybe two. It's been a very long day."

He followed her into the cozy, lightly crowded space. They were shown to a booth that Pallas was surprised to discover felt disturbingly intimate. She shot a couple of covert glances at Ambrose to see if he was experiencing a similar reaction.

He frowned at the menu. "I didn't know this place was vegetarian."

That settled the matter. If there was any intimacy in the atmosphere, Ambrose was immune to it.

"You should have paid closer attention to the front desk clerk when we discussed restaurant options in the neighborhood," she said.

"I was trying to do the gentlemanly thing and leave the decision to you. I should have known better. Apparently no polite deed goes unpunished."

"For future reference, I lean vegetarian."

He looked at her over the top of the menu. He wasn't exactly smiling, she decided, but there was definitely a gleam of laughter in his eyes.

"I'll remember that," he said.

She wasn't sure how to take the casual comment. It seemed to imply that he anticipated they would be eating several more meals together—maybe an indefinite number of meals.

Ruthlessly she squashed the speculation. There was no reason to try to read his thoughts. This wasn't a date.

Stick to business.

"Earlier you said we need to find out more about the patient in room B," she said. "Got any ideas short of breaking into the sleep clinic and trying to find a file on her? Not that I'm opposed to a little B and E in this case. It's just that it sounds a tad risky."

"I don't think there's any point breaking into the clinic. Got a feeling Fenner and crew will have destroyed any evidence relating to the patient in B. But with a little more data, Calvin the Magnificent might be able to come up with some information for us."

"The tech wizard you mentioned?"

"He does research for Failure Analysis."

"That's the security firm you worked for, isn't it?"

"Right. Calvin can do amazing things online, but he needs something to work with. I haven't been able to give him anything he can use, just the fact that there was a woman in room B that night. He did go into the Institute's online records, but he found zilch."

"So how do we get more data?"

The server arrived to take their drink orders. Pallas chose a glass of red wine. Ambrose requested the same. When the server departed he turned back to Pallas.

"I think the next step is to talk to some of the staff at the clinic," he said.

"I saw only two people in addition to Fenner today—the receptionist and the woman who found us in the wrong hallway."

"Jodi Luckhurst."

"I think she's our best bet," Pallas said. "Forget trying to charm the receptionist. She looked mean."

"She did, didn't she?" Ambrose said. "I agree Jodi is a better bet."

"When you think about it, there don't seem to be a lot of people employed at the Institute," Pallas said. "Does that strike you as strange?"

"Not particularly. It's obviously a small operation."

"You said your brother found the Institute online and thought it was a good fit for you," Pallas said.

"Because of its emphasis on dream disorders," Ambrose said.

Pallas paused to drink some wine. "Did you ever tell your family about what happened during your very bad night at the Institute?"

Ambrose snorted. "What do you think?"

"You did not tell anyone, not even your own family, that you're convinced you were a witness at a murder scene in the clinic, because it would make you look even more mentally unstable."

"I've got enough problems with my family," Ambrose said. "I reached out to the *Lost Night Files* team instead."

"Which, if your family ever found out, would make them think you really were in desperate need of a vacation in a locked ward."

"No sense pushing the issue," he agreed.

"What did you tell your family after that night?" she asked.

"That everything was fine. I said I was on medication that was resolving the sleep issues and that I was late on a book and had to drop off the grid for a while in order to focus on getting it done. Told them to contact my assistant if there was a real emergency."

"Did that work?" Pallas asked, intrigued by the idea.

"No."

"I was afraid of that."

"The only option is to block everyone in my family. I can't do that."

"I understand," Pallas said. "Family is family."

"The main reason I haven't tried to block them is because I know it wouldn't work," Ambrose said. "If I really did disappear they would all come looking for me. I'd have even more problems than I've got now."

"I understand. So you are in the rather awkward situation of concealing secrets from the people who love you and are very anxious about your mental health."

"I am, indeed."

"If it makes you feel any better, you are not alone," she said. "Currently my family thinks I'm pursuing yet another harebrained career dream. They're afraid I'm obsessed with becoming a social media star."

Ambrose raised a brow. "They don't see *The Lost Night Files* as a great career move?"

"I've got a long history of being the bad example of career planning in my family. I'm the failure everyone points to when they need an example of what not to do when it comes to achievement and success. I lack focus, discipline, and common sense."

"Yeah?" Ambrose looked interested. "I hadn't noticed."

She sighed. "I come from a long line of doctors, scientists, and academics. In high school I told everyone I wanted to be an artist. They were appalled."

"Too flaky?"

"Well, that and a lack of talent. In college I wandered around taking classes in a bunch of different subjects. Everyone said I had failed to focus. Finally, I signed up for a psych research test that was supposed to help me find the right career. Afterward I talked to a counselor who said the results showed I should become an interior designer. The family was not happy, but they calmed down when it became clear I was good at the work. Then came the business and personal fiasco with Theodore Collier, Architecture and Design. Then came Lucent Springs. Then came my decision to get involved in a podcast that focuses on the woo-woo stuff. In fairness, one can understand my family's concerns."

"Yes," Ambrose said. "One can. Your family sounds like they have a lot in common with my family. I took a career guidance test in college, too. Afterward the counselor said I was doomed to be a writer. My family pointed out that I had better get a day job. I got several of them before I ended up at Failure Analysis. I was doing well there. The family was thrilled. And then I sold my first book and promptly quit my very good job."

"From what I can tell your first book did well, and so did the second one."

"Yes, but my career will fall off the same cliff as yours if I don't finish the third book and the one after that and the one after that."

"I understand," Pallas said. "Believe me."

"We do seem to have a few things in common," Ambrose said.

"Probably just a coincidence."

"I thought I made it clear, writers are not big on coincidence," Ambrose said. "Editors don't approve of them. It's considered lazy plotting."

CHAPTER SEVENTEEN

THE FOG THAT had been lurking off the coast earlier had seeped into town while they were at dinner. By the time they left the restaurant and started walking back to the hotel, the mist had enveloped Carnelian. Ambrose found himself savoring the atmosphere and the feeling of being alone in another dimension with Pallas. He wondered if she felt the same sense of intimacy or if it was all his imagination. Probably the latter.

Dinner with Pallas had not been a date, he told himself—more like rations shared with the woman who happened to be trapped in the same foxhole. They had both needed to eat, so they had eaten a meal together. No big deal. Besides, it was good to talk openly with someone who didn't look at him as if he was delusional.

It was good to be with Pallas Llewellyn.

She stirred something inside him in ways that made him realize he had been alone and lonely for a very long time. It wasn't just the sexual attraction, although that was definitely a serious factor. There was more to the experience—at least on his end—a new and unfamiliar layer of connection. He had never felt anything quite like it.

There were no words for it. Or maybe he was afraid to call up the right words.

One thing was evident: it had been the best evening he'd had since the amnesia episode in San Diego. Granted, San Diego did not set a high bar, but still, the night was a good one and he wanted to enjoy it. He was, therefore, pissed to have the quiet walk back to the hotel interrupted by the realization that he and Pallas were being followed.

He listened to the footsteps echoing in the fog. Whoever was back there was moving deliberately, maintaining a cautious distance. It should have been good news. It indicated that roiling the waters with the interviews had not been a waste of time today. Then again, maybe they were about to get mugged on the main street of Carnelian.

As if she had read his mind, Pallas gave him an inquiring look.

"What's wrong?" she asked.

"We've got company," he said, keeping his voice low.

"Company?"

"Someone is following us." Out of the corner of his eye he saw her aura spike. "No, don't turn around."

"How did you know I was about to—? Never mind. Do you think we're being paranoid?"

"Let's run a little experiment and see what happens."

He took her hand to make sure she didn't stumble when they quickened their pace. Pallas didn't resist. They moved a little faster. The footsteps behind them hesitated and then picked up speed to close the distance.

There was no one else around. The lights of the hotel glowed on the corner of the next block, a long way off if their pursuer proved to be a mugger. They were walking past a row of closed shops, and they were alone on the sidewalk except for the person who was following them.

He tightened his grip on Pallas's hand and moved faster. She kept up with him and did not ask any questions.

"There's an alley up ahead," he said quietly.

She glanced at him but she did not argue. When they reached the dark entrance of the narrow passage he pivoted and hauled her into the dense shadows. She promptly stumbled and uttered a small, choked gasp of alarm.

He caught her and wrapped one arm around her, pulling her close to his side.

"Damn," she whispered.

He decided not to take it personally.

The footsteps got louder. A figure appeared in the light of the streetlamp-infused fog. A woman.

"Nice night, isn't it, Ms. Luckhurst?" Ambrose said from the alley. "What can we do for you?"

Jodi Luckhurst yelped, stopped abruptly, and whirled around to stare, wide-eyed, into the darkness of the alley. Her aura was flashing wildly. She was anxious and scared.

"Who's there?" she gasped.

"Ambrose Drake and Pallas Llewellyn," Pallas said calmly. "But, then, you know that, don't you? We met earlier today at the Institute. Why are you following us, Jodi?"

"You scared the shit out of me," Jodi said.

"Because we don't like being followed," Ambrose said.

Jodi checked the sidewalk on either side and lowered her voice. "I need to talk to you but I have to do it privately."

"This alley is private," Pallas pointed out. "Unless you've got a better idea?"

"No, I guess not." Jodi scanned the sidewalk one last time and then took a few nervous steps into the alley. "This is kind of creepy."

"Yes, it is," Ambrose said. "But here we are. Why do you want to talk to us?"

"You're telling everyone in town that you are here to research the legend of the Carnelian ghosts, but you're really looking into the disappearance of Emery Geddings."

"That's right," Ambrose said.

"I've been looking for him, too," Jodi whispered.

Ambrose got a hit of anticipation. "Two weeks ago Geddings contacted me. Told me he had some information I needed to see. He said he would meet me out at the old asylum but he never showed. Why are you looking for him?"

"He was my boyfriend," Jodi said. "I knew he was supposed to meet someone early that morning. I didn't know that person was you. Emery never returned. I think someone murdered him."

CHAPTER EIGHTEEN

AMBROSE HAD RELEASED her hand, but Pallas did not need the physical connection to sense his icy tension. Her own excitement meter had just shot into the red zone.

"Talk to us, Jodi," Ambrose said.

Jodi responded by flinching and retreating a couple of steps. She was inches away from flight.

Pallas clamped a hand around Ambrose's arm in an attempt to send a not-so-subtle message and took charge of the conversation.

"It's all right, Jodi," she said. "Please don't be afraid. We're not going to hurt you. We really want to hear what you have to tell us."

"You can't record me," Jodi said. "I don't want to be on your podcast. I just want to know what happened to Emery."

"Okay," Pallas said. "No recording."

Ambrose kept silent.

"Tell us about Emery," Pallas said gently.

"The day before he disappeared he told me he was going to meet someone who would pay him a lot of money for some information about what was going on in the Institute," Jodi whispered.

"But he didn't mention me?" Ambrose asked.

"No. He said the less I knew, the better. But today when I heard you talking to Dr. Fenner I realized you were probably the overnight Emery planned to meet."

"Overnight?" Pallas asked.

"That's what we call the sleep study patients," Jodi explained. "Overnights. There haven't been very many of those. I knew something bad happened a month and a half ago on one of those shifts. Emery said there had been trouble. He said he'd cleaned it up for Fenner and that now Fenner owed him. Emery told me that was a good thing."

"Why?" Ambrose asked.

"Emery said it was the big break we had been waiting for. We had plans, you see, but we needed a little more cash. Emery told me he was going to get the money we needed the day he was supposed to meet you. I was all packed and ready to go. I finally realized he wasn't coming back."

"Why didn't you report him missing?" Pallas asked.

"No point," Jodi said. "Everyone who knows him is aware that he's gone. The cops know it, too. It's not a mystery as far as they are concerned."

"What's their explanation for his disappearance?" Ambrose asked.

Jodi sighed. "Most people think he took off because things had gotten too hot for him here in Carnelian."

"What do you mean things had gotten too hot?" Ambrose asked.

Jodi hesitated. "There are those who say he left because he was dealing drugs and he found out the cops were getting ready to arrest him. Others think he was killed by a gang that is trying to move into this territory."

"Did he deal drugs?" Pallas asked.

"He did some dealing when he first got out of the Army," Jodi admitted. "He came back with a habit himself, you see. He was in a bad place. But after he got that job at the Institute he cleaned up his act. Mostly. It was a good job, even if he did have to work nights once in a while."

"What was the information he planned to sell to me?" Ambrose asked, his tone sharpening abruptly.

Jodi flinched and took a step back. "I don't know. Honest. He just said it had something to do with one of the overnight sleep studies."

"Why did he choose the asylum as a meeting point?" Ambrose asked.

"I dunno." There was a shrug in Jodi's voice. "He liked those creepy old ruins. He said something about being able to control the ground. Emery talked like that sometimes. I told you, he used to be in the Army."

"What did you do when you realized he wasn't coming back?" Pallas asked.

"Nothing," Jodi said. "Well, I cried a lot at first. I told myself he'd scored really big and decided to put me and Carnelian in the rear-view mirror. But the more I thought about it the more I couldn't convince myself that was what happened. I told you, we had plans. Today, when you showed up asking about him, I decided maybe he hadn't left me after all. Maybe something bad happened to him."

"What do you think happened to him?" Pallas asked.

"I think he was murdered," Jodi said, her voice breaking.

"What about a body?" Ambrose asked.

"See, that's the part I can't figure out," Jodi said. She widened her hands. "There isn't one. I went out to the asylum and looked. I'm not a cop, but I thought there might be blood or something. On TV the people who buy and sell drugs always use guns or knives. There should have been some blood."

"Maybe the killer cleaned up the scene," Pallas suggested.

"I don't see how," Jodi said. "There's no running water out there. No way to hose down the place. It seems like it would be hard to clean up a lot of blood."

"You're right," Ambrose said. "People who do drug deals don't worry a lot about hiding the dead bodies. They view them as advertising."

"Maybe whoever killed him dumped the body into the bay or in one of the coves," Pallas suggested. "That would be a way of getting rid of the evidence."

"Not for long," Jodi said. "I've lived here all my life. Every year there are a few drownings and suicides. The bodies always wash up onshore. It's the way the currents work along this section of the coast."

"Are you sure you aren't telling us all this because you want to be on the *Lost Night Files* podcast?" Pallas asked.

"*No.*" Jodi flinched again. "I don't want anyone to know I'm talking to you. Why do you think I followed you into this stupid alley tonight? If Emery was dealing and if it turns out he was murdered, the cops will look at me. They'll think I know stuff about his drug business. They might even decide I'm his business partner. That would give me a motive for murder."

"Yes, it would," Ambrose said. "What do you want from us?"

"I just want you to find out what happened to him." Jodi's voice cracked a little. "I need to know if he's dead or if he left me."

"We are going to pursue this investigation," Pallas said.

"I'm glad." Jodi sounded relieved. "Thank you."

"Just to be clear," Ambrose said, "we're not doing any favors here. If you want us to keep you in the loop we're going to need some information."

"What kind of information?" Jodi said. "I just told you everything I know."

"We need the name and address of the other patient who checked in for a sleep study the night I spent at the clinic, the woman in room B," Ambrose said.

"Why?" Jodi asked, bewildered.

"It's part of our investigation," Pallas said, going for a smooth, reassuring tone.

"Oh, okay, I guess." Jodi paused. "We're not supposed to give out any information about the patients."

"We need something," Ambrose said. "A name. An address. A vehicle license plate. A phone number. Anything."

"I don't understand," Jodi said, her voice tightening again.

"We think she disappeared," Pallas said.

"But that's impossible," Jodi said. "It would have been in the news."

"Like Emery Geddings's disappearance?" Ambrose said.

"That's different," Jodi said. "I think."

"We're doing a deal here, in case you haven't noticed," Ambrose said. "We promise to tell you whatever we find out about Geddings's disappearance, but in return we need something we can use to track down the other patient who checked into the clinic that night."

Jodi was silent for a beat. "All right, I'll see what I can find."

Pallas experienced a frisson of dread. "If I were you, I wouldn't mention to anyone that you're trying to find information on the other patient."

"Don't worry," Jodi muttered. "I don't want to get arrested for violating patient confidentiality laws."

"Moving right along," Ambrose said. "Where did Geddings live?"

"Out at the end of Hurley Cove Road," Jodi said. "It's the only house on the cove. You can't miss it. Emery's grandmother left it to him. She raised him after his mom died. After Emery disappeared I drove out there a couple of times to take a look. The first time was the day after he was supposed to do the deal with you, Mr. Drake. The house was locked up. I didn't try to get in, because he told me he had some good security installed."

"You were afraid you would set off the alarms and the cops would respond?" Ambrose asked.

"I wasn't worried about the cops," Jodi said. "I was afraid the place might be booby-trapped. Emery told me he got some special training in explosives when he was in the military."

Ambrose felt Pallas go very still.

"*Explosives?*" Pallas said. "Are you sure?"

"Yeah, but it's okay," Jodi said. "I went out there a second time a few days later. It was obvious someone had broken into the place and trashed it. Nothing had exploded, so I guess Emery hadn't rigged up any traps after all. The door was open, so I went inside. I looked everywhere but I didn't find anything that told me what had happened to him."

Ambrose watched her aura. "Are you certain that there aren't any booby traps at the Geddings house?"

"Positive," Jodi said. "If you go out there you'll see what I mean. Someone tore up the whole house. Whoever it was, they were probably looking for drugs. Like I said, a lot of people assume Emery was in the business."

"How do we contact you?" Pallas asked.

"I'll give you my number." Jodi rattled it off and watched to be sure Pallas entered it into her phone. "Is that all? I have to go now."

"Did you love him?" Pallas asked.

Jodi was silent for a beat. "He wasn't exactly the hearts-and-flowers type, but we were good together. I thought we had a future. I want to know what happened to him. I need to know if he walked out on me."

"I understand," Pallas said.

"Thanks," Jodi whispered.

She turned and went quickly back out onto the sidewalk. Her footsteps faded into the distance. Ambrose watched until her aura vanished into the fog.

"She was telling the truth," he said. "Or what she thinks is the truth. She doesn't believe Geddings booby-trapped his own home."

"She loved him," Pallas said.

"If you say so."

Pallas glanced at him. "You're the one who reads auras."

"You can't see love in an aura," Ambrose said. "At least, I can't. Hate, yes. An effort to lie, yes. Fear and panic, yes. Excitement, yes."

"But not love?"

"Nope."

CHAPTER NINETEEN

THE FOLLOWING MORNING Pallas got out of the car and tried to ignore the tingle of awareness that stirred the fine hairs on the back of her neck. She studied the small, badly weathered house crouched on the rugged bluffs above the isolated cove.

Ambrose climbed out from behind the wheel and came to stand beside her. When she looked at him she saw that he was absently rubbing the back of his neck and scanning the craggy, fog-shrouded landscape.

"I'm getting it, too," she said.

"The feeling that someone is watching us?"

"Yep. I get tired of telling myself it's just my imagination."

He gave her a knowing look. "Get the sensation a lot?"

"Amelia and Talia and I have all been paranoid since we woke up in the Lucent Springs Hotel, but the vibe has been getting worse lately. Stress, probably."

"It's been the same for me since San Diego," Ambrose said. "Maybe the paranoia is a side effect of our new abilities. Our senses are processing more information these days and we're still learning how to interpret the data that's coming in. Hard on the nerves."

"You know what they say. Just because you're paranoid doesn't mean someone isn't out to get you."

"If it turns out someone did run experiments on us, it follows that same individual would want to watch and observe the results," Ambrose said, his voice grim.

"Yes, it does."

Ambrose looked at the fogbound house. "The question I keep coming back to is, why us? I've been writing for a while now. I've had some success but I'm not one of the superstars of the publishing world. Just a working writer. Why choose me for a guinea pig?"

"And I'm a successful interior designer, at least I was, but I'm not a celebrity in my field. I don't do the homes of Hollywood royalty or sports stars or tech lords. Why abduct me for an experiment?"

"Were you paranoid before your amnesia event?" Ambrose asked.

"I used to worry about stumbling into hot spots, but it felt more like clumsiness," she said. "I've always been easily startled. I guess you could say I was risk-averse, because I've worried about tripping over stuff I couldn't see for years. But, no, I wasn't flat-out paranoid, not like I am now."

"We're in Carnelian to get some answers." Ambrose started walking across the graveled driveway, heading for the front door of the house. "Let's see if there's anything to be learned here."

Pallas fell into step beside him. "Geddings liked his privacy," she said, glancing around at the wind-and-storm-lashed landscape. "There's nothing else near this place. If he was dealing drugs this would make a good location for maintaining a low profile."

"A drug deal gone bad would explain Geddings's murder," Ambrose said. "But he wasn't trying to sell me drugs that night. He said he had information."

"He wouldn't be the first person in the history of the world to be murdered in order to keep him from sharing that particular commodity."

"No," Ambrose said.

He stopped at the bottom of the porch steps and waited for her. When she reached his side he took her arm without a word.

"I'm not delicate," she grumbled. "I can manage my talent. Mostly."

"Sorry." He released her arm. "It's just that Jodi Luckhurst said the house had been trashed. I thought that might have left some bad energy."

"Maybe," she admitted. "I didn't mean to snap at you." She took a breath. "Thank you for the offer of assistance."

She knew the words sounded as if they had been dragged out of her.

Ambrose startled her with a quick, knowing smile. "That's right, practice gratitude. It's good for you."

She glared and deliberately switched her attention to the door. "Had a lot of experience breaking and entering?"

"No, but how hard can it be? The good news is that if Jodi was telling us the truth, we won't have to do any actual B and E work. Whoever trashed the place will have done the heavy lifting for us. Theoretically we shouldn't have to worry about booby traps and explosives."

"Theoretically," Pallas said.

"That's why you will wait out here while I go inside and take a look around."

"I appreciate the gallantry, but it's misplaced in this situation," she said.

"Yeah?"

"If Geddings did leave any booby traps behind, I think I've got a better chance of spotting them than you do."

"How do you figure that?" Ambrose asked.

"Setting a dangerous trap, especially one that involves explosives, would require a lot of concentration and, I think, a fair amount of adrenaline. It would leave some serious energy behind. That's exactly the kind of heat I can sense."

"As you trip over it? Not a good idea in this case."

"Okay, I'll admit you have a point. What do you say we go in together? Hand in hand. That way you'll know if I sense something at the same time I do but before I actually fall flat on my face."

Ambrose considered briefly and then nodded once. "Sounds like a plan."

He took her hand, threading his fingers through hers in a fierce grip. She felt energy lift in the atmosphere and knew that he had heightened his other vision to keep an eye on her aura.

Together they crossed the porch to the broken window adjacent to the door and studied what was visible of the front room. The faded, gloom-filled interior was in shambles.

"Jodi was right," Ambrose said. "We aren't the first people to come all the way out here to check on Emery Geddings. If there was a halfway decent security system or a booby trap, whoever trashed the place would have triggered them."

He eased the door open and started to move into the room. Pallas made to follow him, but she paused, one foot inside the space, and gave herself a moment to assess the currents that swirled in the room. Ambrose stopped and waited, not speaking.

She took her time, searching for the pockets of disturbance. The house was old and faded, and so was much of the energy that seethed within it. But there was also a lot of newer, hotter heat. She did not need to go into a trance and draw it to understand what had happened. She had all the context she needed.

"Jodi was right," she said. "Someone tore this place apart."

"Bad guys do that when they're looking for drugs."

They moved gingerly through the chaos. Every item of furniture—sofa, tables, chairs—had been overturned. Yellowed stuffing spilled out of butchered cushions. Closets and drawers and cupboards stood open, the contents scattered across the floor. The braided rug in the living room had been rolled aside to reveal the scarred floorboards.

Ambrose glanced at her, eyes narrowing. "See anything?"

"You can tell when I'm using my other vision?"

"I'm still getting to know you, but I think I've identified some vibes that indicate you are engaging your talent."

"It's a little annoying," she said.

"Your psychic vision?"

"No, yours." She studied the scene. "I'm not sure how I feel about having my aura viewed."

"Sorry." He drew her to a halt in the doorway of the old-fashioned kitchen. "Why is it annoying?"

"I'm not sure," she admitted. "I suppose it has something to do with what you said about being able to see a split second into the future. It feels awfully close to mind reading."

"Not really," he said.

"Yes, really." She tightened her grip on his hand as they moved into the kitchen. "Never mind. I'm getting used to it. We're here for a reason. We shouldn't waste time arguing."

"Right." He studied the canned goods that had been swept out of the cupboards and onto the linoleum floor. "So, I see a house that was torn apart by some people who were probably after drugs. What do you see?"

She concentrated on the seething pools of energy whispering in the atmosphere. "There's a lot of old stuff here and layers of newer energy on top. I'm better at distinguishing the fresh vibes, but what I see doesn't tell me anything we can't tell just by looking at the evidence in front of us. Whoever tossed the place was frustrated. Angry. Looking for something, not just engaging in vandalism for the sport of it."

"Maybe Geddings's competitors dropped by to have a look around when they realized he was no longer in business," Ambrose said, surveying the scene.

"Or?"

"Or whoever killed him at the asylum came here to search for whatever it was Geddings planned to sell to me."

"If you're right it would mean that the murderer didn't find the information on Geddings's body," Pallas pointed out.

Ambrose guided her out of the kitchen and along a shadowed hall. "The beauty of a commodity like information, as opposed to, say, drugs, is that one can make multiple copies and, therefore, multiple deals."

"So maybe the killer came to see if there were any more copies?"

"Right."

They stopped in the doorway of the laundry room. Pallas saw a washer and dryer that were decades out of date. The doors of the appliances had been left open. Ambrose pulled up the flashlight app on his phone.

"What do you sense when you look at the energy I leave behind?" he asked, splashing the light around the interiors of the appliances.

The question caught her by surprise. "If I were to draw your energy I think I would come up with a landscape of fire and ice."

He straightened from a search of the dryer. "What the hell does that mean?"

"I would interpret it as a mix of power and control and determination. You are using all of those elements to fight off exhaustion."

"Think that might translate as mental instability?" he suggested, his voice far too neutral.

"What?" Startled, she turned to stare at him. "No. What makes you ask that?"

"Maybe that for most of my life I've believed I can see human energy fields and eight months ago I experienced a bout of amnesia, after which I concluded that I'm even better at detecting auras. I've got a lot of possibly faulty memories of what happened to me in a sleep clinic a while back and, oh, yeah, my family felt the need to stage an intervention to force me to get treatment for nightmares and sleepwalking."

She raised her brows. "Don't forget your growing paranoia."

"You're not taking this seriously, are you?"

"Wrong." She stopped smiling. "I'm taking you and your new talent very seriously. I take my friends and their talents seriously, too. Actually, I take everything seriously these days—way too seriously. Probably why I haven't had a serious relationship in a very long time. And thanks to my extremely serious approach to life, I now understand why the few serious relationships I have had in the past were doomed from the start."

"Because?"

"Because I'm weird." She widened her hands. "So are you. Want to know what my intuition tells me about you? It tells me that I would not want to get between you and something you wanted very badly. But it also tells me that if I got left behind on a battlefield you're the one who would come back to get me. That's it. That's what my talent tells me about you, and at the moment that is more than enough to make you a trusted partner."

He studied her as if he was trying to figure out where to file her. "Huh," he said.

"What does that mean?" she asked, wary now.

"The first time I got a good look at your aura I came to the same conclusions about you. You're weird but in a really interesting way. I wouldn't want to get between you and whatever you wanted very badly, and you wouldn't leave a friend or a partner behind."

"Glad that's settled," she said.

They went back out into the hall.

"So, *partner,* picking up any other useful information?" he asked.

She thought about reminding him yet again that she was not a search dog, but he had a point. In this situation she was the search dog.

She concentrated on the energy infused into the floor. "I sense a lot of aggression, but not the same kind of panic and rage that I picked up out at the asylum. I suppose the killer might have calmed down before coming out here, but I think that a different person or persons went through this place."

"Did you have to learn how to shut a window or close a door?" he asked.

"Are you talking about my other vision?"

"Yes," he said. "For me it's like a window. When it's closed the glass is fogged up. I can sense that the people around me have auras, but I don't have to see them in detail unless I want to. That's when I open the window."

She stopped at the doorway of a vintage bathroom, complete with claw-foot tub and a badly chipped green sink. Every drawer was open, and so was the medicine cabinet.

"For me it's more like slipping into a waking dream," she said. "I was terrified by my other vision at first." She turned away from the small room. "It was shocking. Frightening. I thought I was going insane. But during the past few months I've gotten a lot better at handling the ability. It almost feels natural now."

"Same with me. It's not surprising when you think about it. We wake up one morning and discover that our rather unusual but not particularly scary sixth sense has suddenly been kicked up several notches. It's like discovering that your normal vision now extends into the UV end of the spectrum or you've developed preternatural hearing. It makes sense that it's taking us a while to figure out how to process the new information we're receiving."

"We didn't suddenly develop our new vision," Pallas said. "Someone conducted experiments on us."

"And someone at the Carnelian Sleep Institute has at least some of the answers," Ambrose said. "Emery Geddings wanted to sell me that information. That's why he was murdered."

Pallas stepped over a pile of towels and sheets that had been hauled out of a linen closet and dumped on the floor.

"Does it occur to you that we're both seriously obsessed?" she said.

"Yep." Ambrose kept his grip on her hand as she led the way into a bedroom. "I wonder if whoever tore this place apart found what they were looking for."

Pallas studied the space with its ancient bed and battered chest of drawers. She shook her head. "I don't think so. All I'm sensing in here is more of what I picked up in the other rooms. Anger and intense frustration."

He surveyed the cluttered, tumbled space. "If there was anything to be found here, it's probably long gone."

The door of the closet was open. Green scrubs, faded camo shirts, and several pairs of cargo pants had been yanked off the hangers and dumped on top of the heavy boots on the floor. The shelf above the hanging rod had been swept clean.

Energy seeped from the back wall. *Excitement. Anticipation. Anxiety.* An adrenaline rush.

"Ambrose," she whispered.

He glanced at her. "Pick up something?"

"There's a lot of heat coming from inside the closet."

Ambrose followed her gaze. "Trapdoor in the floor?"

"Not the floor." She went closer. The energy became more perceptible. "The wall."

She reached inside the closet and flattened one hand against the wooden panels that formed the interior wall. They felt solid to the touch, but the sense of energy got stronger. And there was something else as well. A draft of outside air.

"I think there's something behind the panels," she said.

"Let me take a look," Ambrose said.

She stepped back. He kicked the clothes on the floor out of the way and moved into the closet. She watched him run his fingers around the seams in the wood.

"You're right," he said. "Air is seeping in from somewhere. It looks like the bathroom is on the other side of the closet wall, but I think that's an optical illusion."

Together they moved the remaining clothes out of the way and began a methodical, tactile exploration of the panels.

"Got it," Ambrose announced.

He looked at her, waiting for a verdict.

"It's okay," she said. "But go slow."

He pushed against the seam between two panels. There was a squeak. One of the panels popped open, revealing a dark opening behind the wall. Damp sea air swept into the room.

Ambrose took out his phone and aimed the flashlight into the darkness. Pallas saw a set of worn steps that descended into the depths.

"It's an old smugglers' tunnel," Ambrose said. "Probably dates from the days of Prohibition."

"That fits with the age of the house," Pallas said.

"Jodi Luckhurst told us Geddings grew up in this house," Ambrose said. "He would have known about the tunnel. I'm going to take a look. Stay here."

He started down the steps using the light of his phone.

"Stop," Pallas said. "Let me go first."

Ambrose halted on the second step and looked back, frowning.

She gave him a cool smile. "Partners, remember? Geddings didn't booby-trap the house, but that doesn't mean he didn't protect his secret tunnel."

"I agree. That's why I should go first."

"Be reasonable, Ambrose. I'm the one who can pick up hot energy, and it's a good bet that anyone setting up a trap would have been generating some heat. After all, it's dangerous work."

Ambrose exhaled.

"I know you're not happy, but you also are not stupid," Pallas said.

He stepped aside and let her go first. "Use the flashlight on your phone. Watch for wires or anything that might conceal a wire. The steps are concrete, so I doubt if there's a pressure-sensitive device."

"I'm looking for energy, not blue wires and red wires," she said. "When I'm in my other vision I don't need normal spectrum light."

His jaw tightened. "Right."

He released her hand and rested his palm on her shoulder. The warm, strong vibe steadied her.

She edged downward, moving cautiously, her other vision jacked up to the max. Tendrils of heat drifted on the steps. She ignored the faded stuff and focused on the brighter, hotter pools that were radiant with strange colors.

A nest of scorpions seethed on the sixth step. Even though she had been prepared for a surprise she nevertheless flinched. Simultaneously Ambrose tightened his grip on her shoulder, steadying her.

"Are you okay?" he asked.

"Yes, I think so. There's something wrong on that step," she said, pointing down into the darkness.

Ambrose angled the beam of the flashlight. "Got it."

Light glinted on the nearly invisible wire stretched across the sixth step. She caught her breath. Electrified adrenaline splashed through her.

"Yes," she said. "I see it. Now what?"

Ambrose crouched on the step beside her and studied the trip wire for a moment, using the flashlight to follow it to the wooden wall on either side of the steps.

"Looks basic," he said. "A simple design. I'm sure it requires a man's full weight to trigger the trap, whatever it is. Geddings would not have wanted to take the chance of a rat or some other small animal setting it off."

"How do you know so much about booby traps?"

"I told you, I used to work for a security company. Failure Analysis has a lot of experts on staff. You hang around with them, you learn stuff."

"What do we do now?" she asked.

"You go back to the bedroom. I step over the wire. If nothing happens you can follow me down."

"I told you, we're in this together."

"Exactly," he said. "You've done your part. Let me do mine. We're here because of me, remember? I've got a right to call some of the shots."

One look at his eyes told her he wasn't going to give on this issue.

"I suppose this isn't the best time for someone who is inclined to be a tad clumsy to take charge," she said.

"I wasn't going to say anything."

"I appreciate that."

She went back to the top of the steps and watched from the shadows of the closet.

Ambrose moved over the sixth step, stopped on the one below, and looked back at her.

Nothing happened.

Pallas allowed herself to breathe again. She went back down the steps. When she reached the danger zone Ambrose extended a hand without a word. She took it, her grip very tight, and stepped carefully over the nearly invisible wire. She stopped beside Ambrose and held his hand a few beats longer than necessary. Her heart was pounding.

"Okay, that was scary," she said.

"Yes, it was. My nerves may never be the same."

"Probably a dumbass thing to do," she said.

"Probably," he agreed.

"The fact that we would take such a risk makes you realize just how desperate we are for answers."

"It does," Ambrose said.

They went cautiously downward. The wooden walls of the tunnel gave way to natural rock. The damp and the smell of the sea grew stronger. Pallas kept her senses heightened and Ambrose examined each concrete step with his camera light.

The excavated tunnel abruptly ended at the rear of a cave that had been carved out by the force of the waves. Water splashed in the darkness. Ambrose swept the interior with the beam of his light. Pallas did the same.

A wide stream of seawater washed through the cavern, ebbing and flowing with the rhythm of the waves outside. A two-person kayak had been hauled out onto the stone floor.

"Something tells me Jodi Luckhurst is in for disappointment," Ambrose said. "Looks like Geddings was still dabbling in the drug business."

"Maybe he just enjoyed sea kayaking," Pallas said. "It's very popular here on the coast."

"Call me cynical, but I doubt he went to the trouble and risk of booby-trapping that tunnel just to protect his kayak. See anything worrisome?"

She looked around and shook her head.

"No," she said. "There's definitely a lot of fresh energy down here. I think he came and went this way often, but I don't see any overt signs of violence or anxiety. There's none of the kind of heat I noticed on the sixth step, either."

"Good," Ambrose said. "Let's check out the kayak."

He kept his hand on her shoulder as they crossed the damp, uneven floor of the cave. When they reached the kayak, Ambrose aimed the flashlight into the interior openings. A hefty, military-style flashlight was clipped to the inside of the vessel. A waterproof bag was tucked into a compartment.

Ambrose studied the bag in the beam of his phone's flashlight.

"Any heat?" he asked.

"Some, but nothing that looks dangerous," Pallas said.

Ambrose picked up the bag and handed it to her. She unsealed it. Inside were a change of clothes, a man's wig, sunglasses, and a stack of crisp hundred-dollar bills.

"A go bag," Ambrose said. "Geddings was ready to run on a moment's notice, but he never got this far."

Pallas reached into the bag and took out the clothing and the wig and the money. Underneath there were more items, including a waterproof container about half the size of a shoebox. She removed the lid and looked at the six small glass vials filled with a clear liquid.

Ambrose picked up one bottle and studied the label. "A string of numbers and letters. Must be code for whatever is inside. This stuff looks like it came out of a private compounding pharmacy."

"Looks like Geddings was stealing medication from the Institute and selling it," Pallas said.

"That's how I would have written this scene." Ambrose put the vial back into the container and replaced the lid. He aimed the flashlight into the go bag again. "Jodi Luckhurst was right about one thing. People in the drug trade do like guns." He took out the pistol and checked it. "Loaded. He must have figured that if he ever needed it he would be in a hurry."

"This doesn't make sense," Pallas said. "If his gun is here it means he didn't have it with him when he went to the asylum to meet you."

"Maybe he wasn't expecting trouble that day. But it's more likely he had another gun. He was ex-military and he was dealing drugs. Trust me, he would have been well-armed."

Pallas examined the last item in the go bag, a small black case. She picked it up and opened it. There was one object inside, along with a sticky note.

"A memory card," she said. She held up the tiny digital storage device. "Whatever is on here was valuable enough to be included in Geddings's go bag."

Ambrose picked up the sticky note. "Two initials: *A* and *D*."

"Ambrose Drake," Pallas said.

"There's also a date."

Pallas met his eyes. "Is it—?"

"Yes," he said. "That's the night I spent in the Carnelian Sleep Institute."

CHAPTER TWENTY

EXCITEMENT SLAMMED THROUGH Ambrose. "This is it," he said. "This is what we came here to find."

"Maybe," Pallas said.

"There's no other explanation for the initials and the date," Ambrose said. "Whatever is on the card has to be the information Geddings intended to sell to me."

"If the memory card he planned to sell to you is here in his go bag, what was he going to give you when he met you at the asylum?" Pallas asked.

"A copy. I told you, that's the beauty of selling information. You can duplicate it as often as you want."

"True," she said.

"And why wouldn't he have wanted to keep a copy for himself? After all, if it's worth a lot of money to me, there's a good chance it implicates someone else, someone who could be blackmailed. Fenner, for example."

She whistled softly. "You're right."

He looked at her. "If it hadn't been for you I would never have found this. I owe you."

Her mouth tightened. "We're partners."

"Yes, but that doesn't mean I don't owe you."

"Forget it. This is what I do." She waved a hand in a vague gesture aimed at the smuggling tunnel. "I find hot spots."

She was looking irritated again, but this wasn't the time to try to figure out why. He slipped the small memory card case into the pocket of his jacket and dropped the plastic container with the medication vials inside back into the go bag.

"If we give the meds to the police we're likely to get dragged into a drug case that will screw up our own investigation," Pallas warned. "We might even end up getting arrested. Trust me, I know how these things work."

Her grim tone snagged his attention. He looked at her. "The Saltwood case?"

"Yes." She eyed the tunnel. "There's another problem. Those booby-trapped steps are a serious hazard. It's pure luck that no one stumbled over that trip wire before we got here. What if some transients trying to get out of the rain break in or a couple of local kids decide it would be fun to take a look inside the house and accidentally find the tunnel?"

"Don't know about you, but my skill set does not include the dismantling of explosives."

"Neither does mine," she said. "We don't have any choice, do we?"

"No. We have to talk to the local cops and tell them about that trip wire."

"We'll need a good story to explain what we were doing out here this morning," she said.

"Leave it to me," Ambrose said. "I write fiction for a living."

"You think you can come up with a version of events that will explain everything to the cops?"

"No problem," he said. "We used cover stories all the time at Failure Analysis. I wrote a lot of the scripts for the agents."

"I can't wait to hear the one you write for us."

"We'll talk about it on the way back to town. I don't want to spend any more time here."

"Neither do I." She looked at the tunnel. "Too bad we have to go back up those steps."

"It's not just the trip wire that worries me." He followed her gaze. "I keep thinking about that feeling we got when we arrived."

"That sense of being watched?"

He did not need to view her aura to know that she was feeling as uneasy as he was about a return trip through the tunnel.

"Yeah, that feeling," he said.

"We agreed we've been living with the sensation of being watched for a while now."

"The vibe I got out there in the driveway was a little different," he said. "More intense."

She sighed. "It was pretty strong, wasn't it? You do realize how paranoid that makes us sound?"

"We've already agreed we're on that runaway train," he said.

"Got a better idea?"

He switched his attention to the small craft that had been designed to be a getaway vehicle for a drug dealer. "Maybe. The kayak seats two. We could use it to get out of here, go ashore at that little beach we passed, and walk back to the car. That will give us a chance to take a good look around. If anyone is watching us they'll be focused on the house. They won't see us coming."

"If we're right about Emery Geddings, that kayak is evidence."

"So is the go bag. We've already decided we're going to turn it over to the police. Our concern about tripping the wire on the steps is reason enough to explain why we used the kayak."

She paused, brows lifting a little. "I'm assuming you suggested this plan because you know how to paddle a kayak?"

"I'm not an expert, but I took a class as research for *A Fall of Shadows*," he said. "I wouldn't want to take it out to sea, but I think I can get us out of this sea cave and into the cove."

The crunch of tires on gravel and the slam of car doors stopped him cold. He did not need to look at Pallas to know she had gone still, too.

Another door slammed—the front door of the house this time. Footsteps pounded on the floor.

"Take the kitchen," a man yelled. "I've got the bedrooms." Gunshots boomed. "What the fuck?"

"Thought I saw someone in the kitchen," a second voice called out.

"We know you're in here," the first man yelled. "You're looking for Geddings's stash. It belongs to us. Come out or you're both dead."

Ambrose reached into the go bag and pulled out the pistol.

"They'll see the entrance to this tunnel when they enter the bedroom at the top of the tunnel," Pallas said. "We left the panel open."

"We're fish in a barrel as long as we stand around in here. Help me with the kayak."

He kept the pistol in one hand as they eased the boat into the gentle, slapping water. Pallas waded out a few steps and prepared to climb in with exquisite care. This was no time to lose her balance.

"You down there in the tunnel," the first man yelled. His voice echoed from the top of the steps. "Come out or we're coming in."

"I'll be right back," Ambrose said.

Pallas gripped the side of the kayak, holding it steady in the water. "What are you doing?"

"Hang on," he said.

He went to the lower entrance of the tunnel.

"You don't want to come down here," he shouted up the steps. "Geddings booby-trapped the stairs."

"You think I believe that? Fuck you. You had your chance. I'm coming down."

Ambrose fired two rounds. The shots boomed in the narrow confines of the tunnel.

"Fuck," the first man shrieked.

He sent a volley of shots down the steps.

Ambrose was already loping back across the cavern. He waded into the water and held the kayak steady. "Get in."

Pallas climbed inside and held out one hand. "Give me the gun. I don't know how to paddle a kayak, but I can pull a trigger."

He didn't argue. He got into the small craft, grabbed the paddle, and used it to launch the kayak.

"Flashlight?" he said.

"Got it."

There was a snick as Pallas switched on the big military-style flashlight. A brilliant beam pierced the darkness of the cave. He aimed the vessel toward what, judging by the direction the seawater was flowing, had to be the entrance that opened onto the cove. If he was wrong they were going to have an even bigger problem.

A strange silence fell behind them.

"Maybe they gave up," Pallas whispered.

"I doubt it," he said.

The exit point of the sea cave was dangerously narrow. They had to keep their heads down to avoid getting brained by the rock overhead. Ambrose used the paddle to push the kayak away from the stone walls.

They rounded a crook in the cave and popped out into the cove.

The muffled rumble of the explosion reverberated through the cavern. A couple of heartbeats later the sound was followed by a second, louder roar.

It seemed to take forever for silence to fall.

"He went down the stairs," Pallas said, stunned.

"Yes," Ambrose said.

He focused on maneuvering the sleek kayak across the calm waters of the cove, aiming for the small patch of sandy beach.

"The house is on fire," Pallas said suddenly. "So much for assuming the explosive device was small."

Ambrose glanced back and saw the smoke at the top of the bluffs. He remembered the second explosion. "The first one was small, but it ignited the gas."

They beached the kayak and waded ashore. He collected the go bag and slung it over one shoulder. Without a word Pallas handed him the pistol. They made their way up to the top of the bluffs.

The house was fully engulfed. The drug dealers' car was still parked in the driveway.

"I don't think either one of them made it out," Pallas said. There was a shiver in her voice.

He took out his phone and glanced at the screen. "No signal. We'll have to drive back toward town before I'll be able to call nine-one-one."

"That will give you time to come up with a good story," Pallas said.

"We don't need to invent one. As usual, truth is stranger than fiction. Really, you can't make this stuff up."

CHAPTER TWENTY-ONE

WE WERE SURE Geddings was dealing, but he was smart about it," the detective said. "We didn't know he was stealing from the Institute's medication locker, though. No one reported the thefts."

He had introduced himself as Logan. Excitement hummed in the atmosphere around him. He was young and ambitious and riding an adrenaline high. He had reason to be thrilled, Pallas thought. He was going to get the credit for closing a major drug case.

She and Ambrose were sitting in Logan's office, a small, cramped space that looked out over the town square. The library, fire department, and city hall could be seen from the window. It was noon. She wasn't hungry but she knew she should have something to eat. The only thing Logan had offered was coffee. Ambrose had accepted a cup but she had declined. It was the last thing her nerves needed. She was going to relive the escape in the kayak in her dreams.

"Geddings always looked clean," Logan continued. "No record. Honorable discharge. Until recently he had a steady job at the college. The two who died in the blast were new in the area, part of a gang that has been trying to move into this town. Both had rap sheets a mile long. What made you go out to Geddings's place this morning?"

"As I told you earlier," Pallas said, striving for patience, "*The Lost Night Files* specializes in cold cases that don't seem to be on anyone's radar."

"Geddings wasn't on anyone's radar because no one had reported him missing," Logan said. "What made you think he had disappeared?"

"I had an appointment to meet him," Ambrose said. "He said he had some information for me regarding my medical records. He didn't show up. No one seems to know what happened to him."

Logan frowned. "What kind of medical information?"

"I have no idea," Ambrose said. "I told you, he never showed up. That made me very, very curious, so I contacted *The Lost Night Files*. They agreed to look into the disappearance."

That was the truth, Pallas thought. Maybe not the whole truth, and one could say there were a few lies of omission, but the truth. Mostly.

Logan turned to her. "What made Mr. Drake's case interesting to your podcast team, Ms. Llewellyn?"

"The connection to the ruins of the old asylum, of course," Pallas said. "That, combined with the local legends, made the case very intriguing."

Logan got a pained expression. "Are you talking about the ghosts of Carnelian stories? I can't believe you take that kind of stuff seriously."

"It's the perfect storm for a podcast series," Pallas said. "Abandoned asylum, the ghost of an inmate who wanted revenge on her husband, and now a mysterious disappearance. We specialize in cases like that."

Logan switched his attention to Ambrose. "Let me get this straight. You're the one who suggested that the podcast look into the disappearance, but you're also doing research for a novel?"

"That's right," Ambrose said.

"Uh-huh." Logan did not appear impressed. "All right, you went out to the Geddings place to take a look around. Why did you go into the house?"

"Because it was obvious it had been torn apart," Ambrose said. "We were afraid Geddings might be inside, maybe injured or dead. The door was open. We probably shouldn't have gone in—"

"No," Logan said. "I could charge you with criminal trespass."

"As I said, we had reason to be concerned about Geddings's welfare," Ambrose continued smoothly. "Once we were inside we saw the entrance to the old smugglers' tunnel. It occurred to us that Geddings might have fallen down the steps. We noticed the trip wire on the way down and stepped over it. We were in the cavern, looking around, when the two men with the guns showed up. They assumed we were after Geddings's stash of drugs. They viewed us as competition."

"We realized our only hope was to take the kayak," Pallas added. "Even so, Mr. Drake did try to warn the two drug dealers that the stairs were booby-trapped. Obviously they didn't believe him. You know the rest."

Logan got up from behind the desk, walked around to the front, and angled one hip on the corner. He folded his arms and regarded Ambrose in silence for a long moment.

"You saw a trip wire," he said. "Recognized it for what it was. And you just hopped over it."

"Didn't exactly hop," Ambrose said. "And before you continue with the lecture I can tell you that, while it wasn't the brightest move

Ms. Llewellyn or I have ever made, it wasn't quite as stupid as it sounds. I used to work for a security firm. It wasn't the first time I've seen a trip wire."

"It was a stupid thing to do."

"Yes, it was," Ambrose said.

"Excuse me," Pallas said, "but I think I should point out that if we had not gone down the steps we would have been shot dead by those two drug dealers who stormed into the house."

Logan grimaced. "There is that." He eyed Ambrose. "A writer, huh?"

"For my sins," Ambrose said.

Logan switched his attention to Pallas. "And you're an interior designer who runs a podcast on the side."

"That's right," Pallas said.

Logan squinted. "Any money in that line?"

"The podcast?" she said. "No, at least not for *The Lost Night Files*. We're a small operation. Still building an audience and a brand."

"In other words, you haven't given up your day job?" Logan said.

"No," Pallas said.

Logan nodded. "This podcast thing is just a hobby, then?"

Pallas managed, with an effort, to suppress her irritation. "My associates and I plan to make *The Lost Night Files* a success."

"You might want to think twice about that," Logan said. "It nearly got you and Mr. Drake killed today."

Pallas did not respond. The man had a point.

Logan was silent for a moment and then he appeared to make a decision.

"A new hallucinogen hit town a few months ago," he said. "We had some students turn up in the emergency room and one attempted suicide. We couldn't identify the source. Judging by those meds you found in the kayak, it looks like Geddings was the dealer.

He was stealing from the sleep clinic. I'll talk to the director later today and see if there are any more medications missing."

"Are you going to have the contents of those vials analyzed?" Ambrose asked.

"Not much point, even if we could afford to send a sample out to a fancy forensics lab, which we can't," Logan said. "We're a small department with zero budget for that kind of testing. The vials are still sealed. If the director of the clinic identifies them, that will be all I need. The real question here is, what are you two going to do now that you know Geddings was probably murdered by his competition?"

Ambrose looked at Pallas, letting her take the lead.

"The thing is," she said, "there's no body."

"Good luck finding one," Logan said. "I doubt if the killer or killers dumped Geddings into the bay. Odds are it would have washed ashore by now. But there's a lot of raw land around this stretch of the coast. You could dig forever and never locate a body."

"You're right," Ambrose said. "Our investigation seems to have been closed."

"I'm glad to hear that," Logan said. He stood. "That's all I need from you two. Appreciate your cooperation, but take my advice— don't go looking for any more trouble. Next time you might not get lucky."

CHAPTER TWENTY-TWO

YOU'RE RIGHT, WE didn't need to invent a story," Pallas said. "All we had to do was leave out a few minor details, such as the fact that we think the Carnelian Sleep Institute is conducting illegal paranormal experiments."

"And the fact that I think I witnessed a woman's body being hauled out of the clinic during an overnight sleep study," Ambrose said. "There was no point bringing up either of those things, because Logan wouldn't have taken them seriously."

"We got off lightly today." Pallas shuddered. "After the Saltwood fiasco, I didn't know what to expect from the Carnelian police."

She ate some of her broccoli and cheddar soup and tried not to watch as Ambrose wolfed down a fully loaded hamburger. She told herself that at the moment he needed the protein to help overcome the effects of sleep deprivation and anyway his diet was none of her business. It wasn't like they were planning a future together.

They were sitting at the small table in her room eating the takeout lunch they had picked up at a café near the hotel. She knew they were both trying for some semblance of normal, but the effort wasn't going well. Tension charged the atmosphere, and it wasn't all coming from Ambrose. She was contributing her share. It was going to take time to work through the violent events of the morning.

Their suspicions of what had happened at the sleep clinic were not the only details they had failed to mention to Detective Logan. They had not told him about the memory card they had found in Geddings's go bag. The two items on the card were currently in the process of being imported to Ambrose's phone via her adapter.

"We got lucky with the cops because we had a lot of help from Logan," Ambrose said. "He was very happy to let us skate on the illegal entry charge because he's going to be the headline on the evening news and the morning edition of the *Carnelian Gazette*. Today was a serious résumé builder for him. Two drug dealers have died in a live-by-the-sword kind of way, and some stolen medications will be returned to the Carnelian Sleep Institute. He'll get the credit for closing the case."

"I suppose that's why he let us off with just a warning," Pallas said.

Her phone rang as she was eating the crackers that had come with the soup. She reached for the device.

"That will be Jodi Luckhurst," Ambrose said around a mouthful of fries.

Pallas gave him a wry smile. "Is that an example of your ability to predict the future?"

"No, it's an example of me figuring out that Luckhurst has probably heard the news about the explosion at Geddings's place. She'll want to know what happened."

"We owe her an explanation," Pallas said. "She was the one who warned us about the possibility of a booby trap. She may have saved our lives."

"This is true." Ambrose downed the last of his fries.

Pallas took the call and put it on speaker so that Ambrose could listen in.

"Hi, Jodi," she said. "Mr. Drake and I are both here. We just got back from talking to the police. We were going to contact you."

"Are you both okay?" Jodi said. Her voice was charged with an anxiety that bordered on panic. "What happened? Everyone is talking about the explosion. They're saying they found two bodies. At first I was afraid you and Mr. Drake were the victims. Then I heard a couple of drug dealers had died at the scene. What is going on? Did you find out what happened to Emery?"

"Mr. Drake and I are fine," Pallas said. *Somewhat the worse for wear, but fine,* she added silently.

"Good," Jodi said. "I'm glad. I've been so worried." There was a short pause before she lowered her voice. "They're saying drugs were found in the house."

"Ms. Llewellyn and I came across several small bottles of what looked like medication," Ambrose said. "There was also a bundle of cash."

Jodi sighed. "So Emery was stealing from the clinic. I was afraid of that."

"The fact that he left the drugs and the money behind indicates he probably didn't leave town, though," Ambrose said. "Your theory that he may have been murdered could be correct."

"I'll bet those two drug dealers who died in the explosion killed him," Jodi whispered. Her voice was choked with tears. "They tore his house apart looking for his stash, but they didn't find it, so they kept an eye on the place. When you two went in they figured you were after the drugs, too."

"That's how it looks," Pallas said.

"Now those two bastards are dead," Jodi said. "I'm glad. But you and Mr. Drake could have been killed, too, and it would have been my fault."

"No," Pallas said. "You saved us because you warned us about the possibility of a booby trap. There was one. That was the cause of the explosion. But the drug dealers hit the trip wire, not us."

"We owe you," Ambrose said.

"I'm just glad you're okay," Jodi said. "Do you think the cops will want to interview me?"

"Probably," Ambrose said.

"Shit," Jodi moaned.

Pallas shot Ambrose a *shut up, you heartless monster* look and tried to calm Jodi's panic.

"We didn't mention your name to the police," Pallas said. "But they usually talk to those who knew the victim, and it's no secret that you and Emery were dating."

Jodi sniffed. "No, I guess not."

Ambrose leaned forward a little to speak into the phone. "Logan, the detective in charge of the case, is convinced Geddings is dead, so I don't think he'll push too hard. He's mainly interested in tying up loose ends."

"Emery really is dead, isn't he?" Jodi said, her voice cracking. "He didn't leave me behind like she said."

"Like who said?" Pallas asked.

"Marsha Grove. She's the receptionist at the Institute. She said she watched Emery grow up and he was always shifty. Says I'm better off without him. Thanks for letting me know what happened. Don't get me wrong, I'm sorry Emery is dead, but I guess a part of me is glad he didn't just dump me."

"I understand," Pallas said.

Ambrose cleared his throat. "We had a deal, Jodi."

"What?" Jodi sounded genuinely bewildered. "Oh, right. The name of the patient who was booked for a sleep study the same night you were in the Institute. It's weird. I know there was another patient scheduled for that evening because Emery mentioned he would be looking after two overnights. That was unusual. But I couldn't find any record of the other one. Probably a last-minute cancellation or a no-show. That happens more than you would believe. It always infuriates Dr. Fenner."

"Thanks for trying," Pallas said gently. "I am very sorry about Emery."

Jodi sniffed again. "Thanks. At least I know what happened."

The phone clicked off. Pallas was aware that Ambrose was watching her with a cryptic expression.

"What?" she said.

"You made it sound like you really did understand," he said.

Pallas sat back in the chair. "No one likes to get dumped."

"True. How many times has it happened to you?"

"I try not to keep track," she said. "I've been told I'm complicated, but I think that's a euphemism for scary. I know for a fact that I frightened Theo."

"The architect?"

"Yes."

"I definitely scared my ex a few times before she ended things," Ambrose said. "The sleepwalking was too much."

"To be fair, our exes were right. We are a little scary."

"Yes," Ambrose said. "We are."

CHAPTER TWENTY-THREE

THE IMPORTING PROCESS ended just as they finished lunch. Pallas rose to dump the wrappers and the soup carton into the trash.

"There's a photo and a very long video," Ambrose said, studying his phone. "I'll open the image first."

Pallas returned to the table and sat down. Together they looked at the photo. It was a page that had been ripped out of a logbook. The entries were written in a precise hand. At the top of the page was a name—Brooke Kendrick. There was also an address and a date.

"That's the night I checked in for the sleep study," Ambrose said. "Brooke Kendrick must have been the other patient. This is it, the information I've been trying to nail down."

Energy shivered around him.

Pallas scanned through the log entries. "She was a computer engineer. Age thirty-two; height five feet, four inches; weight one hundred thirty pounds. Blood pressure, pulse, oxygen levels, temperature all normal at ten thirty p.m."

Ambrose studied the page. "Eleven thirty, subject restless. Twelve fifteen, subject awake and agitated. Twelve thirty, agitation increasing. Sedative administered. One twenty-six, subject awake in spite of sedation. Disoriented. Extreme delirium."

"That's all," Pallas said, looking up from the screen. "There aren't any other entries. Does the physical description fit the patient who checked in ahead of you?"

"I admit I wasn't paying a lot of attention to her that night," Ambrose said, "but, yes, the age, height, and weight all match my recollections. We've got a name and an address. Now to see what's on the video."

The footage was not the highest quality, but there was no mistaking the scene of a small, windowless space furnished like an inexpensive motel room. Ambrose slept on the bed, a sheet and a lightweight blanket draped across his waist. Several wires attached to electrodes on his face, head, chest, and legs ran to a small metal box equipped with a handle. The camera was narrowly focused on the bed. Most of the other furnishings in the room were not in the frame.

"You can't see the chair," Ambrose said. "The one I sat in while Fenner cleaned the blood off my hand."

"Or much else," Pallas said.

"So much for the broken video camera story," Ambrose said.

Pallas studied the image. "Why the lie?"

"With luck maybe we'll find out," Ambrose said.

Pallas watched the screen for a long moment. On the bed, Ambrose did not stir. Icy fingertips touched the back of her neck.

"You certainly appear to be deeply asleep," she said.

"I told you, I went out like a light that night," he said. "That is not normal for me."

"But here you are, sound asleep."

"I don't want to sit here watching myself sleep for the next several hours." Ambrose reached for the phone. "I'm going to speed up the video."

An hour slipped by in a matter of minutes. In the video Ambrose scarcely moved on the bed.

A wedge of light abruptly slanted across the bed.

"Slow down," Pallas said quickly. "I think the door opened. Yes. Someone entered the room."

Ambrose adjusted the speed of the video. They watched a familiar figure move to hover over the bed.

"Fenner," Ambrose said. "Watching him watching me gives me a very creepy sensation."

The doctor did a quick check of the sleeping Ambrose, made some notes, and then, evidently satisfied, left.

"You didn't move at all when he leaned over the bed and checked your vitals," Pallas said. "You say you haven't been able to sleep through the night since San Diego, but you are out cold in this video."

Ambrose did not take his eyes off the screen. "I never sleep like that, even on a good night, and I haven't had a good night in a very long time. It's as if I was given a heavy-duty sedative before I got into bed, but I don't see how that would have been possible. I would have been aware of it."

"Did you eat or drink anything at the clinic that night?"

"No. I checked in, undressed, and got into bed. Fenner hooked up the electrodes. I read for a while and went to sleep. I remember thinking I was wasting my time, and that's the last thing I recall until I heard a scream and went out into the hall. Or, at least I think that's what happened."

They went back to studying the sped-up video. Fenner entered the room two more times, but all he did was observe and make some notes. As the night wore on, however, the sleeping Ambrose became somewhat agitated. He changed position a couple of times. There was no audio, but Pallas knew immediately when he heard the scream.

His eyes snapped open. He lay still for a moment and then bolted to a sitting position and swung his legs over the side of the bed. When he tried to stand he lost his balance and collapsed on the floor. The wires that connected him to the black box were ripped away. He lay still on the floor for a couple of minutes before grabbing the side of the bed and hauling himself upright. He took another few seconds to steady himself and then he stumbled toward the door.

He disappeared from the frame.

"I didn't hallucinate that night," Ambrose said, his voice low and fierce. "I wasn't dreaming. I heard a woman scream and I left the room to see what had happened."

"You heard something that you interpreted as a scream," Pallas said gently. "But sounds can invade a person's dreams. The sleeping mind comes up with odd ways to incorporate them into the dreamscape."

Ambrose looked at her, not speaking.

She took a breath. "Okay, I think you heard a scream. But you can't prove it with this video. There's no sound."

"No, but this video is proof that the camera was working that night. I was almost positive that Fenner was not lying when he said it was broken. I must have read his aura wrong. That's beside the point. The question now is, why did Fenner lie?"

They watched Fenner steer the reeling, obviously drugged Ambrose back to the bed. Ambrose collapsed into what looked like a profound sleep. Fenner reattached the electrodes.

Toward the end another man entered the room.

"I assume that's Geddings?" Pallas asked.

"Yes."

After a quick check on the sleeping man he turned toward the camera.

Pallas took a sharp breath. "Look at the stains on his scrubs."

"Blood," Ambrose said. "That explains why Fenner lied about the camera."

The screen abruptly went dark.

"Geddings took the memory card out of the camera," Pallas said.

Ambrose sat back, comprehension heating his eyes. "He stole the card. Probably told Fenner that the camera had failed. *That* explains why Fenner thought there was no video. He was not lying about the camera."

"You didn't misread his aura."

Ambrose got to his feet and went to stand at the window. "The problem is that there is nothing incriminating on the video. Yes, the sleepwalking incident is there, but that just proves that Fenner told me the truth. He was very clear that I had walked in my sleep that night. What made Geddings think I'd pay good money for footage of me sleeping and sleepwalking?"

"It looks like that photo of the page of data about Brooke Kendrick is the only damning evidence on the memory card. Why did Geddings include it?"

"Remember, this is the copy of the card he kept for himself." Ambrose looked down at the little succulents on the windowsill. "I doubt if that page of notes was on the copy he planned to sell to me. Got a feeling he intended to use the photo to blackmail Fenner. It's proof that there was another patient that night and that something went wrong in room B."

"That indicates that Fenner killed Geddings," Pallas said. "Fenner is a doctor. He probably used a lethal drug. That would explain the hypodermic needle you found at the asylum. But we've still got the problem of the body. Geddings was a big man. It's hard to envision Fenner hauling him out of the asylum, stuffing him into a car, and burying him somewhere in an unmarked grave."

Ambrose turned to face her. "Maybe he had help."

Pallas went cold. "We can't rule out that possibility, but it complicates things."

"We need to know more about Brooke Kendrick."

"Assuming the woman named in that picture is the one who checked into the Institute that night, she's probably dead," Pallas said.

"Dead or alive, she's got some of the answers we need."

"I feel like one of us needs to tap the brakes here. In case you haven't noticed, we are a little short on motive. So far none of this makes any sense."

"It does if you remember that drugs are at the core of this thing," Ambrose said. "You saw those meds in Geddings's go bag."

"In that case, our work here is done." Pallas spread her hands apart. "Detective Logan is pursuing the drug angle. You saw him today. He's thrilled with the case. Not only is he enthusiastic, he's got a lot more resources to throw at the investigation than we do."

"So we let Logan work the drug angle and see what he turns up," Ambrose said. "Meanwhile, we find out what happened to the missing patient."

"Got a plan?"

"Calvin is my plan." Ambrose picked up his phone. "If anyone can dig up some useful background on Brooke Kendrick, it will be Calvin."

Pallas picked up her own phone. "I need to call Talia—and Amelia, too, if she's back from Lucent Springs. Talia will be monitoring news out of Carnelian. Sooner or later she'll hear about the explosion. If she does, she'll panic."

"Fortunately, my family doesn't know I'm in Carnelian," Ambrose said. "Neither does my assistant. Everyone thinks I'm hiding out in a hotel somewhere on the coast."

Pallas swept the room with a meaningful glance. "Which just happens to be the truth."

Ambrose smiled, but the smile did not mask the battle he was fighting against exhaustion. He was getting regular meals now, Pallas thought, probably because they were eating together, but the food wasn't making up for his badly disrupted sleep.

"Thanks," he said.

"For what?" she asked, surprised.

"For being here. For being you." He massaged the back of his neck with one hand. "It's a hell of a relief to be able to act as if everything that's happened to me in the past few months is—well, not normal, but real. Weird and disturbing, but real. I'm not quite so worried about my mental health now."

She told herself she ought to be okay with that. And she was. As far as it went. But for some reason it was vaguely depressing to know that he saw her as simply an ally in a battle against a common enemy. Comrades in arms. That should not be a problem. It was how she viewed him, wasn't it?

Well, no. *And what was up with that?*

"Right," she said, going for brisk and businesslike. "Nothing like almost getting killed together to cement a friendship, I always say."

"Exactly."

She clamped her teeth together. Time to move forward. She started to make the call to Talia but hesitated when a thought struck her. She reached into her messenger bag and took out her sketchbook.

"If we're right about any of this," she said, "I think I now know how to interpret my drawing of the staircase at the asylum."

The weariness retreated from Ambrose's eyes. Intense interest took its place. "The picture of the snakes slithering down the steps?"

"Yes." She opened the sketchbook. Together they studied the drawing. "I knew the fact that there are several snakes, not just one, was important; I just didn't know why. Now I think my intuition was trying to tell me that we're not looking for one killer. We're looking at a conspiracy."

Ambrose raised his brows. "As opposed to a drug ring?"

"Obviously drugs are involved, but there is something else going on here. Why would a drug ring run experiments in a sleep clinic?"

Ambrose thought about that for a long moment. "*Conspiracy* is a loaded word."

"Yes, it is, but there is a fundamental rule for conducting an investigation in situations like this: follow the money."

Ambrose gave her a slow, feral smile. She could have sworn his eyes heated with anticipation.

"We need some deep background on the finances of the Carnelian Sleep Institute," he said.

"Know anything about tracking complicated finances?" she asked.

"No, but I know who to call."

"Don't tell me—let me guess. Calvin?"

"He's a one-stop shop for data." Ambrose made the call. He studied the succulents as he waited for Calvin to answer. "There aren't any plants in my room."

"Those don't belong to the hotel," Pallas said. "They're my travel plants. I never leave home without them."

CHAPTER TWENTY-FOUR

"YOU HAVE GOT to get a handle on this situation, Fenner." Hugh Guthrie gripped the arms of his desk chair and pushed himself to his feet. "I can't believe you let things get out of control like this. If the Institute's reputation is destroyed by a drug scandal it will have repercussions that will affect the entire college. *Funding* repercussions."

"Dean Guthrie is right." Margaret Moore adjusted the right leg of her immaculately tailored trousers and tried to conceal her irritation. "I can promise you that if Mr. Knight hears about this he will not be pleased."

The warning was unnecessary. They all understood the importance of not pissing off the anonymous donor they privately referred to as Mr. Knight. She had given their mystery benefactor the name in recognition of his status as the knight in shining armor who had rescued Carnelian College from impending financial disaster. As the director of the Carnelian College Foundation's fundraising department, she felt it necessary to remind Guthrie and Fenner of the danger in which they now found themselves.

Nearly a year ago Mr. Knight had contacted her to inform her that he was prepared to make the largest single gift to the endowment fund in the history of the college. In return he insisted on the establishment of the Carnelian Sleep Institute. He had also stipulated that the fussy, irritating, obsessed Conrad Fenner be hired as director of the new clinic.

Technically speaking, donors were not supposed to be able to control how their money was spent—the administration, in consultation with the faculty council, was tasked with that responsibility. But everyone in the academic world understood that donors always had a say. The larger the donation, the bigger the say. Mr. Knight's donation had saved the college. That meant that when it came to his pet project, the Institute, he got whatever he wanted.

None of them had ever met Mr. Knight in person or spoken to him on the phone. He had contacted her by text to make his generous offer. Aware that scammers, frauds, and pranksters were always a threat in the fundraising business, she had done her due diligence research. In the end, however, she had not been able to find anything solid. Mr. Knight was a man who liked his privacy, and he evidently had the money to buy it.

She and Hugh and the Foundation's board of directors had all held their breath until the first installment of the promised donation was safely transferred into the Carnelian College Endowment Fund. When it arrived and proved to be real, there had been much rejoicing here in Hugh's office. The faculty had been invited to celebrate. Champagne had been brought in for the occasion. After the guests had departed she and Hugh had had sex on the desk. It was the best sex they'd had in a very long time.

"There is no need for panic," Fenner said. He took off his glasses and began to polish them with a small cleaning cloth. "This little brouhaha will go away very quickly."

Margaret looked at him. "In case you haven't heard the news, this little brouhaha includes an explosion at the home of an employee of the clinic—"

"*Former* employee," Fenner snapped.

"Who just happened to be dealing drugs on the side," she said. "It also includes two members of a drug gang, a podcaster who claims to investigate cold cases, and a novelist who just happens to have been a patient at the Institute. Trust me, we have a problem, Dr. Fenner."

Hugh turned away from the view of the campus. "Margaret is right. This is serious. We all know how Mr. Knight feels about his anonymity. He will be furious if he thinks his precious Institute is going to be dragged through the media mud."

"You are both overreacting," Fenner said, impatience sharpening his tone. He put on his glasses. "I assure you everything is under control. When the detective in charge of the case called to confirm that the medication that was found in Geddings's house had been stolen from the clinic I had no choice but to tell him the truth. There is no getting around the fact that the vials were taken from the Institute's medication locker. But I explained that I had let Geddings go precisely because I suspected he was the thief."

"Are you sure he bought that story?" Margaret asked.

"Yes," Fenner shot back. "Logan wanted to know why the Institute hadn't pressed charges. I explained it was because we couldn't prove anything and because Geddings had taken off for parts unknown. If the police want to chase after Geddings, that's their business. As far as we're concerned, it ends here. The Institute is not involved."

Guthrie thought about that for a moment. "You may be right. Given the speed of the twenty-four-hour news cycle, it's possible this will blow over very quickly. No one will care that two low-level drug dealers are dead and a third has disappeared."

"It's the podcaster and the writer who worry me," Margaret said.

Hugh groaned. "They could be a problem."

He went to the window and surveyed his campus empire with a moody gaze. Margaret knew what he was thinking. He, like Fenner and herself, was fully invested in the success of the Sleep Institute. None of them had ended up at the small backwater college by choice. They were here because, for various personal and professional reasons, their careers had been fading for years. They all knew it was too late to reinvent themselves and start over. Carnelian College was the last stop for each of them.

Margaret looked at Fenner. "What happened to the medication?"

"The detective returned the vials and I personally logged them back into inventory," Fenner said.

"What did you tell the detective about the meds?" Margaret asked.

"The truth, of course," Fenner said, exasperated. "I explained that it was an experimental sleep medication and that the Institute was participating in clinical trials."

"Was he satisfied?" Hugh asked.

"Yes," Fenner grunted. "Why wouldn't he have been satisfied?"

Margaret looked at each man in turn. "The police may be satisfied, but that still leaves us with the podcast people. I think we can assume one of two things will happen."

Hugh scowled. "What are you talking about?"

Margaret got to her feet and adjusted the drape of her stylishly cut blazer. "Llewellyn and Drake may conclude that they just hit pay dirt in terms of content for their podcast. If that happens they will hang around Carnelian to ask more questions."

Hugh's jaw twitched. "That will stir up more trouble for the Institute."

Margaret went to the door. "The other possibility is that they will realize there's no story here—or, at least, not one they want to pursue. After all, it sounds like they nearly got killed today. Podcasters are only interested in becoming media celebrities. They aren't real journalists, and they certainly aren't agents of law enforcement. With luck, Llewellyn and Drake won't want to take the risk of getting murdered for the sake of an episode of *The Lost Night Files*."

She opened the door and let herself out into the hall. Llewellyn and Drake might decide to abandon their podcast project and leave town, but she and Hugh and Fenner were trapped in Carnelian. They had fallen to the bottom of the academic pool. Keeping the Carnelian Sleep Institute open and well-funded by Mr. Knight was the number one priority for all of them.

Fenner was obsessed with his experiments. He was happy to run Mr. Knight's clinical trial on the side so long as he could continue to pursue his own trials with the hallucinogen he ordered from a compounding pharmacy that did not ask too many questions. He was convinced the crap was the next miracle cure for insomnia. Hugh was in a state of near-panic at the realization that the money might stop. Neither man could be depended on to handle the crisis.

It was up to her to formulate a strategy for saving the Institute. She needed more information on Llewellyn and Drake. There had to be a weak point. There was always a weak point. All you had to do was look for it.

CHAPTER TWENTY-FIVE

CALVIN SENT THEM the data on the Carnelian Sleep Institute finances shortly before five that afternoon. Ambrose added it to what he and Pallas had gleaned from the newspaper research they had done with the help of the reference librarian at the Carnelian Public Library.

They discussed the findings over wine and dinner at the vegetarian café.

"Here's what we've got," he said, flipping to the first page of his notes. "The Carnelian Sleep Institute was established about a year ago thanks to a major donation to the college endowment made by an anonymous donor. That was front-page news here in town at the time. The money was funneled into the college account by a financial advisory company that handled it for the unknown client. Calvin says he hasn't had any luck identifying the donor, who is concealed behind a million shell corporations. I told him to let that go for a while and focus on Brooke Kendrick. With luck he will have something for us after dinner."

Pallas, seated on the other side of the booth, leaned forward and folded her arms on the table, her expression intent, her intelligent eyes illuminated with energy. Her words whispered in his head again. *Nothing like almost getting killed together to cement a friendship, I always say.*

Okay, that was probably true. A close brush with death was bound to create some sort of bond between two people. But they had shared a lot more than the disaster at the Geddings house. They had each undergone an unexplained spell of amnesia and they had both emerged from their lost nights with a new sensitivity that could only be described as paranormal in nature. They had both worried that they might be on track to take up residence in a psychiatric ward. Bottom line, they had a lot in common, which was a solid basis for a friendship, or at least a partnership, just as she had said.

So why did that bother him?

Dumbass question. He knew the answer. He wanted something more than a friendship or a partnership. He had wanted *her* the first time he saw her, and things had only gotten more complicated. There had been times when he thought he had picked up subtle signals that made him hope the attraction was mutual, but he could not be certain, and he was uneasy about pushing for clarification. It was too soon and they had too many problems.

"According to Calvin, the major players at the college are the dean, Hugh Guthrie, and the director of the endowment, Margaret Moore," he continued. "Both of them were hired before the anonymous donor showed up. They, of course, jumped at the offer of all that free money. So did everyone else. They agreed to the terms, even though the school had no history of having engaged in sleep research. In fairness, they didn't have much choice. Carnelian is a small institution with a shrinking endowment. Enrollment has been falling for years, and the alumni have not been generous."

"Moore and Guthrie must have been thrilled," Pallas said. "The anonymous donor made them look good. They would have gotten the credit for attracting the huge donation. Interestingly, there's no indication the donor was a graduate or had any previous connection to the school. The only reason he rushed to its rescue was because he wanted the Institute opened."

"A sleep clinic that specializes in dream disorders," Ambrose said.

"Maybe he's obsessed with his own sleep disorder so he funded an entire clinic to do research in the field," Pallas suggested.

"It would not be the first time someone established a research facility designed to focus on a disorder or an illness that afflicted the donor or members of the donor's family," Ambrose said. "But instead of bringing in world-class talent, the college hires Dr. Conrad Fenner, who, thanks to Calvin, we now know was quietly forced out of his last job."

Pallas glanced at her own notes. "He was accused of violating research protocols by conducting experiments with a drug that had not been approved for trials."

"So the anonymous donor goes to the trouble and expense of establishing the Carnelian Sleep Institute and then specifies that a disgraced researcher must be appointed director," Ambrose said. "That doesn't seem right."

Pallas looked up. "Fenner might have been accused of violating research protocols, but maybe the donor thinks the drug holds promise. Maybe he was convinced that Fenner was on the right track, an undiscovered genius, and wants to give him the opportunity to continue the research."

"That makes sense," Ambrose said. "But there's another possibility. Maybe our mysterious donor insisted that Fenner be hired as director because he knew he could control and manipulate him."

"To what purpose?"

Ambrose tapped the notebook against the table. "What if Fenner is carrying out research on a drug the donor controls? Think about it. If you developed a dangerous new drug, one that no legitimate, reputable research lab would test on human subjects, how would you go about getting it into a drug trial?"

Pallas frowned. "If you had a great deal of money, you might set up your own research institute and appoint someone you knew you could manipulate to run the experiments."

Ambrose tried to look away from her fierce gaze, but he could not break the spell.

"I need to get inside Fenner's house," he said.

"More B and E?" Pallas said quietly.

She didn't sound disapproving, he decided. Instead she sounded thoughtful.

He lowered his voice even though there was no one seated at the nearby tables.

"It won't be hard to find an address for Fenner," he said. "It's not like he's trying to hide."

THEY LEFT THE café and walked back to the hotel through the damp, streetlamp-infused fog. With his normal vision limited by the mist, Ambrose opened the window in his mind. Auras were visible day or night and regardless of the atmospheric conditions. It was a handy way to watch for trouble on the street.

None of the handful of people on the sidewalk ahead looked threatening. He glanced back over his shoulder. A jittery energy field flared and flashed in an erratic manner. Auras did not indicate gender, but there was no doubt the person was moving quickly, closing the distance.

"You are in your other vision, aren't you?" Pallas said.

He turned back to watch the sidewalk ahead of them. "You can tell?"

"I felt energy shift in the atmosphere. What did you see?"

"Either we happen to be between someone who is very anxious to meet his dealer or we are about to get mugged."

"I'd rather not get mugged." She reached into her messenger bag and took out her Taser. "I think I've had all the excitement I can handle for one day."

"I have, too, but it would be interesting to find out who is behind us."

The hotel was still two blocks away, but the unlit entrance of **Prism: Your destination for all things metaphysical** offered concealment. He pulled Pallas into the shadows.

"Maybe it's Jodi Luckhurst again," Pallas whispered.

"No, it's not Luckhurst," he said. "This is a very different energy field. Promise me you won't use the Taser unless it's absolutely necessary. If you take down some innocent citizen we are both going to end up back at the police station. I don't know about you, but I don't want to spend the rest of the night chatting with Detective Logan."

"Neither do I."

He listened to the footsteps echoing in the fog. They were louder now; moving more quickly. A moment later a figure went past the doorway, aura snapping and crackling.

Ambrose exhaled and stepped out of the doorway. He watched the sparking energy field until it reached the intersection. Instead of continuing across the street, the figure abruptly turned the corner and disappeared.

"Looks like my first guess was right," Ambrose said. "Whoever was behind us was looking for a dealer, not us."

"You're sure?"

"Not the first time I've seen someone in desperate need of a fix. It doesn't make for a stable aura."

Pallas put the Taser back into her big bag. They walked the rest of the way to the hotel in silence. He had no idea what Pallas was thinking but he spent the time trying to decide if it was too early in their relationship to suggest an after-dinner drink in his room.

Definitely too early. Besides, there was a very real possibility she would turn him down. He was not up for the rejection tonight.

The front door of the hotel was locked because of the late hour. He used his key card to get them inside. There was a welcoming fire burning in the lobby. His spirits rose when he noticed that the dark, cozy little bar was still open. Maybe an after-dinner drink in there would work. It wouldn't suggest intimacy the way going upstairs to a room did. An after-dinner drink in a hotel bar was the sort of thing colleagues did. It was a way to decompress after a long day during which they had nearly been killed.

"Don't know about you, but I could use a medicinal glass of something before turning in," he said, going for casual. "What do you say we have a nightcap in the bar?"

Pallas came to a halt in the middle of the lobby.

"Crap," she said.

He took a deep breath. "Okay. Forget I asked."

"I don't believe it," Pallas said.

"It was just a thought."

"This may not amount to stalking, but it is damn close," Pallas said.

"What the hell?" Righteous indignation replaced the pain of rejection. "Don't you think that under the circumstances that's a bit extreme?"

When she did not respond he turned his head to look at her. He didn't need to open the window to see what was happening in her aura. Her voice and body language said it all. She was furious.

"Excuse me," she said. "I'll take care of this. See you in the morning."

He finally realized her attention was fixed on the entrance to the lobby bar. When he looked in that direction he saw a man seated alone at one of the small tables.

Ambrose opened the window and took a quick look at the man's energy field. There was a lot of tension in it, but aside from that there was nothing alarming about it.

"Do you know him?" he asked.

"Theo Collier of Theodore Collier, Architecture and Design."

"Oh, right. The ex."

"Precisely. Ex. He has no business being here. I will explain that to him in very clear terms. Good night, Ambrose. See you in the morning."

She tightened her grip on the messenger bag slung over her shoulder, stalked across the lobby, and disappeared into the shadows of the bar.

Ambrose waited for a moment. When Pallas did not immediately reappear he reluctantly headed for the elevator. He changed his mind at the last minute and took the stairs instead. It wasn't until he was opening the door of his room that he realized what was bothering him.

When Pallas had vanished into the darkness of the bar, her aura had been on fire. Energy was energy. It wasn't always possible to identify the emotion that ignited the flames. She was in a volatile mood, but in this case there was no way to know if she was furious or secretly thrilled to see the ex again.

He ditched his jacket and sat down on the side of the bed, trying to predict what would happen in the bar. Reading emotions was never easy, and it was seriously complicated by physical attraction. There was plenty of the latter going on in this situation, at least on his end. They said nearly getting killed sometimes triggered a primal need to have sex. Something to do with adrenaline and other hormones. Not that he'd needed a close brush with death to make him want to have sex with Pallas.

He needed to stop thinking about sex with Pallas.

He finally decided that the scene downstairs would unfold in one of two possible ways. Either Pallas would tell Theodore Collier to get the hell out of Carnelian or else she would invite him upstairs to her room.

Or maybe not. Maybe there was a third option that he could not visualize because he was a hot mess at the moment.

He pondered the problem for a while. If there was one thing he was pretty good at, thanks to his psychic vibe, it was predicting how people would react under pressure. It was the skill set that had made him valuable to Failure Analysis. But when it came to Pallas there were too many unknowns.

He got to his feet, crossed the room, and opened the closet to take out his duffel bag. Unzipping the bag, he started to remove the devices he used to give himself some peace of mind at night.

He had set out the motion detector and the hotel door lock and was reaching for the coiled length of chain and ankle manacle when his phone rang.

He looked at it, a ridiculous flicker of hope igniting. Maybe things had ended early downstairs and Pallas wanted to talk about it. He dropped the chain into the duffel, picked up the phone, and glanced at the screen. The little rush of excitement faded.

"What have you got, Calvin?" he asked.

"Brooke Kendrick definitely existed," Calvin said. "But six weeks ago she vanished without a trace. The interesting thing is that no one seems to have noticed."

"Hang on, let me make some notes," Ambrose said.

He reached for his notebook and pen. "Okay, I'm ready. Start talking."

He listened closely and wrote quickly.

When the call ended he got to his feet and closed the notebook. His gaze snagged on the open duffel bag. What had he been thinking? No smart woman wanted to sleep with a man who had to chain himself to a bed every night.

CHAPTER TWENTY-SIX

W HAT ARE YOU doing here, Theo?" Pallas said, coming to a stop on the opposite side of the small table. "This looks a lot like stalking."

She had her initial rush of fury under control now. She wasn't yelling. She wasn't making a scene. She was dealing with the situation like a mature adult. A pissed-off adult, but a mature pissed-off adult.

"I am not stalking you," Theo said. "I wanted to talk to you in person because I knew you wouldn't take my calls. I went by your apartment and the manager said you had left town for a few days. She told me you were researching another podcast here in Carnelian."

Pallas groaned. "I should have known. Bev Shaw is a fan. She loves to keep tabs on our investigations."

"I went online to check out Carnelian, and the first thing that popped up was the news of the explosion. One of the reports mentioned that two people from a podcast team barely escaped the burning house."

"So you hopped in your car and drove all the way up the coast from L.A.?"

"I was worried about you. Is that so strange? We're friends, Pallas. Colleagues. Are you all right?"

She watched him for a moment and finally concluded she didn't need Ambrose and his psychic talent to tell her that Theo was nervous. Wary. She still scared him. The only reason he would have come looking for her was because he was convinced he had no choice. So, not a stalker—just a desperate architect.

She sat down across from him and dropped the messenger bag on the floor beside her chair.

There were only a handful of people in the dimly lit space. Two men lounged on barstools and talked sports with the bartender. They were not showing any interest in the attractive businesswoman who sat alone in a booth meditating on a martini.

Theo hadn't changed, Pallas decided. He was still good-looking— toned and fit, stylishly dressed in an on-trend way that managed to walk the line between fashionably edgy and I-don't-give-a-damn-about-fashion. He might be nervous about sitting here with her, but he still had the ambitious, determined vibe. There was, however, something different about him. It took her a few beats to nail the problem.

He still possessed all of the attributes that had attracted her back at the start, but now she knew he was not the man she had believed him to be.

No, that wasn't quite true. He was not the man she had wanted him to be.

Let's be honest. You're not the woman he believed you to be. Not the woman he wanted you to be. Don't blame Lucent Springs. You never were that woman.

"I'm fine," she said.

"I can't believe you almost got killed because of a podcast story,"

Theo said, his jaw tight. "What were you thinking, investigating a drug dealer? You're not an agent of law enforcement."

"I'm aware of that. You've made your opinion of my mental health well-known. I appreciate your concern for my welfare, but we are no longer a couple and we are no longer in business together. You are under no obligation to worry about me. You can go home now."

"Are you serious? It's late. I'm not driving that old highway out of town at this hour."

"Theo—"

He exhaled heavily. "I came here because I was concerned about you, but I also want to talk business with you."

"Of course you had a business reason for making the trip. That explains everything. I always knew you were ambitious. It was one of the things I admired about you. But I'm amazed to find out your need for success is strong enough to make you overcome your fear of me."

Theo's eyes narrowed with sudden rage. He lowered his voice another notch. "I am not afraid of you."

"Yes, you are, and we both know it's because of what happened the day I caught you and Vera in the supply closet."

"Can you blame me? You went off the deep end that day and over-reacted."

Pallas gave him a steely smile. "And scared the shit out of you."

"Damn it, Pallas, I've got a lot at stake here. After the way you walked out on me in the middle of a major project, you owe me."

"No, I don't owe you, but tell me why you're here so that I can say no and then go upstairs and get some sleep. As you are aware, I've had a rather difficult day. What is this business you want to discuss?"

Theo leaned forward, fiercely determined now. "The kind of business that could make a lot of money for both of us. The kind that can get us featured in the big trade magazines."

"No offense, but how did you manage to land a project like that?"

Theo held up a hand. "I'll explain, but first let me buy you a drink."

"No thanks."

"We used to be friends," he said.

"You said you loved me. We talked about marriage. We were sleeping together. I've got news for you—that is not a friendship."

"Looking back, you could say our relationship was a case of partners with benefits," he said.

"Don't you dare rewrite our history," she hissed. "I won't let you do that. The only thing that matters is that I trusted you and you not only concluded I was delusional, you cheated on me."

"Don't blame me for what happened to us," Theo shot back in low tones. "You are the one who blew up our relationship, and you know it. You changed, Pallas. Admit it. After your episode of amnesia you developed an obsession with the paranormal. You decided you had some sort of psychic talent. Just look at you. You're abandoning what could have been a great career in order to work on a podcast that pretends to investigate cold cases. Do you have any idea how bizarre that sounds?"

"If I'm so weird why are you sitting here in a bar in Carnelian trying to get me to work on a commission with you?"

"Look, I realize our personal relationship is complicated."

"No, it's not complicated—it's over."

"Fine," he said. "It's over. That doesn't mean we can't do business together."

"Actually, it does mean that."

"I know you need the money just as much as I do," Theo said. "Neither of us can afford to turn down this commission."

"Is that right? Aren't you the one who told me that interior designers were a dime a dozen?"

"I was angry. Listen to me, Pallas. I know you haven't worked much lately, and there's no money in the podcast, right?"

"So?"

"So hear me out," Theo said. "Please."

"Wow. You are desperate. All right, what is this amazing commission?"

Theo smiled with an air of triumph. "Nothing less than the restoration of the estate of a nineteen twenties–era Hollywood producer named Carson Flint."

"I've never heard of it."

"The original name of the property was Summer House. It sits on a bluff outside of Burning Cove, about a hundred miles north of L.A. Classic example of the Spanish Colonial Revival. It's changed hands several times over the years, and it's been through a lot of renovations. The new owner wants to restore it to its original condition, and money is no object."

"Money is always an object."

"Apparently not in this case," Theo said. "Our client is a tech billionaire. His status in the industry guarantees the project will get a huge amount of media exposure."

"Which tech billionaire are we talking about?"

"He prefers to remain anonymous," Theo said. "At least until we sign the contract. I was contacted by his agent."

"Theo—"

"That's not unusual when you're dealing with high-end clients," Theo said quickly. "You know as well as I do people like that never handle this kind of thing personally. They always have staff to manage every aspect of their lives."

"I know." And with that she felt the energy of her anger drain away. A sense of calm resignation and acceptance took its place.

There was nothing personal here. It was business, just as Theo said. All she wanted to do now was go upstairs to her room. She was about to collect her messenger bag, get to her feet, and head for the door when a thought stopped her. "Why me?"

Theo looked wary again. "What do you mean?"

"One of the last things you said to me was that it wouldn't be hard to replace me. Why come looking for me for this project?"

Theo shrugged. "The client toured the Callaway Hotel and was impressed with the interiors. According to his agent, he thinks you captured the dramatic, nineteen twenties glamour aesthetic but transcended it with a warmth and grace that will appeal to the modern sensibilities of today's upmarket travelers and vacationers."

Pallas wrinkled her nose. "I love it when the client talks dirty."

Theo flashed her his trademark grin, the one that had once had the power to make her believe they had something deep and meaningful together.

"So do I," he said.

"I appreciate the offer." Pallas reached down and gripped the strap of the messenger bag. "But I'm afraid I'm too busy with the podcast to take on a major project like the one you're talking about."

"A podcast investigation?" Theo's voice got tight. "That's not a job. It's not even a hobby. And I'll tell you what else it isn't. It isn't healthy. You should be talking to a shrink about your obsession with these so-called paranormal cold cases. There is no such thing as the paranormal, and you are not investigating real murders or disappearances. You're chasing conspiracy theories. Rumors. Ghost stories."

"*The Lost Night Files* is not interested in hauntings," Pallas said. "We do disappearances and unexplained deaths. Good night, Theo."

He bolted upright out of his chair and grabbed her arm. "Just think about this Burning Cove commission. Please. That's all I'm asking."

She looked down at his fingers wrapped around her arm and then raised her eyes to meet his. "Let go."

His eyes widened. He released her as if he had received an electric shock and took a quick step back.

"Please say you'll think about coming in on this project," he said through tight teeth. "Name your price. Whatever you want, it's yours. I'm begging you, Pallas."

He was telling the truth. Her intuition pinged.

"Why?" she asked.

Theo scowled. "What do you mean, why? I thought I made it clear. This is the biggest, most important commission I've ever been offered and I need you to make the client happy. Don't tell me you couldn't use the money. Think of the boost to your reputation. We both know you haven't had any important work since . . . you know."

"Since I developed my little obsession with the paranormal? Is that what you were going to say?"

"It's true, isn't it?" he said. "You haven't done anything except some small condo remodels for months."

"I appreciate your concern for my financial welfare, but something tells me there's more going on here. Are you in trouble, Theo?"

He got a mutinous look. For a moment she thought he wasn't going to respond. Then he visibly deflated. He shoved his fingers through his hair, which fell neatly back into place, just as he had known it would.

"After you left I took out a loan," he said. "A big one."

"I see. That explains a lot. I did wonder how you were able to move your business into that sparkling new building and hire your own in-house design team."

"You know how the real world works," Theo muttered. "You've got to look like a winner if you want to attract the attention of winners. I'm good, Pallas. You know that. But reputation is everything in this business. I need the Carson Flint commission to take my firm to the next level. You aren't in great shape, either, business-wise. I know your last serious client fired you after the Saltwood incident hit the press. This is a chance for both of us to recover before it's too late."

Business was business. He was right, there was no money in the podcast—not yet, at any rate—and her career was, at best, in a precarious state. Saltwood had done a great deal of damage. Theo was right about something else as well—she had been distracted since the Lucent Springs experience. The result was that her career was in free fall. If she didn't take drastic action soon she would be looking for another line of work.

"When do you need an answer?" she said.

Hope flared in Theo's eyes. "As soon as possible. I can stall the client's agent for a while but not indefinitely."

"I need to think," she said. "And right now I'm too exhausted to do that. I'm going to bed."

"While you're thinking try to focus on the future," Theo said. "Not the past. Don't let our personal relationship stand in the way. Going forward it will be strictly business between us. You and I will be partners in this venture."

"Right. Strictly business. Partners." She started toward the door but hesitated. "Where are you staying?"

"Here." Theo looked wary. "And, no, I wasn't stalking you. There aren't a lot of options in this town."

"No, there aren't," she said.

She went briskly toward the door and did not look back until she was about to turn the corner into the elevator lobby. She caught movement inside the dimly lit bar. The woman who had been sitting alone in a booth was on her feet. A weary business traveler on her way upstairs to bed.

But she did not follow Pallas out into the lobby. She stopped at Theo's table.

Pallas stepped into the elevator. It looked like Theo would not be spending the rest of the night alone in the bar. She watched the doors close and asked herself how she felt about that.

She realized she did not give a damn. If she did agree to a partnership with Theo it really would be strictly business. That understanding lifted her spirits for all of two seconds. That was how long it took to remember that a business partnership was what she currently had going with Ambrose Drake.

"Right," she muttered as she swiped herself into her room. "And how's that working out for you?"

THEO LOOKED AT the woman who had just sat down at the table. She was attractive in an austere, professional way. Crisply tailored business suit. Black high heels. A little discreet gold jewelry. A successful business exec, he decided, maybe an academic recruiter or a wealthy alumna in town to give a sizable donation in exchange for having a building named after her.

Under other circumstances he might have been interested in a casual, no-strings-attached hookup, but not tonight. It had been a long drive, and while the conversation with Pallas had left him with a little hope, a satisfactory outcome was still in doubt. His future was riding on her decision—the decision of a woman who was in the process of sacrificing her once-promising career in favor of chasing a wild conspiracy theory. The decision of a woman who had once sent a chill of primal terror through him. He shivered at the memory.

"Let me introduce myself," the woman on the other side of the table said. "My name is Margaret Moore. It looks like you've been abandoned. I think we have a few things in common. The friend I was supposed to meet here tonight never showed. You're almost finished with that drink. Can I buy you another one?"

What the fuck. It wasn't like he had anything better to do tonight.

"Thanks," he said. "I could use the company. Theo Collier."

"In town on business?" Margaret asked.

"Yes," he said. "You?"

"I live here," Margaret said. "I'm with the college."

He eyed the tailored suit. "You don't look like a member of the faculty."

"I'm on the financial side of things. I oversee the endowment."

Warily he raised one hand, palm out. "If you're looking for a donation from me, don't waste your time. I am not in a charitable mood."

Margaret's chuckle was soft and not without sympathy. "I don't blame you." She signaled the bartender and turned back to Theo. "I know who Ms. Llewellyn is. By now, I think everyone in town is aware of her. She and some writer named Ambrose Drake are here doing research for a podcast. Are you a member of their crew?"

He choked on the last swallow of his drink. "Fuck, no."

"Did you know that Pallas Llewellyn and the writer nearly got killed today?" Margaret asked.

He grimaced. "Yeah. Saw it online. It's all over the local news. I warned Pallas that she was taking too many risks for the sake of the podcast."

Margaret smiled. "You and I have a lot to talk about."

CHAPTER TWENTY-SEVEN

THE TEXT FROM Ambrose came in just as Pallas opened the minibar.

I have news but it can wait until morning if you're busy.

She hit reply.

A polite way of asking if I'm alone. The answer is yes. Come on up.

There were two tiny bottles of after-dinner liqueurs in the minibar. She removed both, grabbed a couple of glasses, and set everything out on the table. Ambrose announced his arrival with a soft knock.

She was surprised by the rush of relief she got when she opened the door and saw him standing in the hall.

"Come on in," she said. "I was just about to have a drink. Join me?"

"Sure." He walked into the room and closed the door. "Everything okay? Or should I not ask?"

"You can ask." She flopped down on the desk chair and waved him to the large padded reading chair. "But the answer is complicated. The short version is that Theo wants to bring me in on a major project. Evidently the client saw my work at the Callaway Hotel and is insisting that I lead the design team that will be handling the interiors of an old estate he just bought."

"Huh."

She twisted the cap off one of the little bottles and splashed the contents into a glass. "What's that supposed to mean?"

"Does it strike you that having your ex show up here in Carnelian is a rather interesting coincidence?"

Startled, she paused in the act of removing the cap from the other bottle. "No. Theo is very anxious to land this particular commission. He's got a big loan to pay off. Also he's convinced that the job would do wonders for both of our careers. To be fair, he's right."

"Okay," Ambrose said, lowering himself into the oversized reading chair. "I'll be the first to admit that I tend to question any and all coincidences these days."

She finished uncapping the bottle and poured the liqueur into the other glass. "You are not alone. But if you knew Theo you'd realize that his presence here in Carnelian is a perfectly logical business move. He's got a true artistic vision, and he believes in that vision. He's also ambitious. In addition, he's in financial trouble, and he sees a way out that happens to involve me."

"How did he know you were in town?"

"He asked the manager of the apartment complex where I live." Pallas picked up her glass, sat back, stretched out her legs, and crossed her ankles. "It's not like I'm trying to hide. He could have tracked me down without Bev Shaw's help. *The Lost Night Files* is a small podcast, but it has a loyal following. Everyone in Carnelian knows I'm here doing research for a series. So the news that I'm in town and that I almost got killed today is readily available."

"I should have known it would be impossible to keep this investigation quiet."

"The Lost Night Files isn't Failure Analysis," she said. "We don't do clandestine work. We don't try to stay in the shadows. In the podcast business, most publicity is good publicity."

"I get it." Ambrose drank some of the liqueur and lounged deeper into the padded chair. "Fortunately for me, no one seems to remember the writer who nearly got killed along with the podcast investigator. On second thought, that's probably not a good omen for my career. Moving right along, I had an interesting conversation with Calvin the Magnificent tonight."

She stilled. "Your text said you have news."

"Brooke Kendrick lived alone in an apartment in San Jose. No close family. No friends. She was a software engineer and up until eight months ago made a good living doing contract work for various companies. Apparently she was very, very good at online security. I could tell Calvin was impressed."

Pallas raised her brows. "What happened eight months ago?"

"She suddenly stopped doing the consulting work and, as far as Calvin could tell, became a full-time Internet gambler. Shortly thereafter she booked appointments with a string of online therapists and sleep counselors. Six weeks ago she walked out of her apartment carrying a backpack, used an app to call a ride, and was never seen again. The manager of the apartment complex figured she had lost a lot of money because of the gambling and had skipped out on the rent."

"That's it?" Pallas said. "She just vanished?"

"Apparently."

"That's hard to do in the modern world."

"No," Ambrose said, "it's not hard to do if no one is looking for you."

Pallas thought about that. "Just as no one searched for Geddings. I see what you mean. You did say Brooke Kendrick was a loner."

"Evidently no one except the apartment manager realized she was missing. Calvin is going to do a deep dive into Kendrick's past to see if she ever reported an episode of transient global amnesia."

Pallas caught her breath. "Regardless, we know she wound up at the Institute. Judging by that page that was torn out of a logbook, she had a bad reaction to whatever medication Fenner gave her. Fenner killed her."

"Or Geddings. We can't say for sure."

"Regardless, Emery Geddings took care of the body and helped clean up the scene. But there was a witness. You."

"Let's face it, I'm a lousy witness," Ambrose said. "All I saw was a laundry cart being wheeled down a hallway."

"You saw blood on the floor."

"Which Fenner will deny. Supposedly I was sleepwalking, remember? Dreaming." Ambrose swirled the liqueur in his glass. His eyes burned. "What is going on at that sleep clinic?"

"We know what's going on. Fenner is running experiments on people. The real question is why?"

"Maybe I'll find some answers tomorrow when I take a look around his place."

"I'll go with you," Pallas said.

Ambrose shook his head. "Not a good idea. This isn't like the Geddings situation. It will be straight up B and E, the kind of stuff that can get you arrested."

"We do this together. We're partners. Besides, I'm the one with the talent for identifying hot spots, remember?"

Ambrose didn't look pleased, but he didn't argue. They sipped their drinks in silence for a while.

"Think you'll go back into a partnership with Collier?" Ambrose asked eventually.

"From a professional standpoint it would be the smart thing to do," Pallas said. "Theoretically I ought to be able to put the personal crap aside and focus on the opportunity. My career has been mostly on hold since Lucent Springs. I'm burning through my savings at a pretty fast clip."

Ambrose watched her with a knowing look. "I sense hesitation."

She smiled. "Did you come to that conclusion by analyzing my aura?"

"No aura reading necessary. It's all there in your voice and your body language."

"Yes, well, I wasn't trying to hide my feelings. I am conflicted."

"But leaning toward turning down the offer."

"Yes," she said. "The thing is, I really don't think I can put the personal crap aside. I am going to be seriously annoyed every time I look at Theo. I can't do my best work under those conditions. In addition, I am currently obsessed with finding out what happened to my friends and me in the Lucent Springs Hotel. On top of that, I want to find out what happened to you here in Carnelian. The bottom line is that I won't be able to focus on restoring that old estate."

"Just like I can't focus on finishing my book."

"I suppose so. Besides, it's not as if Theo has changed his opinion of me. I can tell he still thinks I am at least semi-delusional. And there's another issue."

"What?"

Pallas set the empty glass down on the table. "I told you, I scare him."

Ambrose nodded in understanding. "The same way I frightened Maureen."

"Your ex?"

"Yeah. Hell, I managed to scare my whole family."

"In my case it's a little more complicated, but it comes down to the same thing."

"Think you and Collier would still be together if it hadn't been for that lost night in Lucent Springs?" Ambrose asked.

"Good question. I've thought about it a lot lately. The answer is no. It's true we had our work in common. That is a huge bond. And we enjoyed a lot of the same things. Until the happy chickens and cows and pigs debacle, we got along quite well. But on some level I always knew he would walk away in a heartbeat if the going got tough or if something better came along."

"I get the picture," Ambrose said. "Commitment issues."

"I also knew deep down that it would not be the end of the world if he left. We never moved in together. We used to joke that we had to live apart because we would never be able to achieve a design aesthetic in a shared residence that would satisfy both of us."

"But that wasn't the real reason," Ambrose said.

"No. There was always something missing. We blamed it on the fact that, like a gazillion other people, we are both children of divorce. The therapists tell you that the experience can result in commitment and trust issues. But I prefer to think that's just psych-speak for what amounts to being saddled with a realistic view of human nature at an early age."

"Maybe. I've come to the same conclusion but I don't have the same excuse. My family is close and I'm pretty sure my parents are still in love. But, yep, I've definitely got commitment and trust issues these days."

"What happened with you and Maureen?"

"We were together for a few months but we never moved in together," Ambrose said. "We told each other we needed our space, but as you said, there always seemed to be something missing. Our relationship was on shaky ground before San Diego. It would have ended sooner or later."

"It's us, not them, isn't it? Do you think our psychic vibe makes us risk-averse?"

"Asks the woman who stepped over a trip wire that was connected to a small bomb," Ambrose said.

"There are all kinds of risks. Some, like that booby trap, can be calculated, especially given our talents. Others, not so much."

"True." Ambrose gripped the sides of the big armchair, preparing to get to his feet. "It's late. It's been a hell of day. I'd better go back to my room and let you get some sleep."

"I doubt if I'll sleep much tonight." She watched him. "What about you?"

"With luck it will be the usual—a string of short naps and the opening clips of some bad dreams. Don't worry, I've taken steps to make sure I don't wander the halls of the hotel. Wouldn't want to frighten the locals."

She hesitated, telling herself she would probably regret what she was about to do but knowing she was going to do it anyway.

"You don't need to leave on account of me," she said. "I wouldn't mind having company for a while. When was the last time you had a decent night's sleep?"

"Before San Diego."

"What happens when you try to sleep?"

For a moment she thought he wasn't going to answer, but after reflecting on the question he responded.

"I feel like I'm sliding into another dimension, a dreamscape," he said. He watched the night on the other side of the hotel room window as he spoke. "It's not just the sleepwalking that scares me, although that's bad enough. What I'm really afraid of is that I'll go into a dream and never come out of it."

"Is it always the same dreamscape?"

"I think so," he said. "But who knows? I don't dare enter it. In addition to being afraid that I'll get trapped in it, I'm worried I'll sleep-walk again. I've somehow conditioned myself to wake up if I sense that I'm going too deep, but the result is that even on a good night I just nap for about twenty to thirty minutes at a time. I wake up, make myself sit on the side of the bed or get to my feet to break the spell, and then go back to sleep. If I can. Sometimes I do, sometimes I don't."

She studied him for a long moment, trying to make a decision.

Ambrose watched her. "What?"

"I think I can help you get a few hours of calm sleep," she said.

"If you're talking about sex, I appreciate the offer, but I don't think—"

"*No.*" She stared at him, horrified.

He groaned and closed his eyes. "Shit. I just went down a very bad road, didn't I?" He opened his eyes. "I'm sorry. I don't know what else to say."

His regret and pain and, above all, his soul-deep weariness broke through her shock. She relaxed and put her hand on the table.

"No sex involved," she said, going for light and reassuring. "I was going to suggest that you let me try to balance your energy field."

"What does that mean?"

"I'm not sure," she admitted. "But I've had a few experiences that make me think I can temporarily calm a person's energy. I might be able to help you go to sleep and stay asleep."

"How?"

"I don't know. The first time I did it was in Saltwood. The killer grabbed me, intending to slit my throat. The instant he touched me I felt his sick vibe and I somehow flattened it. The media and the police said he appeared to have suffered a stroke or a heart attack. I didn't try to correct that impression but I knew that wasn't what really happened."

"What do you think happened?" Ambrose asked.

"I'm not sure, but I could feel him lose consciousness. It was as if I had flipped a light switch. You want the truth? I think I might have killed him."

To her astonishment, Ambrose looked amused.

"Is that supposed to reassure me?" he asked.

"I'm trying to explain that there may be some risk involved."

"Any other practical experience?"

"Yes, one other incident you should know about. I told you that I found out Theo was cheating on me."

"I remember."

"It was a rather dramatic moment. I opened the supply closet to get some new sketching pencils and I discovered Theo and one of the junior architects inside. Let's just say they were not talking about the differences between the Rem Koolhaas and Frank Lloyd Wright aesthetics."

"Understood," Ambrose said.

"What followed was a massive quarrel. At one point Theo grabbed my arm and wouldn't let go." Pallas hesitated. "I . . . made him release me."

"With your energy-balancing vibe?"

"Yes. I didn't take it as far with him as I did with the killer in Saltwood, but I'm sure I could have achieved the same result. What's more, Theo knew I was doing something to him. I could see the shock and fear in his eyes. That's the real reason he's scared of me now. He doesn't understand what really happened. I'm sure he tells himself it was his imagination. But deep down, yes, I terrified him."

"Are you proposing to knock me out?" Ambrose said, his tone very dry. "Render me unconscious? I don't think that constitutes a good night's sleep."

She smiled. "No, I'm suggesting you let me balance your energy field the way I would the energy in a house or a room. I'll just re-arrange the furniture. Repaint a couple of the walls. You'd be amazed how much difference a fresh coat of paint can make."

He stretched out his hand. "Why not?"

She threaded her fingers through his, gripped his hand very tightly, and heightened her talent.

CHAPTER TWENTY-EIGHT

CONRAD FENNER UNLOCKED the front door of the small house, walked into the hall, turned on the light—and stopped short when he saw the package on the floor. It was wrapped in brown paper, just as the other shipments had been. No address. No postage. No shipping label. It had been hand delivered.

Just like the other shipments.

The relief hit him so hard it left him feeling shaky and light-headed. He set the briefcase on the floor and used both hands to pick up the package. He carried it into the kitchen and placed it carefully on the round wooden table.

He sat down and took a moment to catch his breath. The research trial would go forward. The anonymous donor he and Moore and Guthrie had dubbed Mr. Knight apparently did not yet know that Ambrose Drake and a podcaster named Llewellyn were in town asking questions. Or maybe he wasn't concerned because the situation was under control.

They had all had a very close call.

It had been one thing to make the problem of the patient in room B go away six weeks ago. No one had come around asking about Brooke Kendrick. All the records relating to her appointment at the clinic had been destroyed. The patient in room A had been the only witness, and his memories were fractured and distorted because of the drug.

Geddings's disappearance had been somewhat more complicated, but in the end no one except Jodi Luckhurst had cared. She had been convinced that her boyfriend had deserted her for greener drug-dealing pastures.

Everything had been under control until Drake and his podcast pal, Llewellyn, had arrived in town. In spite of nearly getting killed in the explosion and regardless of the fact that they had no proof to confirm their suspicions, they showed no signs of giving up their so-called investigation. Something had to be done about them, but that was Moore's and Guthrie's problem.

Fenner stared at the package on the table, savoring the relief, temporary though it was. He knew what was inside—the same items that had been in the previous two packages—the drug that he would use on the next unwitting research subject Mr. Knight sent his way.

The brief flash of relief faded. He was eager to move forward with his own experiments with the insomnia drug, but he dreaded having to deal with the next patient Knight referred to the Institute. The disaster with Brooke Kendrick had left him badly shaken. But running Knight's trial was the price he paid to continue with his own cutting-edge work. The insomnia medication still had some quirks. The hallucinations were a serious problem. But he was making progress. He just needed time.

He got up to make himself a cup of tea. He had no doubt but that in the end, his years of research in the field of insomnia would be validated. He would not let his future be destroyed by the likes of

Llewellyn and Drake. He had come too far and risked too much to see it all burned down by the podcast bitch and the writer.

He was sitting down to drink the tea when he heard the sharp, demanding knock on the door. Between one breath and the next his anxiety level shot sky-high. His heart raced. He could hardly breathe. Something was wrong. No one called on him. He never invited staff or members of the college faculty to visit. He had chosen to rent the house in which he was living precisely because there were no nearby neighbors.

He rose, went into the front hall, and peered through the peephole. Bewildered, he opened the door.

"What are you doing here?" he said. "I assume you have news. You had better come in."

He turned to lead the way back into the kitchen. He never saw the syringe in the killer's hands. The needle pierced his upper shoulder where it curved into his neck. Shocked, he started to turn around, but the world was already getting blurry.

The killer took his arm and steered him across the living room and into the kitchen. He collapsed on a chair. It occurred to him that there was something wrong with the light. It was fading.

A moment later he toppled off the chair and sprawled on the floor. He listened to the killer moving around in the kitchen. They said that hearing was the last sense to go. He realized in a rather vague way that he would never receive recognition of his pioneering work. He was doomed to be a forgotten footnote in the history of sleep research.

The last things he heard were the soft sounds of the killer picking up the package wrapped in brown paper and the closing of the front door.

A moment later there was nothing.

CHAPTER TWENTY-NINE

AMBROSE OPENED HIS eyes to the smell of freshly brewed coffee and a rainy dawn. The fragments of a dream whispered through him. Not a nightmare, for once; instead he recalled the feel of a warm, soft, gently curved female body snuggled against him. A familiar scent still clung to the pillow propped behind his head. It was a scent he recognized, a scent he would forever associate with Pallas.

"What the hell?" He sat up suddenly, struggling to orient himself. There was no muffled clanking from the chain that bound him to the bed. Something was wrong. Had he somehow succeeded in unlocking the manacle while sleepwalking?

He finally realized he was still in the padded armchair in Pallas's room. His unchained ankle was propped on a footstool. There was a blanket draped over him.

Pallas was no longer holding his hand. She was at the console, pouring coffee into a cup. She glanced over her shoulder and smiled.

"Good morning to you, too," she said.

Memory and reality slammed through him. He checked the view

outside the window, confirming the sunlight. Then he looked at his watch, trying to remember when he had come upstairs, calculating how long he had been asleep.

"About seven hours," Pallas said. She crossed the room and handed him the coffee she had just poured. "That's what you want to know, right? How long you were asleep? I doubt if it's enough to make up for all the bad nights, but maybe it will help."

He took the coffee. "I don't understand."

"You needed the rest. After I calmed your energy, your body took control and sent you straight to sleep. As far as I could tell, you didn't have any nightmares. You definitely did not sleepwalk."

He frowned. "You were awake the whole time?"

"No, but I slept very lightly. Dozed for the most part. Woke up several times to check on you."

He glanced at the bed. It was still made up.

"Where did you sleep?" he asked, confused.

"You and I shared that chair most of the night. I thought it best to maintain physical contact even after I was sure you were sleeping peacefully. That way I would know immediately if you became agitated or tried to sleepwalk."

"Shit."

"Yes, well, you're quite welcome."

He groaned. "Sorry. I didn't mean it that way."

"I know. You're pissed because you're a little embarrassed, or maybe you think you owe me. It's okay. We're partners, remember? You saved my life yesterday at the Geddings house. If I'd gone down those stairs on my own I would have hit the trip wire." She paused for emphasis. "And I would have gone down those stairs."

"Partners," he said.

He drank some coffee while he tried to come to grips with the word; tried to understand why it still felt off somehow. Not wrong, but not right, either. He was probably overthinking things.

"How do you feel?" she asked, studying him with a critical eye.

"A lot better than I probably look." He raised one hand to the side of his face and grimaced when he felt the stubble. "I need to shower and shave."

"Sounds like a plan." She checked the time. "Why don't I meet you downstairs in about half an hour? We'll grab some breakfast and then figure out how we're going to break into Fenner's house. It's still early. I assume we will want to wait until we know for sure he's at the Institute."

"Right." He finished the last of his coffee, set the empty cup on the table, got to his feet, and headed for the door. "Thanks."

She watched him cross the room, frowning a little in concern. "Are you sure you feel all right?"

"Yes," he said, aware that he had spoken much too sharply. He had no reason to be irritated. He needed to take the advice he had given her and practice gratitude. "I know I look like hell warmed over, but I feel fine, really."

"I'm guessing you're not a morning person," she said, amused.

He ignored that, but a thought intruded. He paused, one hand wrapped around the doorknob. "That was the first good night's sleep I've had since San Diego. Thank you."

"You're welcome."

"Any idea how long the effects will last?"

"No. Sorry. For obvious reasons I haven't had much opportunity to run experiments with that particular side effect of my talent. Turns out balancing a person's energy is a little more complicated than adjusting the energy flow in a room. It's also a lot more unpredictable, because the individual keeps generating fresh energy."

"Makes sense," he said.

He moved out into the hall, shut the door, and went downstairs to shower and shave. Time to focus on the day's agenda: break into Conrad Fenner's house, take a look around, and don't get arrested. Also, it would be good to have a plan B.

He realized that for the first time in a very long while he actually was able to focus. It was amazing what a good night's sleep could do for a man.

CHAPTER THIRTY

S O MUCH FOR plan A," Ambrose said. "Fenner didn't go into the office today. Looks like we'll be going with plan B."

Pallas studied the car parked in the drive in front of the house that Fenner had rented. When she and Ambrose had realized that Fenner was still home they had decided on a confrontation instead of B and E. Their car was now also parked in the drive. She was surprised Fenner had not emerged from the house to demand an explanation.

"Do you really think he'll let us in, offer us coffee, and tell us what's going on at the Institute?" she said.

"What I think," Ambrose said, "is that we'll get some information out of him when we tell him we know that Brooke Kendrick was the other patient booked into the clinic the night I was there and that she disappeared and we want a statement from him before we go live with the podcast."

"In other words, we're going to threaten him," Pallas said. "You're hoping he'll panic and tell us everything he knows."

"Maybe not everything, but, with luck, something."

They started toward the porch. The house Fenner had rented

stood alone at the end of a side road on the outskirts of Carnelian. It was desperately in need of fresh paint and some carpentry work. The wooden railing around the front porch was broken in places, and the lawn had long since been colonized by some aggressive weeds. Faded curtains drooped across the windows. The only thing that looked remotely new was Fenner's late-model car parked in the driveway.

There was no doorbell. Ambrose raised his hand to rap on the flaking wood panels. "I'm guessing Fenner doesn't do a lot of entertaining at home."

Pallas shuddered. "Having met him, I think I can safely say the man is not the sociable type."

"And I thought I was an introvert."

There was no response to the knock. Ambrose tried again. Pallas listened closely but there were no muffled footsteps. No one called out. Cautiously she heightened her senses a little.

A faint frisson of cold energy sparked across her nerves. She shivered.

"Something is wrong," she said.

"I agree." Ambrose tried the doorknob. It turned easily in his hand. He pushed the door open a few inches. "Dr. Fenner? Ambrose Drake here. Ms. Llewellyn is with me. Some new information has come to light that reflects negatively on the research you're doing at the Institute. We would like to have your response to the material before we record the podcast."

Silence.

Ambrose pushed the door wide and moved into the gloom. "Fenner?" When there was still no response he took a couple more steps inside. "Wait here," he said.

He vanished into the gloom. A moment later he spoke again.

"Damn," he said. "One problem after another."

"Ambrose?"

"Fenner's dead."

Pallas got a grip on her nerves, clutched the messenger bag with both hands, and moved gingerly into the hall. The precautions helped but they were not enough to completely dampen the jolt delivered to her senses by the spiderweb of icy energy she stepped into.

She flinched violently. "Ouch. Shit. Damn it."

She took a hasty step back, lost her balance, and fetched up hard against the wall. She managed to keep her hold on the messenger bag, but just barely.

Ambrose appeared at the other end of the hall. "Are you okay?"

"Yes." Flattening her back against the wall, she edged cautiously past the invisible spiderweb. "Just walked into some bad stuff."

"I'm not surprised. I'm pretty sure Fenner's death is not from natural causes."

Pallas shuddered. "Murder."

It was not a question. She knew then that she had blundered straight into the spiderweb of violent energy that had been spun by the killer.

Spiderweb. Why did that image come to mind? Why not a storm or snakes or fire or scorpions? She needed to draw.

"Looks like whoever killed Fenner wants the authorities to think it was an overdose," Ambrose said. "There's a needle and an empty vial."

"I want to draw the energy in the hallway, but I should look at the body first," she said. "The more context, the more useful the picture."

Ambrose eyed her with a wary expression. "Are you sure?"

She steeled herself. "Unfortunately, yes. I rarely get an opportunity like this. The podcast does cold cases, remember? The body is always gone by the time we get there."

"Have you ever seen a corpse?"

She clutched the messenger bag with both hands, holding it in front of her like a shield, and straightened her shoulders. "I've attended a few open casket funerals."

"This is different. Very different."

"I know. I have to do this, Ambrose. The sooner I get it over with, the better."

He looked like he was going to argue but instead he nodded once, accepting her right to make the decision. Without another word he turned and led the way across the small, parlor-like living room. The entrance to the kitchen was on the far side of the space.

She took a steadying breath, unsure what to expect. Without a word Ambrose rested a hand on her shoulder, silently offering her whatever support and comfort he could with physical touch. She felt the reassuring heat of his energy.

"Thanks," she said.

He kept his hand on her shoulder as they walked into the kitchen and stopped a few steps away from Fenner's body. It was crumpled facedown on the floor beside the kitchen table. There were an empty glass and a bottle of whiskey on the table. Next to the bottle were a small vial and a used hypodermic needle.

"He looks smaller in death than he did when he was alive," Pallas whispered.

"When they do an autopsy they'll probably find some of whatever was in that vial in his blood," Ambrose said. "And maybe that is what killed him. He certainly wouldn't be the first medical professional to get addicted to drugs."

"But you don't think that's what happened."

"No. I think he was murdered."

"So do I," she said.

She kicked up her senses and slipped into her other vision. Waves of energy oscillated in the kitchen, much of it old and faded. She tuned it out and focused on the new currents. The icy, glistening strands of a nearly invisible web littered the kitchen.

"The scene I need to draw is out there, just inside the front door," she said.

"All right." Ambrose took his hand off her shoulder and pulled out his phone. "While you do your thing I'll call nine-one-one and make sure Detective Logan gets the news. He'll be excited. He's probably already submitting his résumé to one of the big-city police departments—or, hey, maybe the FBI."

"What if he decides we're suspects?"

"If he does, we may have a problem," Ambrose admitted. "But if it turns out that Fenner died during the night we should be in the clear. The hotel security cameras will show us entering the lobby when we got back from dinner. They will prove we didn't leave again until this morning. Relax. As far as Logan is concerned we're just a couple of reckless podcast investigators who are in a position to give him a real career boost."

"Right."

She carried the messenger bag back into the other room, set it on the scarred wooden floorboards, and reached inside for her sketchbook and a pencil. She crouched very close to the strongest pool of energy and went into her other vision.

She proceeded slowly and carefully, trying to limit the worst of the jolt, but a spiderweb was a spiderweb. Brushing up against one, whether real or the product of a trance vision, always came as a shock to the senses and sent a frisson of primal horror across the nerves.

Resisting the urge to retreat, she studied the glittering strands, searching for the pattern. For a moment it eluded her. And then the scene became startlingly clear. There was something in the web . . .

She began to draw.

Some time later, the feel of Ambrose's hand resting lightly on her shoulder yanked her out of the trance.

"What?" she gasped.

"Sorry to disturb you," he said. He hauled her lightly to her feet. "But Logan and his officers will be here any minute. It would not be a good idea to have him catch you sketching the scene."

Belatedly she became aware of the blaring sirens in the distance. "You're right. Let's get out of here. I'll take a closer look at the drawing when we're alone."

She dropped the sketchbook and pencil into the messenger bag.

They were waiting on the front porch when the first police vehicle slammed to a halt in front of the house. Logan climbed out of the passenger seat and strode toward them, a man on a mission.

"You two ever consider that you might want to look for another way to make your mark in social media?" he said as he came up the steps.

"That thought has crossed my mind more than once lately," Ambrose said.

Logan pulled on some disposable gloves as he headed for the doorway. "You're sure Fenner is dead?"

"Yes," Pallas said.

Logan grimaced. "The college authorities are not going to be happy about this."

"I can see where having an esteemed member of the faculty get murdered wouldn't be good for the image of the college," Pallas said. "Parents might have some understandable concerns about campus security."

"I don't know how esteemed Fenner was," Logan said. "From what I hear he was a loner who was generally considered to be an arrogant asshole. As for the concerns of the parents, they pale in comparison to the real problem the college is going to be facing."

"Which is?" Pallas asked.

"Follow the money," Ambrose said.

"Oh, right," Pallas said. "The funding from the anonymous donor was tied to Fenner and the Institute. It wouldn't be surprising if the Institute shuts down once word gets out that the director is dead."

Ambrose got a thoughtful look. "If the anonymous donor cuts off the funding it could mean the end of Carnelian College."

"Yep," Logan said. "And if that happens, this town is going to be in serious trouble. The college is the biggest employer in these parts. Without the students and the staff, most of the businesses in the area will close. The bottom will fall out of the real estate market. Carnelian will fall on very hard times. By the way, I'm going to need statements from both of you, so don't leave town."

He disappeared inside the house. Two uniforms hurried after him.

Ambrose looked at Pallas. "What are you thinking?"

"I'm thinking the donor who funded the Institute doesn't give a damn about the future of the college or the town," Pallas said. "It was just a convenient cover for the experiments. There's only one reason why someone would murder Fenner at this particular moment."

"He screwed up," Ambrose said. "Fenner made some mistakes and attracted too much attention. He put the whole project in jeopardy, so the anonymous donor shut down the Carnelian Sleep Institute."

CHAPTER THIRTY-ONE

PALLAS STUDIED THE picture she had drawn in the front hall of the house Fenner had rented. She shuddered.

"It was cold-blooded murder," she said. "Not that we had any doubts."

They were in the front seat of Ambrose's car, which was parked at a scenic overlook on the cliffs above the bay. The sketchbook was between them. The image she had drawn showed an intricately woven web. Some of the silken strands were badly frayed. A few hapless insects appeared to be trapped in the web. A small spider crouched in a corner, barely visible.

"Unfortunately, Ace Detective Logan needs something more than a psychic drawing," Ambrose said. "What does the picture tell you beyond what we already know?"

Pallas studied the web for a moment. Her intuition pinged. "The murder was a necessary business decision, but there was a lot of emotion involved. The killer is frustrated and furious."

Ambrose glanced up from the drawing. "Angry at Fenner?"

Pallas hesitated. "Not in a personal way. Fenner is one of the trapped insects in this drawing. The killer viewed him as a tool that had failed to perform as expected, and because of that failure the entire project was a disaster."

"We're the ones who fired up an investigation that threatened Fenner's experiments," Ambrose said. "Why not come after us?"

Pallas looked up. "Because we don't know enough to be dangerous. We're just flailing around, asking questions. The killer probably considers us annoying but not a threat. Fenner, on the other hand, must have known a lot more about the experiments."

"Once the spider made the decision to shut down the project, Fenner had to be silenced." Ambrose rested one hand on the steering wheel and looked out over the sun-bright bay. "It will be interesting to see who quietly packs up and leaves town in the near future."

"Yes." Pallas stared at the drawing, her intuition pinging again. "You're right. Whoever was running what was obviously a very complicated project at the Institute had to be nearby, close enough to keep an eye on all the moving parts."

"Close enough to step in quickly and pull the plug if things went south," Ambrose said. He tapped one finger against the wheel. "A project manager. Someone Fenner knew."

"Think so?" Pallas asked.

"If we're right, if Fenner was murdered, he must have opened the door to the killer last night. There was no sign of a struggle."

"Not until the killer was inside the front hall, at any rate. Whatever happened there happened fast." Pallas sank back into the seat. "We've still got a town full of suspects. Damn. We were so close. Now we'll never know who was running those experiments."

"I think we can narrow the list," Ambrose said. "I doubt if we're looking for one of the locals. The project manager is more likely to be someone who moved into town at about the same time the anonymous donor made the offer to fund the clinic."

"Maybe there are two project managers," Pallas suggested. "Margaret Moore and Hugh Guthrie took control at the college about a year before the Institute was opened. They were in a position to make all the important financial decisions."

"They have to be involved somehow," Ambrose said. "The question is, how and why?"

"Money always makes a good motive," Pallas said.

"Yes, but this is about more than money. I'm sure of it. We're talking serious paranormal research and illegal experiments with an unknown drug."

"I agree that the anonymous donor appears to be interested in something more than making money, but that doesn't mean whoever it is can find a lot of dedicated employees who are willing to risk jail time by engaging in illegal pharmaceutical research."

"True." Ambrose shifted his gaze away from the bay and looked at her. "You go into an illegal research project with the staff you've got—not the loyal, well-trained professionals you wish you had."

"Guthrie and Moore aren't the only ones closely involved with the clinic. Jodi Luckhurst was also conveniently positioned to keep an eye on the project. And then there's the mean-looking receptionist."

Ambrose thought about that and then shook his head. "If Luckhurst was running this operation she would not have gotten emotionally involved with a loose cannon like Geddings. It doesn't make sense. He put the whole project in jeopardy with his drug-dealing side hustle."

"Maybe she thought she could use him and discovered too late that he was stealing drugs and selling them on the side." Pallas hesitated, remembering the sadness in Jodi's voice when she was told that Geddings had apparently not skipped town. "Or maybe she really was in love with him."

"I think we can rule out both Luckhurst and the receptionist," Ambrose said. "They seem to have lived in Carnelian for years. We're looking for someone who is relatively new to the area."

"I keep coming back to Guthrie and Moore."

"I see them as pawns, not management."

"Insects caught in the web?" Pallas said. "Like Fenner?"

Ambrose put on his sunglasses and started the car. "We may be too late. The killer is probably gone or preparing to leave soon, but we might be able to get a few more answers, or at least a little more context."

"How?"

Ambrose drove onto the old highway. "Back at the start the librarian at the public library suggested we talk to the caretaker out at the town cemetery. She said he was an expert on the history of Carnelian."

CHAPTER THIRTY-TWO

I'VE BEEN LOOKING after this cemetery since I got out of the Army a couple years back." Ron Quinn leaned on a shovel and regarded the well-tended grounds of the Carnelian Memorial Gardens with an air of satisfaction. "The place was real run-down when I took over. Weeds growing everywhere. Graffiti on the headstones. Grass was mostly dead. Nobody visited. No one left flowers."

"It's very peaceful now," Pallas said. "Very calm."

Ambrose looked at her, surprised by her reaction. In spite of her assurance that she could deal with the energy at a cemetery, he had been worried. He had anticipated that, at the very least, she would find it deeply disturbing to walk through a place populated by the dead. He had offered to conduct the interview on his own, but she had insisted on accompanying him. He reminded himself that she investigated cold cases on a regular basis.

Ron Quinn had been digging a fresh grave when they arrived. He had immediately identified himself as a fan of *The Lost Night Files* and made it clear he was delighted to meet Pallas. *The Lost Night Files* might be a small operation, but it was clearly establishing a brand,

Ambrose thought. According to his publicist he needed to get busy and do that. And he would—right after he finished the next Jake Crane book. Right after he got over his writer's block. Right after he got his life back.

His to-do list was getting longer and longer.

But in the meantime, his status as "just the writer" had some serious advantages. It freed him to take a closer look at certain things without drawing attention, and one of the things that he found interesting was a certain vibe in Quinn's aura.

"I like to think of this cemetery as a meditation garden now, a place where people can spend a few hours figuring out how to deal with loss," Ron said. "It usually takes a while to learn how to say goodbye."

"Yes," Pallas said. She looked around. "Not that there's anyone left to say goodbye to."

"Nope," Ron agreed. "The dead move on right away. Cemeteries are constructed for the living, not the dead."

The investigation was veering off track, Ambrose thought. They were not here to get a gravedigger's take on the meaning of life, death, and cemeteries. He tried to think of a way to get things headed in the right direction again, but before he could speak, Pallas continued her conversation with Ron Quinn.

"There is so much history in a cemetery," she observed.

"That's a fact," Ron said. He swept out one heavily gloved hand to indicate the graveyard. "The history of Carnelian is all right here. All you gotta do is walk through the place. People do that a lot these days. Some are looking for ancestry information. Others want to get ideas for names for a baby. Some just want to sit for a while."

He and Pallas stood quietly, contemplating the grounds. Ambrose took a quick look at their auras. Both appeared unaccountably

serene, as if they would be content to spend the rest of the day standing here, absorbing the atmosphere. It was time to take charge.

He cleared his throat to get their attention.

"We're curious about the Carnelian family crypt," he said, an-
gling his chin at the large gray stone burial vault that dominated the
scene. "Background research for the podcast."

Ron and Pallas made a visible effort to pull themselves out of
their reverie.

"Right, *The Lost Night Files*," Ron said, waxing enthusiastic. "I
never miss an episode. That was good work you did in Saltwood, by
the way, Ms. Llewellyn. I couldn't believe it when they accused you
and your friends of being frauds. Said you were just out for publicity.
That sick sociopath would still be murdering people if he hadn't been
dumb enough to try to kill you."

"Please call me Pallas," Pallas said. "I have to tell you, it was a
little awkward there for a while in Saltwood."

"I can imagine." Ron snorted in disgust. "In the end they still
didn't figure out what really happened. Probably just as well they assumed the monster had a stroke. The authorities wouldn't have believed the truth."

Ambrose had been in the process of examining the names and
dates on the Carnelian vault. Ron's observation made him turn
around.

"What truth?" he asked, very curious now.

Ron winked. "Everyone who pays attention to *The Lost Night Files*
knows the killer didn't just keel over on account of bad blood pressure or a clot. It's no secret Pallas put him out like a light. But most
people wouldn't believe it, even if you told 'em. They'd want proof
and more proof and even then they'd say it was all a trick. How do
you prove something like that?"

"I see," Ambrose said. "You believe in the paranormal, then?"

Ron shrugged. "Be a fool not to. Expect you believe in it, too, or you wouldn't be here in Carnelian with Pallas trying to figure out what is going on at the Institute."

Ambrose looked at Pallas. She was focused on Ron.

"You know we're looking into the disappearance of Emery Geddings?" she said.

"It's no secret," Ron said. "Doubt if you'll ever find him, though. Pretty sure he was dealing there at the end. That kind of employment usually results in a short life span."

"You think he's dead?" Ambrose asked.

"Yeah." Ron shook his head. "The cops are convinced Geddings's competition took him out, but I don't think that's who killed him. More likely the doctor who's running the Institute murdered him when he discovered that Geddings was stealing drugs. They weren't just ordinary sleep medications, you see. The doctor had them made up special. Geddings didn't talk much about it but we went back a long way. Both of us were born and raised here. Both went into the Army. Afterward we used to get together for a beer a couple of times a week. He let a few things drop."

"What, exactly, did Geddings say about the medications he was stealing?" Pallas asked.

"He said the stuff was some kind of hallucinogen that Fenner had made up in a special kind of pharmacy. It was supposed to cure insomnia. Geddings said as far as he could tell the shit didn't help anyone sleep better but the college kids loved the stuff. He also told me that wasn't where the real action was at the Institute."

"What do you mean?" Pallas asked.

"Geddings said there was something else going on there, something that might be worth a lot of money. He was trying to figure out what Fenner was up to. That was a couple of months ago. But Geddings didn't come around much after that. When I texted him to see if he wanted to go out for pizza and a beer he said he was busy. The last thing Geddings told me was that he was going to have to leave town."

"Did he say why?" Ambrose asked.

"He wouldn't talk about it," Ron said. "I knew something had happened at the Institute but when I asked him about it he said it was better if I didn't know anything. Then, a couple of weeks back, he vanished. At first I figured he took off because he found out the cops were getting ready to arrest him for drug dealing. But that didn't feel right."

"This morning, Ambrose and I went out to Fenner's place," Pallas said. "We wanted to ask him a few more questions. He was dead."

"No shit?" Ron said, clearly startled. "Huh. Someone kill him?"

"On the surface, it looked like an overdose," Ambrose said. "The cops are at the scene now. We'll see what they come up with."

Ron whistled in amazement. "Did not see that coming. There really is something weird going on at the Institute, isn't there?"

"We think so," Pallas said.

"Do you mind answering a few more questions?" Ambrose said.

Ron squinted at him. "Someone said you were a writer."

"Yep."

"What name do you write under?"

"My own," Ambrose said.

"Huh. I've never heard of you."

"I get that a lot," Ambrose said. "About our questions."

"What kind of stuff do you write?"

"Thrillers," Ambrose said.

"Cool," Ron said. He paused. "I don't read a lot of fiction."

"You'd be amazed how many people tell me that," Ambrose said.

Ron's eyes lit with excitement. "You know what? I've been thinking about doing a book about the history of Carnelian. Lots of great stories. You could be my ghostwriter."

Ambrose ignored the laughter in Pallas's eyes.

"Thanks," he said. "But I'm tied up with my current contract. About our questions."

"Sure," Ron said. "What do you want to know?"

"There were some major changes at the college shortly before an anonymous donor funded the Institute," Ambrose said. "Guthrie was appointed dean and Margaret Moore was hired to manage the endowment. Did Geddings ever mention those two?"

"He knew them because they paid a lot of attention to the Institute, but he didn't consider them friends, if that's what you mean," Ron said. "He didn't think too highly of them, I can tell you that. He mentioned once that he was sure they were sleeping together and had been for a long time."

"Moore and Guthrie are a couple?" Pallas asked sharply.

"According to Geddings," Ron said. "He suspected they are working a scam of some kind, probably skimming off the college endowment. He didn't think it was the first time they had played that game. In his opinion, they are a couple of grifters. But, hey, the college authorities think they are brilliant because they brought in that big donor. Hard to argue, given the size of that donation."

Pallas looked at Ron. "You've been very helpful."

"No problem," Ron said. His eyes lit up. "Think you'll get a podcast out of Geddings's disappearance?"

"Maybe," Pallas said. "If we do I'll be back to record an interview with you, assuming you're up for that."

"Absolutely," Ron said. "Does that mean you're not interested in our local ghosts, Catherine and Xavier Carnelian?"

"Ghost stories are not a focus of *The Lost Night Files*," Pallas said. "As a faithful listener I'm sure you're aware that we try to stick to more unusual cold cases."

"Right," Ron said. He looked around with pride. "But the Carnelian ghosts are special to those of us who grew up here. After all, if it hadn't been for the fact that Catherine Carnelian haunted her bastard husband to his death, her sister, Eugenia, would never have inherited the fortune. There would have been no Carnelian College, no hospital, no library. Hell, there probably wouldn't be a town if not for her."

Pallas went closer to the impressive gray crypt and studied the list of names on the plaque. "The last name on here is Alexander Carnelian. The date is eighteen ninety-five. I don't see Catherine's name, or Xavier's."

"That's because neither of them was buried in the family crypt," Ron said.

"I can see why Eugenia didn't want Xavier buried inside," Pallas said. "But why isn't Catherine here?"

"There was no way to identify the body," Ron said. "She died inside the asylum. Back in those days the deceased patients were buried anonymously. They were identified with just a number. The number corresponded to a record of names that the director of the asylum kept locked up. Supposedly it was done that way to protect the family's privacy."

"Wouldn't want potential marriages threatened by gossip about insanity in the family line," Ambrose said.

"That was the official reason," Ron said, "but I wouldn't be surprised if the director of the asylum was running a lucrative sideline blackmailing the families."

Pallas looked grim. "I'll bet you're right."

"In the end it didn't matter," Ron said. "The record of the names of the deceased and the corresponding numbers on the coffins was destroyed in a fire. That meant there was no way to identify Catherine Carnelian's body so that it could be moved here to the family crypt."

"I doubt if Catherine would have wanted to be buried in the Carnelian crypt," Pallas said. "She must have hated her husband for having her locked up."

Ambrose studied the monument. "Where is Xavier Carnelian buried?"

Ron chuckled. "Eugenia saw to it that the asshole who had her sister committed was buried in a numbered coffin out at the old asylum. Pretty much the working definition of an unmarked grave."

"And Eugenia?" Pallas asked.

Ron pointed to an elegant monument in the center of the cemetery. "That's her resting place. She wasn't a Carnelian, but even if she had been, she wouldn't have wanted to be buried in the family crypt."

A HALF HOUR later Ambrose got behind the wheel of the car and slipped on his sunglasses. He sat quietly for a moment, watching Ron Quinn disappear into the gardening shed.

"I think Quinn might have a psychic vibe," he said. "Something about his aura."

Pallas fastened her seat belt. "You can tell that from his energy field?"

"Maybe." He started the engine, put the vehicle in gear, and drove out of the small parking lot. "I told you, I'm still working out how to read auras. It's not like there's a YouTube video with step-by-step instructions I can watch."

"It's the same with me," Pallas said. "I'm still trying to understand how to interpret my automatic drawing."

Ambrose turned onto the road that would take them back into town. "Mind if I ask you a personal question?"

"Considering what we've been through together in the past few days, you're entitled. What do you want to know?"

"I've been wondering why it didn't bother you to walk through the cemetery. You just strolled along as if you were in a park. All that death underfoot and it didn't bother you at all, as far as I could tell."

"The energy in a graveyard isn't worse than it is anywhere else. In my experience, it's usually more balanced, in fact. The mourners leave the usual baggage behind, but for the most part it isn't hard to tune out."

"I was thinking about the psychic vibe from the graves. A lot of the people buried under those stones probably died unpleasant deaths. There must have been the usual assortment of car crashes, accidents, and acts of violence. Some would have endured the pain and suffering of a long illness. And then there's the despair of suicides. Sadly, most of us don't get to die quietly in our sleep."

"Ah, I see what you mean," Pallas said. "The thing is, those people didn't die in the cemetery."

"Well, no, not right in the cemetery, but—"

"Everyone buried in the Carnelian Memorial Gardens died somewhere else," Pallas said. "That other location is where the violence and pain disturbed the energy flow. By the time a body arrives in a cemetery the recycling process is well underway. Nature is processing the remains and making sure things are restored to a state of harmony."

"That's an interesting view of the cycle of life."

"Ron Quinn is right," Pallas said. "Cemeteries are for the living. The dead don't need them."

CHAPTER THIRTY-THREE

D ETECTIVE LOGAN IS on a roll, career-wise," Ambrose said. He clicked off the phone and dropped it into the pocket of his jacket. "According to the latest tweets from the Carnelian police, he is going to get the credit for exposing the drug ring that Fenner and Geddings were operating out of the Carnelian Sleep Institute."

Pallas forked up the last bite of the cauliflower steak she had ordered. They were eating dinner at the vegetarian restaurant she favored, because when the decision of where to dine had come up Ambrose had been too busy talking to Calvin the Magnificent and checking police tweets on the phone to participate. He had not looked up from the device until the entrée she had ordered for him had been set in front of him.

"What is Logan's theory of the crime?" Pallas asked.

"What you'd expect at this point," Ambrose said. "Dr. Conrad Fenner was a disgraced sleep expert who was addicted to some of the drugs he ordered for the clinic. To pay for the habit he decided to sell some of the stuff to the college students. Emery Geddings was already in that market. When he found out that Fenner was trying to horn in on his business he offered a joint venture."

"Logan thinks Fenner and Geddings were in business together?" Pallas asked.

"It makes sense as far as it goes," Ambrose said. "Logan suspects there was a falling-out between the two and Fenner probably murdered Geddings, but without a body and some evidence there's no way to prove it. If Fenner was the killer, it's a moot point now because he's dead. As far as Logan is concerned, it's all nice and tidy."

"What about Margaret Moore and the college dean, Hugh Guthrie?'

Ambrose picked up his fork and finished the last of the mushroom bourguignon she had selected for him. "No mention of them in the police tweets."

"Hmm." Pallas put down her fork and thought for a moment. "What do you think they'll do?"

"Moore and Guthrie?" Ambrose shrugged. "They'll skate. Even if they are embezzling I doubt if anyone will be able to prove it, and of course they will deny all knowledge of the drug dealing."

"*The Lost Night Files* isn't interested in an embezzlement case, either," Pallas said. "All we care about is what was going on at the Institute."

"It occurs to me," Ambrose said quietly, "that with the death of Conrad Fenner, there won't be much going on at the Carnelian Sleep Institute. It's not even a crime scene, because Fenner's death is being attributed to an overdose."

"I think I know where this is going," Pallas said.

"I want to take a look around before someone decides to clean out the desks and archive the files."

"Tonight?"

"No. Campus security or a passerby would notice a flashlight inside. I doubt if Jodi Luckhurst or the mean-looking receptionist will be at work tomorrow. With Fenner dead, the Institute is out of business. But just in case, it would be best to go in early in the morning. If someone sees me I can always say I'm a patient and had a follow-up appointment."

"I don't think that will work for both of us."

"It won't," Ambrose said. "That's why I'm going to go in alone. If I'm caught I can talk my way out of it."

"I don't like it."

"Got a better idea?"

She reflected briefly. "No."

He looked down at his empty plate. "What was that?"

"Beef bourguignon without the beef."

"Is that a thing?"

"It is if you lean vegetarian."

"I didn't used to lean vegetarian until I met you," Ambrose said.

"Believe it or not, I figured that out pretty quick."

"Probably your psychic vibe in action."

"Probably."

CHAPTER THIRTY-FOUR

THEY WALKED BACK to the hotel through a muffling cloak of damp fog. When Ambrose reached for her hand, Pallas gave it to him without comment. She told herself he was just being nice. Polite. Gracious. He understood her tendency to stumble over unseen storms of energy and was literally offering a helping hand.

As if she was a fragile little old lady who needed help crossing the street. Damn.

She yanked her hand out of his and shoved her fingers into the pocket of her coat.

Ambrose came to a halt. "What's wrong? Are you okay?"

"Yes, I'm okay," she shot back, suddenly furious for no reason. She stopped and glared. "I'm not frail. You don't have to hold my hand because you're afraid I'm going to trip and fall at any moment. I managed to survive the side effects of my other vision before I met you. I'm capable of walking down a sidewalk without you."

"Where's this coming from? A few minutes ago we were having a nice dinner—okay, it was a vegetarian dinner, but it was still nice—

and now you're acting like I insulted you. I think I deserve an explanation."

She groaned and closed her eyes. "You do. I know it appears as if I'm behaving irrationally."

"I wasn't going to mention it. I may not be the brightest member of the Drake family, but I'm not that dumb."

She opened her eyes and glared. "That is not funny."

"It was a statement of fact. Do you want to tell me why you acted as if I burned your hand?"

"I appreciate your consideration," she said. "I admit that my other vision makes me clumsy at times. But it's embarrassing to know that you feel you have to take my arm and escort me down the street so that I don't fall flat on my face."

"So that's what this is about." Ambrose took a step toward her, closing the distance between them. "Allow me to clarify things. I don't need to hold your hand to know if you're about to stumble. I can sense it in your aura. I was holding your hand because I like touching you."

"Oh," she said. She tried to think of something more intelligent to say but nothing came to mind.

He liked touching her.

The energy in the atmosphere between them always felt charged with a unique vibe. She had been aware of it from the moment of that first chaotic meeting in the ruins of the asylum. Their relationship was layered and complicated with many different elements, but here and now in the darkness it was the energy of a thrilling sexual attraction and the promise of intense intimacy that dominated.

"Pallas, I need an answer," Ambrose whispered. "Would you rather I didn't touch you?"

For a heartbeat or two she no longer required oxygen. She could live on this kind of energy. She raised one hand and stroked her fingertips along the side of his face.

"I want you to touch me and I want to touch you," she whispered. "I just want us to touch each other for the right reasons."

His eyes burned in the shadows. Without another word he caught her face in his hands and pulled her close. When his mouth came down on hers she could have sworn she had been struck by lightning. The night exploded.

Dazzled, she threw herself into the searing embrace. The kiss overwhelmed her senses. She had never experienced anything like it.

"Does that feel like the right reason to you?" Ambrose said against her mouth. "Because it sure does to me."

"Yes," she said. "This feels right."

His mouth came back down on hers. She would have been content to stand there in the middle of the sidewalk kissing Ambrose for the rest of her life, but reality slammed home in the shape of youthful voices.

"*Get a room, you two. That's what adults do.*"

"*Faculty. Always trying to pretend they're still cool. It's sad, really.*"

"*What do you want to bet he's cheating on his wife?*"

"*Wait, I think that's the podcast team. They actually are sort of cool. I heard they found the body of that creep who was running the sleep clinic today. Hey, Ms. Llewellyn, did you find any paranormal evidence at the scene?*"

Ambrose broke off the kiss. "We're setting a bad example for today's youth. What do you say we take their suggestion and get a room?"

"Good idea," Pallas said.

Ambrose grabbed her hand. She tucked the messenger bag under one arm and together they ran the final half block to the hotel, laughing, and escaped into the lobby.

Several heads turned when they burst through the front door. Pallas caught a glimpse of a familiar figure in the bar. Theo was sitting alone at a table. Evidently he had not given up and left town. He saw her and started to get to his feet. There was no mistaking the shocked look on his face. In fairness, everyone in the lobby had turned to stare.

Pallas decided to ignore all of them. She was riding a wave of excitement and anticipation. She could not abide the idea of waiting for the elevator. She tightened her grip on Ambrose's hand and headed for the stairs.

Ambrose gave her a wicked smile and took the heavy messenger bag. She did not argue.

"My room or yours?" Ambrose said when they reached the third floor.

"Mine," she said, struggling to catch her breath. "I won't have to redecorate."

"Right. We have to stop at my room first, though."

"Why?"

"Condoms." He paused on the third-floor landing. "Unless you brought some?"

"No. Wait. You brought some?" She wasn't sure how to take that.

"I'm hoping there are a couple somewhere in the bottom of my duffel left over from the old days when I used to have a sex life."

"Right, you'd better get them."

She waited in the hallway outside his room while he disappeared into the darkness. When he returned, he had his duffel in one hand. Her heavy messenger bag was slung over his shoulder. By the time they reached the fourth floor he was breathing hard, proving he was human, after all.

She got the door of her room open, grabbed a fistful of his jacket, and pulled him into the shadows. Neither of them bothered to grope for the light switch.

Ambrose kicked the door shut, slammed the lock home, dropped the duffel and the messenger bag, and reached for her. They fell together across the bed.

CHAPTER THIRTY-FIVE

THIS WAS WHAT passion was all about, Pallas thought. She had known pleasant interludes with others, but in the past the experiences had been mild, fleeting, and so remarkably unmemorable that she had sometimes wondered if she was the problem.

Her doubts about her own ability to respond could now be cast aside forever. What she was feeling now might be fleeting, but it was definitely not going to be mild or unmemorable. She would remember this for the rest of her life even if things didn't get any further than they had right now. This sensation was nothing short of amazing.

Ambrose rolled her under him and came down on top of her, crushing her into the quilt. "I've been wanting to do this since the moment I saw you," he said against her throat. His voice was husky and urgent.

"Me, too," she gasped, fighting to get her hands inside his jacket.

"Liar." He kissed her, his mouth hungry and desperate. When he raised his head his eyes were ablaze. "You wanted to zap me with your Taser."

"Okay, maybe I wasn't thinking of doing this exact thing the first moment I saw you, but I started thinking about it very soon afterward."

"Good," he said. He brushed his mouth across hers. "That's very good."

How would they explain this to themselves and each other in the morning? she wondered. Adrenaline overload, maybe; an elemental, hormone-driven response to the need to decompress from the stress of the past few days.

She decided she did not give a damn. She would worry about explanations and rationalizations if and when it became necessary. All that mattered was what was happening right now.

She managed to peel off his jacket and hurl it aside. He eased his hands under the hem of her sweater and pushed the garment up over her head. They undressed each other in a rush of heat, caught up in the volatile energy and power of desire.

Ambrose wasted a precious few minutes searching for a condom in the duffel, and then, finally, they were tangled in each other's arms, setting fire to the sheets.

She thrilled to the feel of his furnace-hot body. His hands were warm and strong and tender and he was rock-hard. He seemed to know exactly how and where to touch her. Then again, she was sure he could touch her anywhere and in any way and she would respond.

And he was responding to her touch. He wasn't afraid of her.

When she reached down and captured him in one hand he groaned, shifted onto his back, and pulled her astride his thighs.

"I need to be inside you," he rasped.

She guided him slowly into her core and took a sharp breath when she realized the sensations she was experiencing hovered between pleasure and pain. She was so tightly wound she was amazed she did not fly apart.

"So *good*," Ambrose groaned.

He sounded as if he, too, was riding the same exhilarating wave of pleasure-pain. Before she could analyze the experience, her body took control. It was all pleasure after that. The climax cascaded through her, leaving her breathless.

Ambrose gripped her thighs, uttered a muffled roar of satisfaction, and followed her over the edge. Together they sank into the depths.

CHAPTER THIRTY-SIX

A YELP OF DISMAY followed by the unmistakable thud of a body hitting the edge of the bed, bouncing off, and sliding to the carpeted floor brought Ambrose out of the glorious aftermath. He sat up very quickly, his eyes and the window in his mind open.

"Pallas?"

"Shit," she muttered. "Shit, shit, *shit*."

She was sprawled on the floor beside the overturned duffel. Her aura blazed with shock and annoyance.

"I'm so sorry." Ambrose stood, switched on the lamp beside the bed, and reached down to help her to her feet. "Are you okay? Did you hit your head? Anything feel broken? This is my fault. I should never have left the bag there. I was in such a hurry to get that other condom. I was careless."

"Yes," she said. "You were. I'm fine, I think, but for the record, I have enough problems stumbling over the unseen stuff; I don't need any additional trip hazards."

"I know, I'm sorry." He pulled her into his arms. "Are you sure you're okay?"

"Yes." She pushed her hair out of her eyes and grimaced. "Can't blame bad energy this time. I was returning from the bathroom. Didn't see the bag."

"I'll take care of it." He released her and glanced at the clock on the table beside the bed. He groaned when he saw the time. "It's after one. I need to get dressed and get back to my own room."

He was reaching for his trousers when he heard the familiar clank and rattle of a metal chain. He froze.

Pallas cleared her throat. "Something you want to mention about your taste in sex toys?"

He spun around. She was holding the ankle manacle of the chain that had fallen out of the duffel.

"I can explain," he said. He could feel himself flushing from head to toe. "I told you I take some precautions because of the sleep-walking."

"It's okay," she assured him. "I'm very open-minded about these things."

"You're laughing at me."

"With you, not at you," she said.

He shook his head. "Nope. You're laughing at me."

"Maybe a little. But I must admit the thought of you chained to a bed does present a very interesting visual."

"Is that right?"

"Why don't you spend the rest of the night here in my room and we'll try out some possibilities?"

He tossed the trousers over the back of the armchair and crossed the room to take her into his arms.

"What did you have in mind?" he said.

"You're the one who writes fiction. I'm sure you can come up with something creative."

He reached out and took the manacle from her. "Now that you mention it, I think I'm over my case of writer's block."

CHAPTER THIRTY-SEVEN

THE TEXT FROM Theo came in just as Pallas was preparing to make herself another cup of coffee. Ambrose had slipped out of the hotel nearly an hour ago, headed for the Institute. She had been drinking coffee, pacing the room, and expecting bad news along the lines of I've-been-picked-up-for-burglary-please-come-to-the-jail-and-bail-me-out.

Oddly enough, the message from Theo was even more unnerving. We need to talk. Someone is asking questions about you. Meet me in the hotel lobby.

She didn't hesitate. Grabbing her messenger bag, she headed for the door. There were two possibilities, she thought. Either Theo was trying to trick her into giving him a second chance to plead his case or else he really did have some information. Regardless, there was no risk in hearing what he had to say. There were few places more public than a hotel lobby.

Out in the hallway a woman in an immaculately tailored suit was waiting for the elevator. Her face was averted, her attention focused on the door. She glanced at her watch, her body language signaling tension. Late for a meeting, no doubt.

Pallas hesitated, trying to decide if it would be faster to take the stairs. The elevator bell chimed and the doors slid open. The business traveler stepped inside, reaching back to hold the door.

"Thanks," Pallas said.

Decision made, she moved into the elevator. There was one other person inside, a man. He pressed the button for the garage. There was something vaguely familiar about him.

"I'm going to the lobby," Pallas said.

When she stepped forward to press the lobby button he looked at her, his eyes stone-cold.

"No, you're not," he said.

Pallas's intuition slammed into overdrive, but it was too late. The business traveler was already in motion.

Pallas felt the needle bite into the curve of her shoulder. She tried to scream but her voice was already gone. She managed to turn far enough to glimpse the face of the woman who had held the door for her.

"You've caused us enough trouble," the business traveler said. She dropped the hypodermic needle into her handbag.

Pallas finally realized she had never met either of the two in the elevator but she had seen photos of them in the course of the research she and Ambrose had done lately. Margaret Moore, the director of the Carnelian College Endowment, and Hugh Guthrie, the dean.

Snakes on a staircase, she thought. *One used the needle on Geddings. One handled the body.*

The light went out.

CHAPTER THIRTY-EIGHT

S HE OPENED HER eyes to a dreamscape of fog lit by undulating waves of auroras. Wild visions came and went in the mist, sending sharp frissons across her nerves. *You've been here before. You know what to do.*

This was how the automatic drawing trances always began, but she usually entered her other vision intentionally. That way she was able to maintain control. She had been slammed into her other senses without warning this time. It was disorienting and unnerving.

The trick to channeling the visions and hallucinations was to draw. She put out a hand, instinctively reaching for a pencil and a sketchbook. Her fingers scrabbled across cold stone. Nothing. No pencil. No sketchbook.

The unnerving frissons flared into sparks of panic that electrified her nervous system, threatening to overwhelm her senses. In response, the visions became more vivid; more intense. She was not gaining control. She was losing it. If she did not master the hallucinations she would be lost forever in the dreamscape.

Frantically she pulled hard on her other vision, struggling to find the source of the chaos. The hallucinations retreated but they did not vanish. She tried to transfer out of the trance state into her normal vision.

Darkness immediately engulfed her, absolute and terrifyingly claustrophobic. The darkness of a tomb.

The panic rushed back. Desperate, she intuitively retreated back into her trance vision. The space around her was once again lit by auroras, but this time the hallucinations were under control, more or less. When she concentrated she was able to make out some of the details of her surroundings.

Cold, cracked concrete everywhere. Floor, walls, ceiling. A dank smell infused the atmosphere. She thought she caught the tang of the ocean.

Then she saw the caskets.

For a horrifying moment she thought she was seeing another round of hallucinations. That would indicate she had lost control of her other vision. Maybe she really was trapped in a nightmare this time.

She took a deep breath. Her nerves steadied. The caskets were real, and there were a lot of them.

They were stacked in rows at the rear of the space. Made of cheap wood, many had partially rotted and collapsed. In several cases the contents had spilled out onto the floor. A clutter of rib cages, long bones, and skulls was piled in one corner as if someone had kicked them out of the way.

She was in an underground crypt.

In addition to the caskets there were two long black bags on the floor against one wall. She shivered, not because of dark energy but because her intuition told her what was inside the bags.

The only body bags she had ever seen were in the news media

and in films, but she knew immediately what she was looking at. The two bags were not empty.

She looked around, hoping to find her messenger bag. She longed for her phone, with its handy flashlight app. Even more importantly, she wanted to get her hands on the Taser.

There was no sign of the bag.

She had to move. To act. She could not stay where she was, waiting for disaster. She managed to get to her hands and knees. Keeping the hallucinations at bay while simultaneously using her trance vision to navigate the absolute darkness proved to be a complicated juggling act. It was as if she had one foot inside a dream and the other foot outside.

You know this sensation. It's the feeling you get when you're in the place between sleep and the waking state.

Once again the panic welled up, threatening to drown her.

"*Shit,*" she whispered.

For some reason the expletive had a steadying effect on her nerves. She had to stay focused on escape. There was fresh air coming in from somewhere. If she found the source, she might discover the way out. She also needed a weapon, something—anything—she could use to defend herself.

She got cautiously to her feet and took a moment to regain her balance. Moving through a dreamstate was hard. In a sense, she was lucid dreaming and sleepwalking at the same time.

In spite of the caskets and the body bags she wasn't picking up the heavy energy of on-site violence, pain, and fear. The remains of the dead had been stored there, but the deaths had occurred somewhere else.

She pushed some flickering visions aside and was able to make out a flight of concrete steps. They led up from the floor of the crypt and ended at a wooden door.

Given her luck today, there was a high probability that the door at

the top was locked, but what if it wasn't? Maybe the kidnappers assumed the drug would keep her unconscious. Or maybe the door
was locked on the other side but not on this side.

Buoyed by that faint spark of hope, she concentrated on the steps
and made her way toward them with painstaking care. Separating
the visions from the reality of the paranormal-lit crypt took consid-
erable effort.

When she reached the bottom of the concrete stairs, her pulse
was pounding. There was no handrail. She stopped, appalled by the
thought of trying to climb all the way up to the door while in her
other vision without the security of a handrail. If she fell she could
easily break some bones. Her neck, for instance.

She put one foot on the bottom step, took a breath, and moved
her other foot to the next level. A wave of panic brought on another
surge of disorienting visions. She had to worry about trip hazards
even when she wasn't trapped in a crypt and fighting drug-induced
hallucinations. This was a nightmare.

She retreated back down to the floor and tried to come up with a
strategy. There was a door at the top of the steps. She had to find a
way to open it.

When she had her senses under some semblance of control, she
went down on her hands and knees and experimented with edging
her way up the steps in crablike movements.

The technique worked, but it took forever to make it to the top of
the steps. When she finally arrived at her destination she was trem-
bling. She took a moment to catch her breath and then rose on her
knees and tried the doorknob. Unlocked.

She could not believe her good luck. She twisted the knob and
pushed it open. The door moved a scant couple of inches before en-
countering a solid barrier.

Should have known I wouldn't be able to just walk out of this place.

The frustration was crushing. It was also infuriating. She wanted to scream her rage to the universe, but she had to do something else first. She had to crawl down the terrifying concrete steps. The process proved just as unnerving as climbing up them.

When she reached the floor she almost collapsed in relief, but that was a luxury she could not afford. It didn't take any psychic talent to know that the kidnappers did not intend for her to walk out of the crypt alive.

Ambrose would be looking for her. Sooner or later he would find her because he was Ambrose and because they were partners. It was her job to keep herself alive until help arrived.

She staggered upright and forced herself to focus on the next objective. She needed a weapon, any object that might give her an edge. She started to explore the eerie shadows of the crypt. There were no guns, knives, or palm-sized chunks of rock lying conveniently nearby, but there was something else. A body.

"Theo," she whispered.

He wasn't in a bag. He was alive.

She crouched beside him. He was unconscious but she could not find any visible wounds. The kidnappers had probably drugged him, too. She wondered if she owed him an apology and then reminded herself that it was not her fault he had landed in the middle of her investigation.

"I told you to leave town," she said.

But it wasn't that simple, she thought. The fact was, Theo would not be lying unconscious on the cold concrete floor of a crypt if it wasn't for her. Okay, his professional ambition was certainly a contributing factor, but still.

Deciding she would worry about the ethics of the situation later, assuming they both survived, she went back to searching the crypt. There were no handy blunt objects on the floor. With a groan, she made herself cross the space to the ranks of stacked caskets. Maybe she would find something useful among the jumble of rotting wood, tattered fabric, and bones.

She took a deep breath before she walked into the maze of coffins stacked higher than she was tall. She had no issues with the energy in the space. The dearly departed had, indeed, departed. But it felt wrong to prowl through the clutter of human remains and the boxes that had been used to store them. The patients of the Carnelian Psychiatric Hospital for the Insane had been disrespected enough in life.

"I'm sorry," she said. But she knew even as she said the words that she was speaking to herself, not the dead.

She discovered the chest of woodworking tools when she turned a corner at the end of a pile of caskets. The lid of the chest opened on squeaking hinges. Inside was an array of hammers, saws, chisels, and pliers—the tools needed to build the caskets. All were coated with rust, and the wooden handles were cracked and splintered, but a vintage tool made of heavy steel and stout wood was a formidable object and, therefore, a potential weapon.

She picked up a hammer and quickly realized it was far too heavy to wield effectively. She was not Thor. She put it back into the chest and experimented with some pliers. She was reaching for a large chisel when she heard the muffled groan of heavy hinges. The sound reminded her of a garage door opening. It came from the top of the concrete steps. She grabbed the chisel and went very still behind a stack of caskets.

Footsteps echoed on the concrete steps. From where she was hiding she could not see anyone, but a narrow slant of murky daylight angled into the crypt. It wasn't anywhere near enough to illuminate the cavernous space, but it relieved some of the oppressive darkness. She heard a couple of snicks. Two flashlight beams appeared.

"Hurry," Hugh Guthrie said. "We need to clean up this fucking mess and get out of here."

"There's no reason to panic." Margaret Moore was tense, impatient, angry, and maybe something else. She sounded as if she was unnerved. "The situation is under control."

CHAPTER THIRTY-NINE

AMBROSE CLOSED THE last drawer of Fenner's desk and straightened to take one more look around the office. Whoever had searched the place before he had arrived—presumably the killer—had done a thorough, professional job. If there had been anything that might have pointed to the identity of the anonymous donor or the person overseeing the Carnelian Sleep Institute project, it had been removed.

Fenner's office had not been left in chaos. Whoever had gone through his files and records had been careful not to leave any obvious tracks except when it came to the medication locker. The door of the locked closet had been forced open and there were some empty places on the shelves. It was the only space in the Institute that looked as if it had been searched. That was not an accident, Ambrose thought. The killer had wanted to make it appear that someone had broken in to steal drugs. Just another add-on to the media story of a drug ring operating out of the Institute. No loose ends.

Ambrose headed for the rear door. He had spent too much time searching the old mansion. He needed to get back to Pallas. He could no longer ignore the frisson of dread that was icing the back of his neck.

CHAPTER FORTY

I T WAS RAINING when Ambrose braked to a violent stop in front of the entrance to Carnelian Memorial Gardens. Ignoring the downpour, he ran to the caretaker's cottage and pounded on the front door.

Ron Quinn opened the door and stared at him, first in surprise and then in concern. "You're the writer, the guy who is helping Ms. Llewellyn with the podcast investigation. What's wrong?"

"Where were the asylum patients buried?" Ambrose asked.

"What?" Ron looked past Ambrose and saw the car. He frowned. "Is Ms. Llewellyn okay?"

"No. She's been kidnapped."

Ron looked stunned. "Who would want to grab her?"

"Got a feeling we're dealing with Moore and Guthrie," Ambrose said. "They have to be involved in this thing. I think they're panicking. My best guess is that they will try to make Pallas disappear the same way they did Emery Geddings. The same way Geddings made Brooke Kendrick vanish."

"Who is Brooke Kendrick?"

"Later," Ambrose said. "The point is the bodies of Geddings and Kendrick were never found. People assume Geddings left town to escape his competitors in the drug business. Nobody even noticed that Kendrick had vanished. I think they were concealed in the one place no one would think to look. The asylum cemetery."

"I don't understand."

"You said the inmates who died at the hospital were buried in numbered caskets and the only way to identify the dead was with a directory that had been destroyed in a fire. You told Pallas and me the deceased were now in the equivalent of unmarked graves."

"That's right."

"Where is the asylum cemetery? I've been out there a few times and I never saw a graveyard."

Comprehension lit Ron's eyes. "Because there wasn't one. The dead were stored in a crypt in the basement of the hospital."

"There's a basement?"

"The entrance was concealed behind the main staircase. It connected to one of the old smugglers' tunnels. Why are you so interested in it?"

"I think someone is using it to make people vanish."

Ron's eyes narrowed. "You think whoever kidnapped Ms. Llewellyn will take her to the crypt?"

"It seems like the most likely scenario. People tend to stick with whatever worked in the past."

"Any idea how many people we're talking about here?"

"Two, I think, Moore and Guthrie."

Quinn watched him intently. "Ms. Llewellyn may already be dead."

"No," Ambrose said, very certain now. "I'd know if she was dead. But time is running out. I need to move fast."

Ron nodded, accepting the statement as fact. "I've been inside the hospital a few times over the years. I know where the door to the crypt used to be, but like I said, it's been walled."

"There must be a way in," Ambrose said. "I'm sure Geddings used the crypt on a regular basis for his drug-dealing business and maybe to hide Kendrick's body."

"Huh." Quinn got a knowing look. "If you're dealing with a couple of kidnappers, you don't want to go in through the front door. They'll use Ms. Llewellyn as a hostage."

"Got a better idea?"

"Like I said, that old crypt connected to a smuggling tunnel. We'll use that entrance. Hang on, I'll get my weapon."

"Will we need a boat?" Ambrose said. "A kayak?"

"Not now. The tide is out."

[260]

CHAPTER FORTY-ONE

N O, THIS SITUATION is not under control," Guthrie snarled. "We would not be down here dealing with the podcaster and the architect if it was under control. And when we're finished here we'll have to deal with the writer. The whole project is a fucking disaster."

"Shut up," Margaret said, her voice tight with fury and tension. "None of this is my fault. I'm not the one who thought it would be a good idea to bring in Geddings."

"We needed someone who knew the local community. It was a smart strategy."

"Right up until he decided to blackmail us because of the screwup with the Kendrick woman."

"That was Fenner's fault," Guthrie roared. "Fuck, where's Llewellyn?"

"You're the one who carried her down here," Margaret said. "Where did you put her?"

"Over there, next to that wall. Fuck. The drug must have worn off already. It should have held her. The architect is still out. You fucked up."

"I gave her the same dose I gave Collier," Margaret said.

"We should have used the stuff Fenner gave us to use on Geddings," Guthrie said.

"We don't even know what that crap was," Margaret said. "Fenner cooked it up for us. We're lucky there was a supply of the sedative in your office."

"Nothing is going right," Guthrie whined. "We had to move too fast this morning. No time to plan."

"What else could we do? If we hadn't spotted Drake leaving the hotel we would still be trying to figure out how to get a handle on the situation."

"If only we hadn't had to go back to the house for the guns."

"Don't be an idiot," Margaret said. "It's not as if the dean and the head of the college Foundation can be seen walking around campus carrying pistols. Now where is she? She has to be down here. There's no way out."

"The caskets," Guthrie said. "She must be hiding among them. How did she find them? She wouldn't have been able to see anything. I found her phone and Taser when I searched her bag. It's still upstairs."

"She must have blundered into that section of the crypt. I'll deal with her." Margaret raised her voice. "Pallas Llewellyn, it's going to be okay. We're here to help. We know you're hallucinating. We'll take you to the emergency room. Just follow the beam of my flashlight. Can you see it? Open your eyes and look for the light."

Pallas gripped the handle of the chisel and waited, trying to remain motionless. She was horribly aware of the sound of her breath and the pounding of her heart.

"I know you're confused," Margaret said. "I can explain everything. I'm afraid you walked into a clandestine drug trial that is being run by the government. It's all highly classified. For obvious reasons the authorities don't want you exposing the project on your podcast. If you will sign some papers swearing that you won't discuss the trial, you'll be free to go."

[2 6 2]

The footsteps were coming closer. Margaret was working her way deeper into the maze of jumbled caskets. The beam of her flashlight bounced around in the dense darkness. Pallas found the light disorienting. She had to focus even harder in order to stay in her other vision.

She experimented with closing her eyes and concentrating on her sense of hearing.

Margaret was closer now. Her footsteps echoed on the concrete as she threaded a path through the stacks of burial boxes. Her shoe struck some bones. They skittered across the floor of the crypt.

"Fuck," Margaret hissed. "I hate this place."

She was in the adjacent aisle now. Pallas held her breath.

"You and Drake are here because of what happened to the Kendrick woman, aren't you?" Margaret said. "Fenner told us she had been identified as a good candidate for the drug, but she experienced a psychotic break. She went mad. Attacked Fenner. He grabbed the lamp to defend himself. Geddings got rid of the body. We had no choice. We couldn't have that sort of bad publicity. We would have been ruined. I'm sure you understand. It was unfortunate, but no one was to blame."

Margaret was on the opposite side of the stack of burial boxes. Pallas dropped the chisel and used both hands to push the top two caskets into the neighboring aisle.

Wood cracked and creaked, screeched and splintered. Margaret screamed as the disintegrating caskets and their contents cascaded down on her. The roar of a gunshot boomed in the darkness.

Margaret's shriek of shock and horror was abruptly cut off. The beam of her flashlight was extinguished beneath the rubble of bones and fractured wood.

"What the fuck?" Guthrie's voice rose in near-panic. "Margaret? Where are you? What happened?"

He swung the flashlight around in wild, sweeping arcs, trying to make sense of the scene. Pallas dropped to her knees behind the remaining casket and grabbed the chisel before crawling to the end of the row.

No sound came from beneath the fallen caskets.

Pallas gripped the chisel and waited. She would not be able to hide and evade Guthrie indefinitely, but if she could hold out just a little while longer—buy a little more time—maybe, just maybe, Ambrose would find her before it was too late.

Footsteps approached the maze of jumbled caskets. Guthrie was nervous, moving warily.

"Why did you have to go and fuck up everything?" Guthrie shouted.

Pallas didn't know if he was talking to her or to Margaret Moore.

"This was the score of a lifetime," Guthrie continued. "If you and the writer hadn't come to Carnelian, we wouldn't be here now."

Okay, he's talking to me, Pallas thought.

She waited, chisel in hand.

The glare of a powerful flashlight exploded across the crypt.

"Nobody moves," Ambrose ordered.

"*Fuck,*" Guthrie yelled.

He squeezed off a string of gunshots, firing blindly. It occurred to Pallas that people got killed all the time by ricochets and stray bullets.

"There are two of us," Ambrose said. "This is over. Drop the gun."

"He's right," another man said. "This ends here. We don't like outsiders coming into our little town and causing trouble."

Pallas recognized the voice: Ron Quinn, the cemetery caretaker.

"Pallas," Ambrose shouted. "Where are you?"

"Back here," she said. "Guthrie and Moore were in this together. She's here, too, but I think she's unconscious."

"Put down the gun and come out, Guthrie," Ambrose said.

Pallas heard bones clatter across the concrete. She turned quickly.

Guthrie was standing directly in front of her. He pinned her in the glare of his flashlight. In his other hand he clutched a pistol.

"Come here, bitch, or I swear I'll kill you right now," he hissed. "I've got nothing to lose. Nothing. It's all fucked because of you and the writer."

She realized he intended to use her as a hostage. He was desperate. Frantic. If he were still rational he would be throwing down his gun and calling for a lawyer, but instead he was sliding into a full-blown panic.

"All right," she said, struggling to keep her voice calm and non-threatening. "I'll go with you."

"Drop the chisel."

"Sure." She set the tool on the floor and got to her feet. Guthrie clamped a fist around her upper arm and yanked her into position in front of him. The physical contact sent a nerve-shattering flash of electricity across her senses, briefly setting off another round of hallucinations. It was all she could do not to scream. She swayed, but Guthrie did not appear to notice. He clutched her arm as if she was a life preserver.

"I've got her," he yelled. "We're coming out together. Put the guns down and move into the light so I can see you."

There was a short, seething silence and then Ambrose spoke.

"Pallas?" he said.

"It's okay," she said. "He has a grip on my arm. He's touching me."

"I understand," Ambrose said.

"Shut up," Guthrie raged. "Drop the fucking guns."

There were a couple of muffled clunks, the unmistakable sound of metal on concrete.

"Ron and I are unarmed," Ambrose said. "You've got a clear path to the door, Guthrie."

Satisfied, Guthrie wrenched Pallas toward the concrete steps. It was clear that he hoped to use her as a shield until he got as far as the door. Once there he would push her down the steps, lock the door, and take off.

Instead of trying to shut out the disturbing vibes of energy he was generating, she made herself focus on them. When she had the fix she deliberately began to dampen them.

Guthrie stumbled over a skeleton that was partially shrouded in a ragged, rotting sheet. A skull rolled out and bounced across the floor. Guthrie yelped and jerked back a couple of steps.

"Try that again and you're a dead woman," he gasped.

For a shocked instant she thought he had realized exactly what she was doing.

"I didn't—" she began.

"You think I don't know you tried to trip me?"

He used his sleeve to wipe his forehead. He hand tightened around her arm. If she lived, she would have some bruises. She heard a faint noise in the shadows and knew that Ambrose was trying to edge closer to the concrete steps.

"Don't try it," Guthrie shouted. "I'll kill her. You know I will. Nothing to lose."

"I understand," Ambrose said. "Pallas?"

"Almost there," she said.

"Stop talking," Guthrie rasped.

They were at the foot of the steps. Guthrie started up, hauling her awkwardly behind him. She knew that if they made it to the top it would be too late.

He was on the second step now. She was on the first. Last chance. She steeled herself for the effort and unleashed everything she had into stilling the violent energy he was radiating.

"What the fuck?" he whispered, his voice raw and weak. "Something's happening to me. It's *you*. You're doing this."

Eyes wide with horror, he stared at her as if hypnotized. He was on the third step now, trying to raise the gun and aim it at her. But in the next second he lost his grip on the pistol and pitched forward.

She realized his trajectory would bring him down on top of her. They would land on the unforgiving concrete, but she would get the worst of it, because she was destined to be on the bottom. She tried to scramble aside, but it was hopeless. Instinctively she squeezed her eyes shut and tried to brace herself.

And then, somehow, Ambrose was there, deftly snatching her out of the path of the falling man. There was a bone-jarring thud when Guthrie hit the floor.

Pallas opened her eyes and saw Ron Quinn bending over to retrieve the pistol that Guthrie had dropped.

She suddenly had a million questions, but she could not ask any of them, because Ambrose had wrapped an arm around her and was crushing her against his chest.

She discovered she would have been content to remain there, pressed close into his heat, indefinitely, but a familiar voice interrupted.

"Guthrie's out cold," Ron announced. "He hit his head when he lost his footing on the steps."

"What's going on?" Theo mumbled from the shadows.

"Well, will you look at that," Ron said. "There's another one."

He angled his flashlight across the space. Theo had levered himself up to a sitting position. He had a hand clamped to his head. He stared into the beam of light, dazed.

Pallas reluctantly pulled free of Ambrose's grip. "I almost forgot. Margaret Moore is over there somewhere buried under a bunch of caskets. I don't know if she's alive. She had a gun."

"I'll find her," Ambrose said

Pallas hurried after him. "She's under that pile over there."

Ambrose smiled a little. "Your doing?"

"I was desperate."

"Nice work." Ambrose stepped over a shattered casket, ignoring the bones. "I see her. Looks like she's semiconscious. Here, hold the flashlight."

Pallas took the light and watched Ambrose dig through the rubble. Margaret groaned when he freed her. She stared at him, shocked.

"Well, fuck," she said. "It's the writer."

"I get that a lot," Ambrose said. He leaned down and retrieved the gun that she had dropped. "Can you stand?"

"No," Margaret said.

"In that case, you can sit there on that pile of bones until the cops get here."

Galvanized by the realization that she was sitting on a bone pile, Margaret scrambled to her feet.

"I hate this place," she muttered.

"Move," Ambrose said.

Margaret stumbled through the clutter of caskets and bones. Pallas was about to follow her, but she stopped when she saw an envelope on the floor.

She reached down and picked it up. The stationery was yellowed with age. She could sense the energy infused into the paper. *Excitement. Rage. Triumph.*

"What is it?" Ambrose asked.

"It must have fallen out of one of the caskets when they crashed on top of Margaret Moore," Pallas said. "No address, but there's a letter inside. I'll read it later."

CHAPTER FORTY-TWO

EMERY GEDDINGS WAS in one of those body bags in the crypt," Ron Quinn said. "The coroner thinks he was given a fatal dose of some drug. The dead woman in the other bag has been tentatively identified as Brooke Kendrick. She was bludgeoned to death."

Pallas watched Ron pour tea into three mugs. "Have you always known about the old smuggling tunnel under the asylum?"

"Oh, yeah," Ron said. He carried the mugs across his vintage kitchen and set them on the table. "I grew up here, same as Emery. Poor guy. He couldn't bring himself to get out of the drug business. The money was just too easy."

Ron handed a mug to Pallas and one to Ambrose and sat down.

Pallas inhaled the bracing aroma of the green tea. She and Ambrose and Ron were gathered at Quinn's house because they wanted privacy, and at the moment there were not a lot of options in Carnelian. The events in the crypt had gone down a few hours earlier and by now the entire town was aware that something dramatic had occurred in the ruins of the asylum. It would have been impossible to find a bar or a restaurant where they could have talked without attracting attention.

"That tunnel was built at the same time the asylum was constructed," Ron said. "A hospital for the insane was the perfect cover for a smuggling operation. As you discovered, it did double duty as a crypt for the patients who died on the premises. The smuggling along this section of the coast was focused on liquor. The business came to an end in the early nineteen thirties, and the hospital was closed a few years later. Over time people mostly forgot about the old tunnel."

"Geddings obviously knew about it," Ambrose said.

Ron chuckled. "His family was in the trade for generations."

"He made the mistake of going into business with Moore and Guthrie," Ambrose said. "Logan told me Guthrie is awake. He sustained a concussion but he'll live. He and Moore are asking for their lawyers, but Logan says he's got all he needs to hold them on charges of murder, attempted murder, embezzlement, drug dealing, and kidnapping. After they grabbed Collier they used his phone to send the text. Evidently that wasn't the original plan but they changed course when they saw him in the garage. Collier had his phone out and was about to send you a message, so they took advantage of the opportunity."

"So they admitted they killed Geddings and Fenner?" Ron asked.

"Logan says they aren't admitting to any of the deaths but he's sure he can tie them to the murder of Geddings. They claim they had nothing to do with Fenner's death, however, and can prove it. He's planning to check out their alibis but he admitted that murder charge may not hold up, because it looks like an overdose."

Pallas shuddered, remembering the spiderweb of bad energy she had stumbled into in the hall of Fenner's rental. "He was murdered. I'm sure of it. The killer was in the house that night."

Neither man argued with her.

"Moore and Guthrie were already skimming off the endowment," she continued, "but they got greedy. They couldn't resist the prospect of going into the drug trade, and they had their very own doctor who could use his license to order the hallucinogen from a compounding pharmacy. Geddings realized they were moving into his territory here in town and offered them a partnership. They grabbed the opportunity."

"They all needed Fenner," Ambrose said. "Not only because the anonymous donor had insisted on having him appointed director of the Institute but because he was the source of the hallucinogen. Fenner's only interest was in conducting his own experiments and those he was running on the side for the donor. Brooke Kendrick's death was the disaster that threatened all of them. An investigation would have exposed Fenner's illegal experiments, as well as the drug dealing."

"Up until that point Guthrie and Moore were probably just a couple of low-rent con artists with fake academic credentials who specialized in embezzling the endowment funds of small, struggling colleges," Pallas said. "But here in Carnelian they got in over their heads."

Ron exhaled deeply. "One thing's for sure—this whole mess will be the end of the Institute. The anonymous donor will pull the plug on the funding, which will probably be the final nail in the coffin of the college, too. This town is going to take a real financial hit."

"It's safe to assume the mysterious donor will disappear," Pallas said. "But I'm not so sure the town will collapse. This is a beautiful location. You know what the real estate people always say—you can't go wrong with waterfront property."

Ron snorted. "Let's hope you're right. I own a chunk of this town."

Pallas looked up from her tea. "You do?"

"Yep." Quinn chuckled. "Geddings's people weren't the only ones in the smuggling business back before World War Two. But my relatives were a hell of a lot smarter when it came to investing the money. They bought up most of what is now Main Street. Looks like I'd better take a few steps to protect my assets."

"How do you plan to do that?" Ambrose asked.

Ron drank some tea and lowered the mug. "I think I'll run for mayor. Taylor has been telling me I need to find a new purpose in life."

"Who's Taylor?" Pallas asked.

"The reference librarian at the public library. We've been seeing each other ever since I got out of the Army. I've been trying to convince her to marry me for ages. She said I'm just drifting through life out here at the cemetery. Says I need to find a purpose. I think I just did."

Pallas smiled. "Maybe it's time we read the letter that fell out of one of the caskets."

She reached into her messenger bag, which she'd found on the first floor of the asylum, pushed aside her phone and the Taser that Detective Logan had recovered, and took out the yellowed envelope. Once again she got the whisper of energy that told her that whatever was inside was going to be interesting.

She removed the sheet of stationery from the envelope, unfolded it carefully, and concentrated on deciphering the faded, old-fashioned cursive handwriting.

To Whom It May Concern:
If you found this letter it means you opened my casket and
discovered that I am not inside. A year ago my husband had

me committed to the Carnelian Psychiatric Hospital for the Insane. He did so not out of concern for my mental health but because he wished to be free to consume my inheritance. He will pay for his cruelty.

I have had a year to compose my vengeance. Tonight I will be declared dead. My casket will be assigned a number and carried down into the crypt beneath this terrible place. The records will be destroyed.

In the weeks to come my husband will be troubled by my ghost. He will never know another peaceful night. When he is gone I will return as my long-lost twin sister to reclaim my life and my fortune.

Yours in Vengeance,
Catherine Madison Carnelian

Pallas smiled. "She did it. She escaped the asylum, took revenge on her evil husband, and reinvented herself as her twin sister so that she could regain her fortune."

Ron grinned. "And then she made Carnelian a real community."

"Brilliant," Ambrose said. "Couldn't have written a better ending myself."

CHAPTER FORTY-THREE

'M SO SORRY you got caught up in this mess, Theo," Pallas said. "Are you sure you're okay?"

Theo grimaced. "I've still got a headache, but it's clearing up. The doctor said I was okay to drive. I won't try to make it all the way home tonight but I want to get started."

"How did you happen to get in the way of Moore and Guthrie?" Pallas asked.

She and Theo were sitting at a table in a coffeehouse near the hotel. Ambrose was at the police station having another conversation with Logan. It had turned into a very long day, she thought. Given all the excitement of the morning, it was hard to believe it was only midafternoon.

She had been in the lobby when Theo returned from giving his statement. Determined to apologize, she had invited him for coffee.

"I explained everything to Detective Logan," Theo said. "It was a classic case of being in the wrong place at the wrong time. I checked out this morning. I was in the garage putting my suitcase in the car when I saw that woman, Margaret Moore, getting into an elevator. I suddenly remembered that she had bought me a couple of drinks the night you and I had that argument in the hotel bar. It bothered me."

"Our argument?"

"No, the memory of how that woman had asked all those questions about you."

"She talked about me?"

"I had a couple of drinks while I waited for you and she insisted on buying me a few more. When I woke up the next morning I didn't even think about the conversation with her. I just assumed she was a business professional who had been stood up. But when I saw her in the garage with that guy—"

"Hugh Guthrie."

"Yeah, Guthrie, I started thinking that something seemed off. I remembered the conversation with Moore and I decided to text you to let you know that some stranger had been asking questions about you. But Moore saw me when she and Guthrie started to get into the elevator. I could tell she didn't like the idea that I had noticed her. She said something to Guthrie. The next thing I know they were both coming toward me. I honestly don't remember anything after that until I woke up in that damned crypt."

"Moore knew you had recognized her and that you would be able to place her and Guthrie in the hotel on the day I vanished. They were both unnerved by the way things had gotten out of control. They panicked and decided to grab you as well as me."

"Like I said, wrong place, wrong time."

Impulsively she reached out to put her hand on his arm. "You were trying to warn me. Thank you."

She stopped talking because she realized that Theo had gone still. He stared at her hand on his arm. She let go immediately and sat back.

"Sorry," she said.

"It's okay," Theo mumbled.

"No, it's not okay," she said. "It's never going to be okay between us again."

He sighed. "Not on a personal level, but that doesn't mean we can't do business together."

"Theo—"

She broke off because the door had opened and Ambrose was walking into the coffeehouse. She smiled and raised her hand to get his attention. He had already spotted her and was making his way to the table where she sat with Theo. When he arrived he leaned over and brushed his mouth lightly across hers. Theo watched with a mix of disbelief and fascination.

Ambrose did not appear to notice. He sat down and nodded at Theo. "How are you feeling, Collier?"

"I'll live," Theo said. He cleared his throat. "You two really stirred up some shit in this town."

"*The Lost Night Files* is good at that," Pallas said. She looked at Ambrose. "Did Detective Logan have any new information?"

"Some," Ambrose said. "He's sure now that he can't pin Fenner's death on either Moore or Guthrie. Their alibis checked out. The county coroner established time of death as sometime between eight and ten p.m. Moore and Guthrie attended a faculty event that night. Plenty of witnesses saw them. Logan says it's possible one managed to sneak away long enough to murder Fenner, but he is convinced he can't prove it, especially since the coroner called it an overdose with no signs of foul play."

"Someone killed Fenner," Pallas said.

Ambrose looked grim but he did not say anything.

Theo glanced at his phone, checking the time. "I'd better hit the road. Pallas, my offer is still open. Give it some thought."

He walked quickly across the restaurant and disappeared through the door.

Ambrose watched the exit with a bemused expression. "He seemed to be in a hurry."

"I accidentally scared the hell out of him. Again."

"Yeah?" Ambrose said, amusement flashing in his eyes. "How did you do that?"

"I put my hand on his arm. I wasn't thinking. I just wanted to thank him for trying to warn me about Margaret Moore. But he suddenly remembered exactly why I made him nervous."

Ambrose smiled a wicked smile. "Oh, right. You've got the magic touch. No wonder you scared him."

"I don't scare you," Pallas said.

"Nope, but if you ever do I'll just get out my manacle and chain."

"That sounds . . . kinky."

"Yes, it does, doesn't it?"

CHAPTER FORTY-FOUR

H E AWOKE TO the luxurious warmth of Pallas' soft, sleek body curled against him. He draped an arm around her waist, trying to draw her closer yet. He told himself he should go back to sleep, but he made the mistake of opening his eyes. There was still a lot of night on the other side of the window, but he could perceive the subtle light of impending dawn.

Pallas stirred. "What?"

"Didn't mean to wake you," he said.

"Too late. I'm awake." She turned onto her back and stretched her arms overhead. "So why are we both having this conversation at"—she paused and turned her head to look at the clock on the bedside table—"four ten in the morning?"

"I dreamed about the video of my night in the Institute." He levered himself up on his elbow. "We're missing something in it."

"What makes you so sure of that?"

"The fact that Guthrie and Moore murdered Geddings to keep him from selling it to me."

"They didn't want the drug experiments and the dope dealing exposed," Pallas said. "Sounds like a motive for murder to me."

"That's just it." Ambrose pushed the covers aside and sat up. "There's nothing on that video that exposes the experiments or the dealing. It shows me going to sleep, waking up, climbing out of bed, and walking toward the door. Then we see Dr. Fenner getting me back into bed. Yes, I'm sure he gave me a sedative out in the hallway when I got up to see what was going on, and afterward he sat me down in a chair while he wiped the blood off my hands, but there's nothing on the video that shows that. The video doesn't incriminate anyone. What made Geddings think I would pay for it?"

"Maybe he thought he could scam you, tell you there was some actual evidence on it," Pallas said. "He was in the drug-dealing business. By definition he was good at lying. He was planning to leave town. He probably thought that by the time you were able to view the video he would have disappeared."

"Maybe." Ambrose swung his legs over the side of the bed and reached for his trousers. "But there's something else that's been bothering me about that video."

Pallas sat up. "What?"

He pulled on the trousers and got to his feet. "I went to sleep so damn easily that night."

"You said Fenner told you that was often the case when people underwent sleep studies."

"It shouldn't have been the case, not with me." Ambrose picked up his phone and looked at her. "And even if I did somehow magically go to sleep that easily, I should have awakened after about twenty or thirty minutes. But that night I went out and stayed out until Brooke Kendrick screamed. That was around two in the morning. When I did get out of bed, I wasn't dreaming; I was in my other vision. It was disorienting."

She watched him carry the phone to the table and sit down. "What are you going to do?"

"Watch that damn video we found in Geddings's go bag again. This time I need to pay more attention to the details at the beginning. Maybe I missed something the first time around."

Pallas got out of bed and pulled on the plush hotel robe. "I'll watch it with you. Let me get my sketchbook and make some coffee."

"Thanks. But why the sketchbook?"

"When I draw things I see them in a different light. Literally."

AN HOUR LATER Pallas sat back and positioned her sketchbook on the table so that they could both see what she had created. Ambrose studied the images. They were all scenes of Dr. Fenner reattaching the electrodes that connected to the black box. The images reminded him of the drawings done by courtroom sketch artists—minimalist pictures designed to capture the emotion and drama of the moment.

"Fenner looks very, very intent," he said.

"More than intent," Pallas said, studying her drawing. "He's . . . feverish. He's got a real mad doctor vibe. That explains the heavy layers of anxiety I picked up in your room. I told you I didn't think they had come from you."

"Well, he was in the process of covering up the death of a patient who had died in the middle of an illegal drug trial. Makes sense he was more than a little anxious." Ambrose turned back to the video. "Huh."

"What?"

"Something about his body language seems off. As you said, he's got a real mad doctor vibe. It's as if he's never attached electrodes before and is worried about getting it right."

"He was rattled by what had happened to Kendrick," Pallas said. "But I see what you mean. Nothing about hooking you up to those electrodes looks routine, yet he must have done that procedure countless times."

Ambrose did not take his eyes off the screen. "Attaching electrodes to a patient is a common procedure. It's done all the time for various tests, and the job is often handled by an assistant. But Fenner handled that task personally—both times, in my case. Look, I'm already out."

"Probably because Fenner gave you that injection when he found you in the hall." Pallas watched the screen. "But you're right. He spends a great deal of time and care attaching the electrodes again."

"He had to repeat the entire process because the sticky parts of the original electrodes wouldn't adhere to the skin very well after being yanked off." Ambrose stopped as understanding slammed through him. "That's how he did it. That's how he administered the drug that knocked me out so quickly and kept me out for hours."

Pallas looked up from the screen, frowning. "He used the electrodes? But they don't work that way."

"The hardware doesn't, but the sticky patches could have been infused with the medication and administered through the skin like a nicotine patch. There's a word for delivering drugs that way."

"'Transdermal,'" Pallas said.

"Right. That's what Geddings meant when he assured me he had evidence of what was going on in the clinic. Maybe he planned to sell me a sample patch as well as the memory card when we did the deal at the asylum. Moore and Guthrie must have grabbed the evidence when they murdered him."

Pallas sat back, eyes narrowing. "We're assuming a lot here. I don't see anything on that screen that proves you were given an illegal drug. And even if we could prove it, the man who did it is dead."

"Conveniently." Ambrose looked at her. "Case closed, as far as the local law is concerned."

"But not for *The Lost Night Files*," Pallas said. "We're still looking for the anonymous donor who funded the Carnelian Sleep Institute."

CHAPTER FORTY-FIVE

THE WOMAN'S SCREAM brought him to the surface of the nightmare but not out of it. Ambrose knew that he was in the in-between place, the borderland between the dreamstate and the waking state.

In the dream he was in bed at the Institute, hooked up to a black box data recorder by a dozen electrodes.

The part of him that was awake and aware that he was dreaming understood he was in bed with Pallas in the hotel room, but the urge to get up was powerful. Overwhelming. There was something he had to do, something important.

In the dream he gets out of the bed and starts across the room. The sticky patches that connect the electrodes to the data recorder rip off, leaving a maze of wires scattered across the sheets.

The door opens. A woman is there but she is standing in deep shadow. He can't see her face, but he knows he should recognize her. Why can't he identify her?

"What are you doing here?" he asks.

"You're in this place because of me," she says.

"Who are you?" he asks.

"Ambrose, wake up," Pallas said.

He felt her hand on his shoulder. Her calming energy whispered to his senses. He yanked himself out of the dream. The vision of the Institute sleep room vanished, taking the woman with it.

He realized he was on his feet beside the bed. Pallas was in front of him. He groaned and squeezed his eyes shut for a few seconds.

"Shit," he said, opening his eyes. He stared at Pallas. "I was sleep-walking again, wasn't I? I should have set the alarms. Used the damn chain. Thanks for waking me before I wandered out into the hall in my underwear. My publisher would not be happy with that kind of branding."

"It's all right," she said. "You're awake now."

"I can't go on like this," he said. "I can't spend the rest of my life worried that I'm going to walk off a cliff in the middle of a dream."

She watched him, her eyes unreadable in the deep shadows. He opened his inner window a little. The sight of her aura, strong and bright and stable, was reassuring. His attempt at sleepwalking hadn't thrown her into a panic. Yet.

"Who were you talking to in your dream?" Pallas asked.

"I'm not sure. I think I was supposed to recognize her, but I didn't." He grimaced. "Before you ask, there was no sex involved."

Pallas got a knowing look. "In that case we should find out why she showed up tonight."

"It was a dream, Pallas. They don't follow the rules of waking logic."

"No, but they have their own logic. You've been in the process of recovering your memories for the past few weeks. Maybe this is your intuition trying to tell you something."

"Like what?" he asked, frustrated.

"I don't know. Has the woman appeared in any of your previous dreams or sleepwalking episodes?"

"No." He hesitated. "Well, maybe. I think there has been someone hiding in the shadows all along, but I never paid attention because in the dream I was always focused on the woman's scream and the blood."

Pallas watched him with her sorceress eyes. "Do you want to try to find out why the woman showed up in your dream tonight?"

"How? Are you going to draw my dream?"

"I'm not sure if it will work," she said. "As we keep reminding each other, there's a steep learning curve when it comes to this psychic thing. But I think we should try to find out why an unknown woman showed up in your dream."

CHAPTER FORTY-SIX

I T WAS THE psychic vibe of your dream that woke me," Pallas said. She put her sketchbook down on the table. "I could calm those wavelengths so that you could go back to sleep, but that won't give us any new information. If we can get you back into your dream, however, I might be able to get a better picture of what was going on."

"Do you really think you can put me back into my dream?"

"Maybe." She opened the sketchbook. "What I know is that I can calm and rebalance certain wavelengths of an individual energy field. Those wavelengths appear to be related to sleep. Maybe I can manipulate them in other ways."

"Do you have any idea how scary that sounds?" Ambrose asked.

She was in the process of reaching into the messenger bag for a pencil. She straightened very quickly and looked at him. He was watching her with a slight smile. His eyes were very intent.

"It does sound scary, doesn't it?" she said. "If you'd rather not run this particular experiment, I understand, believe me."

"Let's do it."

She smiled. "You're not scared of me."

Ambrose stretched out his hand. "I trust you, partner."

"Thanks." She took a breath and let it out slowly. When she was ready she threaded her fingers through his. "Here we go."

She kicked up her other vision and focused gently. This time she was not trying to achieve balance or harmony. This time she was an observer.

"Tell me about the dream," she said.

"It started the way it always does. I was in bed, hooked up to the box. Lots of wires. I heard the woman scream. I got up. I'm in the underwater shadow world. Maybe I'm hallucinating—"

She felt him slide back into the dream. It was a strangely disorienting experience for her. She could not see what he was viewing but she could feel his reactions.

"You are not hallucinating," she said. She tightened her grip on his hand, feeling her way into the dream storm. "You are not sleepwalking. You know you are dreaming. You are searching for information. Tell me what you see."

"I walk toward the door as I always do, but this time it opens before I get to it. There is someone standing in the shadows. A woman. I can't see her face but she is holding something in her hand. I ask her what she is doing there."

"What does she say?"

"She says, 'You're in this place because of me.'"

Pallas turned the words over in silence for a moment, trying to make sense of them. "Is the woman your mother?"

"No," Ambrose said. Very certain.

"Your sister?"

"No."

"Is the woman your ex?"

"No."

"Can you see her aura?"

"No."

"Why can't you see her aura?"

"I don't know."

"What is she holding in her hand?"

"A phone," Ambrose said.

"Ask her why she is holding a phone."

Ambrose went silent, but she knew he was struggling to ask the question. It was clear he was meeting resistance, because the energy of the dream abruptly became even more chaotic. The storm metamorphosed into a full-blown hurricane.

Horrified by the possibility that she was losing control and that she might send Ambrose into a permanent dreamstate—a coma—Pallas struggled to rebalance the violently oscillating wavelengths.

"I can't see her aura," Ambrose said from the depths of the dream. "I can't identify her until I see her aura." His agitation got worse. He was suddenly on his feet. *Why can't I see her aura?*

Pallas tightened her grip on his hand and leaped out of the chair.

"Ambrose, wake up," she said, fighting to keep her tone calm but firm. "You must come out of the dream now."

He looked at her then, really looked at her. She knew he was no longer in the dream trance, but a dangerous energy burned in his eyes.

"I've been a fool," he said.

"Why?" she asked.

"She answered my question," Ambrose said. "She told me why she was holding the damned phone."

"Why?"

"She said that with today's tech you can run the world with a phone."

"Why is that important?"

"Because it's not the first time she's said that—or, rather, texted it," Ambrose said. "There's only one person in this mess whose aura I have never viewed. For most of the past year she has run my world with tech. I think the woman in my dream is Iona Bryant, the perfect virtual assistant."

CHAPTER FORTY-SEVEN

GUESS YOUR TALENT isn't as useful as one might think," Pallas said.

"I can't view auras through a computer screen." Ambrose stalked across the room to the console that held the small coffee maker. He selected a premeasured packet of coffee and dropped it into the machine. "Or in an email or a text message."

"You had no reason to be suspicious of Iona Bryant," Pallas said.

Ambrose had calmed down but he was still in a savage mood. She knew he was blaming himself for a failure of judgment.

"Technically, I still don't." Ambrose stepped into the bathroom and filled the coffeepot at the sink. He reappeared a moment later. "When you think about it, nothing in the equation has changed."

"I disagree," Pallas said. "Something has changed. Your intuition has a lot more information to work with now. Context."

Ambrose poured the water into the reservoir of the coffee maker. "It's rather breathtaking when you think about it. If Iona is the one pulling the strings it means she lied to me from the start. And I fell for every single lie."

"That brings up an interesting point," Pallas said, determined to keep the discussion on track. "When did you hire Iona?"

"About a month after the San Diego writers' event." Ambrose groaned. "I can't believe I was that . . . what? Dumb? Stupid? Unobservant? Naive? There aren't enough adjectives."

"Let's forget the negative self-talk. It's a waste of time. One month after your amnesia episode you were a man dealing with an extraordinary new vision. You were trying to process a whole new level of sensory input. You were disoriented and off-balance. On top of that, you wondered if you were losing your mind."

Ambrose glanced at her. "Just like you and your friends?"

"Yep." Pallas sighed. "Talia and Amelia and I frequently tell each other that the only reason we didn't end up in a locked ward was because the three of us were able to support and reassure each other. You had to face all the dreams and doubts and fears on your own. I can't even imagine the nightmare you've been living."

Ambrose watched the coffee drip into the pot with a brooding expression. "Makes you wonder if there are others like us."

She shivered. "Good question. Do you think Iona Bryant is the anonymous donor who funded the Institute? Maybe she's responsible for everything that has happened to us. Our amnesia, our new psychic abilities, the experiments here in Carnelian. The whole damned nightmare."

"Maybe," Ambrose said. "But I doubt it."

"Why? And please don't tell me it's because she's a woman."

"A woman who made me look like a fool," Ambrose said. "Don't get me wrong, I'm sure Bryant is involved in this thing, but I don't believe she's running the show."

"Why not?"

"For one very simple reason." Ambrose poured two coffees. "She really is a great virtual assistant."

"I'm not following you."

"Think about it. If we're right, Iona Bryant spent a huge chunk of the past year keeping an eye on me and, probably, on Brooke Kendrick. She was monitoring Fenner and the Institute. But there are a lot of moving pieces in this thing. For instance, who is keeping watch on you and Talia and Amelia?"

Pallas went cold. "That is a very disturbing question. It would explain the low-grade paranoia, though."

"For all we know there are other unwitting research subjects out there." Ambrose carried the coffees back to the table and sat down. "I think we're looking at an organization. Yes, there must be someone in charge, but every smart leader knows how to delegate. Got a feeling Iona Bryant was the project manager on this operation, not the boss."

"How did you find her?" Pallas asked. "Were you searching for a virtual assistant and just happened across her name?"

"After San Diego I was in bad shape. My world seemed to be falling apart. I had trouble writing. My nightmares were getting worse. Maureen walked out. I was making my family nervous. I was trying to hold it all together and pretend I was okay. It occurred to me that I needed a virtual assistant. I went online and found Iona Bryant."

"Did anyone recommend her to you?"

Ambrose went very still, his eyes stark. "No. I can't remember why I settled on her. Everything about her just seemed, you know, perfect."

"Sometime in the weeks after San Diego you decided you needed an assistant and almost immediately you found Ms. Perfect online. I hate to say this, but that does not sound like a coincidence."

Ambrose massaged his forehead with one hand. "Call me paranoid, but I am inclined to agree. What does it sound like?"

"A delayed hypnotic suggestion that was implanted during your lost night in San Diego?"

"I was afraid you were going to say that."

"It's just a hypothesis," Pallas said. "You told me your family gave you the number of the Carnelian Sleep Institute when they staged the intervention. You said your brother did an online search and found the clinic."

"I know where you're going with this. Yes, Iona Bryant is very, very good with tech. Yes, it's possible she hacked into my computer and manipulated my search results when I went looking for a virtual assistant, and yes, it's possible she invaded my brother's computer and manipulated the results when he went looking for a sleep clinic."

"We need to find her," Pallas said. "Do you know anything about her that is personal?"

"Not much. We communicated by text and email. She was always friendly but professional. At one point when I complained that my family wouldn't stop bothering me she said she understood what it was like to deal with family. I got the impression she had a brother and a sister but that they weren't close. I think she mentioned her father once, but she didn't say much about him."

"Maybe your pal Calvin the Magnificent could help us locate her."

"There's no time to bring in Calvin," Ambrose said. He was suddenly on his feet, heading for the door. "We need to move fast if we're going to find her before she leaves town."

"What makes you think she's in town? You said she's very good with tech. She probably ran the whole project with a laptop and a phone."

Ambrose paused at the door. "You are the one who insists that Fenner was murdered."

"I'm sure of it."

"And I agree with you. If we're right, he wasn't killed from a distance, and afterward the killer definitely did not search the Institute by remote control. Both of those were hands-on jobs, and they were done on very short notice. The project manager had to be in position to move fast once the decision was made to shut down the project."

"Good point."

"There's something else that indicates whoever was responsible for the operation is local," Ambrose said. "The goal was to conduct illegal experiments with a very unique drug. That must have involved special protocols for handling and delivery. It's not the kind of thing you entrust to the post office. Someone had to provide the meds to Fenner, and that same individual would have wanted to monitor results personally. You don't run off-the-books drug trials without a lot of supervision and control."

Pallas took a breath. "Agreed."

"She had to be here in town. She knew her way around. I think she's been here all along."

"Jodi Luckhurst? The receptionist?"

"No, the timing doesn't fit. They've lived here for years. We're looking for a newcomer to the community. I think we need to talk to someone at the local tech shop."

"Why?"

"Because I just remembered one bit of personal information that she let slip in her emails. She's obsessed with video games."

———————

HIS NAME WAS Jason. He worked at Tech Magic on Main Street. He was plugged into the local gaming community and he knew exactly who fit the profile Ambrose had created.

"She moved into town about a year ago," Jason said. "Rented the Atherton place out on Bridge Road. I helped her get set up. Fiber optics. Gigabit speed. Badass gaming computer. I remember thinking it was a lot of juice just to sell crystals and candles online."

CHAPTER FORTY-EIGHT

"A RE YOU SURE Serenity is gone for good?" Ralph Atherton frowned. "I know her car is gone but I figured she went to see friends or maybe take a couple of days off. She's been real busy with that store in town and her online shop. She probably needed a little vacation. Retail is a tough business."

Ralph had answered the door a short time ago when Pallas and Ambrose had arrived. He was in his seventies and had the enthusiastically friendly air of a man who had retired too soon and was now bored and eager to chat with strangers, even if they did show up on his doorstep asking personal questions about his tenant.

"We're sure she's gone for good," Ambrose said. "She's not answering her phone or responding to email. The shop is closed."

That was the truth, Pallas thought. What Ambrose had not clarified was that the woman who had called herself Iona Bryant had also vanished. There had been no response to the texts and emails he had sent.

Ralph squinted at him, alarm sparking in his eyes. "You're the podcast crew, aren't you? Seems like you're lighting a real fire under this town. Haven't had this much action since the big landslide a few years back. Why do you want to find Serenity?"

"Follow-up interview," Pallas said, going for smooth and professional. "She was kind enough to answer some questions when we first arrived, and now that the drug ring has been exposed we'd like to thank her for her help and maybe get a little closure for the series."

It wasn't a complete lie, she thought. The part about trying to get some closure was certainly true.

"Huh." Ralph looked as if he wasn't sure what to make of that. "Well, I can't help you." He angled his chin at the small house across the street. "You can see for yourself she's not here."

Ambrose got a deeply troubled expression. "To tell you the truth, we're more than a little worried about her."

"Why?" Ralph asked, bewildered. Then his eyes widened in shock. "You think she's part of that drug gang? Not a chance. I can guarantee you she's not into anything like that. She's a damn good tenant and a hard worker. Pays her rent on time. Doesn't party. Doesn't have men stay overnight. Hell, she doesn't even date, as far as I can tell."

"You don't understand," Ambrose said. "We're concerned about her safety. As Ms. Llewellyn said, Serenity went out of her way to help us at the start of our investigation. Now we're concerned that someone involved in the drug dealing found out that she was helpful."

There was a lot to be said for a writer's imagination, Pallas thought.

"Well, shit," Ralph said, genuinely alarmed now. "You think they might have killed her because she knew too much about what was going on there at that damn sleep clinic?"

"We don't have any proof of that," Pallas said quickly. "We just want to talk to her and make sure she's okay."

"But she's not here," Ralph said.

"It might be a good idea for you to go into the house and have a look around," Ambrose said. "See if things look normal. As her landlord, you have every right to make certain she's not in danger."

"Now you've got me worried," Ralph said. "Hang on. I'll get the key."

He disappeared through his front door and returned a moment later, key in hand. "I'll just take a quick look around."

He hurried across the narrow road and went up the steps. Pallas and Ambrose followed at a respectful distance. They waited on the front porch while Ralph rapped on the door.

"Serenity?" he called. "Are you in there?"

When there was no answer, he opened the door and moved into the front hall. Ambrose went to the entrance but he did not cross the threshold.

"What the hell?" Ralph shouted from somewhere inside the house. He reappeared at the far end of the hall. "She's gone. Pulled a midnight move-out. I'll be damned. Never saw that coming. Just didn't seem like the type, y'know? She owed me a month's rent."

"Are you sure she's gone?" Ambrose asked.

"See for yourself," Ralph growled. He gestured vaguely at the interior of the house. "Closet is empty. Nothing left in the bathroom."

Ambrose did not wait for a second invitation. He moved into the hallway and disappeared.

Pallas took a step inside the hall, intending to follow him . . .

. . . and put one foot right into the heart of the small storm of dark energy. *Rage. Frustration. Fear.*

"Damn it," she yelped.

She veered to the left and managed to bump up against the wall.

"Whoa," Ralph said. "Are you all right, Ms. Llewellyn?"

"Yes, thanks." She pushed her hair out of her eyes, embarrassed. "I tripped. New shoes."

"So long as you're okay."

"I'm fine. Really."

Ambrose appeared at the far end of the hall. He gave her a quick, concerned look, and when she nodded to assure him she was okay, he vanished again. She realized he was trying to take a look around without attracting Ralph's attention.

She pulled herself together and gave Ralph her best client smile. "This is a very interesting house. Has it been in the family for a long time?"

"Yes, indeed." Ralph perked up immediately, delighted to chat. "My great-grandfather built it."

"I'm an interior designer by training," Pallas said. "Just looking around I get the impression that almost everything is original. It's an excellent example of pre–World War Two architecture. I'm surprised it's in such good condition."

"I paint occasionally and polish the floors, but that's about it." Ralph patted a nearby wall affectionately. "Solid as a rock. They just don't build 'em like they did in the old days."

"What about the kitchen?" she pressed, leaning into an air of enthusiasm.

"Well, some new appliances, of course. Had to take up the old linoleum. But the tile work on the counters is all original. I'll show you."

Pallas followed him into the charming, old-fashioned kitchen, de-termined to keep up the comments and questions so that Ambrose would have an opportunity to finish the search.

"The tile work is fantastic," she said, admiring the backsplash. "And it's in excellent condition."

"I have to do some grout work occasionally, but that's about it," Ralph said.

Pallas heard Ambrose coming back down the hall. Relieved, she turned toward the kitchen doorway. The glint of sun sparking on glass caught her eye. She looked up and saw a small crystal pyramid on top of the refrigerator. It had been carefully positioned to catch light and reflect it in a subtle way.

Ambrose appeared. "We should be going."

Ralph abruptly switched gears.

"Do you think I should call the police?" he said.

"Not much point," Ambrose said. "It's obvious our concerns were misplaced. You were right. Looks like she bailed on the rent. I wouldn't be surprised if her shop on Main Street is in trouble. She probably couldn't handle the lease, so she left town."

Ralph sighed. "She seemed so nice."

They trooped back across the street, said goodbye to Ralph, and got into Ambrose's car. Pallas looked at him.

"Well?" she said.

"She's gone, all right." Ambrose put on his sunglasses, fired up the engine, and drove back toward town. "She left plenty of stuff behind but nothing of a personal nature. She had her exit strategy planned ahead of time. I'll see if Calvin can pick up any leads but I'm not hopeful. She knew we were closing in on her and she decided to dis-appear. What did you stumble into in the front hall?"

"Rage," Pallas said. She shivered at the memory. "A lot of it. There was also a sense of frustration and, I think, some fear. It felt like the same kind of emotional heat I picked up in Fenner's house."

"She's the one who killed him," Ambrose said.

"I think so. There's something else as well. When she walked out the front door of the Atherton house, she wasn't just walking away from a failed business project. She was fleeing a major personal disaster, and she was very upset about it. I need to draw."

Ambrose braked for a stop sign at an intersection. He glanced at her.

"One thing I've been wondering about," he said.

She gave him a rueful smile. "You want to know why I didn't pick up any of her emotional turmoil the day we visited her in her little shop on Main Street."

"Just curious," he said.

She thought about the crystal pyramid on top of the refrigerator. "Energy is energy. It isn't good or bad. It's what you do with it that matters. If you know what you're doing, you can manipulate it so that it feels balanced and harmonious. Iona Bryant may be a criminal mastermind and a killer, but credit where it's due. She knows how to handle energy. I'm going to have to look into the potential of crystals when I get home."

SHE WAITED UNTIL they were back in her hotel room before she dug out the sketchbook and a pencil. She took a few seconds to slip into the trance—it was getting easier now, more natural—and then she went to work.

The drawing came together quickly. When it was finished she

showed it to Ambrose. He studied it for a long moment and then looked up, his eyes grim with a dark comprehension.

"A gathering storm?" he said.

"Serenity was the spider in the web here in Carnelian," Pallas said. "But you were right. This thing is bigger than the Carnelian Sleep Institute project."

CHAPTER FORTY-NINE

W HAT WE DON'T have is a motive," Ambrose said.

"What do you mean?" Pallas said. "Guthrie, Moore, and Geddings were running a drug ring."

Ambrose stacked his heels on the hassock and drank some coffee. When he lowered the cup his eyes were thoughtful.

"I'm not talking about a motive for the drug operation here in Carnelian," he said. "Those three were in it for the money, and Fenner was obsessed with his insomnia drug experiments. But none of that explains the Institute. What was the anonymous donor's motive?"

"People—heck, governments—have been running experiments in the paranormal for generations. The U.S. has a long history of that sort of research."

"But usually with a well-defined purpose," Ambrose said. "In this case, we know the donor was willing to spend a lot of money, commit murder, and take serious risks to conduct off-the-books experiments. What we don't know is why."

"Money is a huge motivator, and everyone knows there's a lot of it in the drug business, both the legal and the illegal sides," Pallas said. "Just imagine how much you could make if you came up with a drug that gave people psychic talents." She paused, thinking. "Or enhanced someone's low-level psychic vibe, as it did with us."

Ambrose shook his head. "We're not dealing with some standard-issue drug lord trying to make a lot of cash."

"Then why experiment on us?"

"The most valuable commodity in the modern world is information," Ambrose said. "You and I have the ability to collect data that is invisible to most people. We have unique talents for gathering intelligence about individuals that could be used by corporations, cartels, law enforcement, government agencies, or the military. I would make a very good spy, and I have the ability to predict other people's actions before they take place."

She shuddered. "I could be the perfect assassin." She realized her cup was shaking a little. "The deaths would look like natural causes."

Ambrose said, "You are not an assassin, and you never will be."

She ignored that. "Do you think that you and I and Talia and Amelia are proof of concept for whoever did this to us? Are we successful experiments?"

"No," Ambrose said. "We're failures."

"Why do you say that?"

"Because the anonymous donor is about to learn the lesson that Dr. Frankenstein learned."

"Right." Pallas relaxed a little. "If you set out to create monsters you had better be prepared for them to turn on you."

CHAPTER FIFTY

THE CARNELIAN PROJECT was a failure.

Cutler Steen shut down the laptop. It took every ounce of control he possessed to resist the urge to hurl the damn machine against the nearest wall.

He crossed the high-ceilinged room, went through the open French doors, and stepped out onto the wide veranda. He gripped the teak railing and contemplated the paradise of lush tropical gardens and sparkling ocean. The island offered everything a man in his profession could want—discreet offshore banking and government institutions designed to accommodate the requirements of successful individuals such as himself. The local police did business the old-fashioned way—by bribery. The infrastructure was state-of-the-art. The airstrip could handle the fastest corporate jets, and the harbor was equipped to service those who preferred to travel by private yacht.

It all came at a price, of course, but he and the handful of elite entrepreneurs who ran their empires from the island were happy to pay for the priceless commodity of privacy.

He checked the time. Four thirty. The jet carrying his younger daughter was due to land in fifteen minutes. An hour from now she would join him and her brother and sister for drinks on the veranda and a debriefing. It was important to analyze the failure and learn from it.

Motion in the gardens below drew his attention. He looked down and saw Jenkins, a member of his security team, patrolling a winding path. The agent was wearing a floppy-brimmed hat, sunglasses, a loose-fitting, short-sleeved shirt, and a pair of khaki trousers. He could have been mistaken for a tourist, but there were no tourists on this half of the island. If you looked closely you could see the earpiece. The pistol and knife were tucked out of sight under the shirt.

Sensing that he was being watched, Jenkins looked up and inclined his head respectfully. "Good afternoon, sir. I'm told Ms. Celina's plane is on time. There is a vehicle waiting for her at the airport."

"Excellent," Steen said. "I'm looking forward to having the family together for drinks and dinner this evening. It's not often that all three of my children are on the island at the same time. They lead very busy lives."

"I understand, sir. It's always good to be with family."

"Yes," Steen said.

Neither of them mentioned that Jenkins did not have any close family. None of the members of Steen's security detail did. None were married. Steen hired carefully vetted loners, and he took good care of them. For the most part, they rewarded him with loyalty.

He turned and walked back into the vast great room of the villa. Each of his children had their own villas situated on the grounds of the sprawling estate. There was ample room for all of them here in the main house, with its many bedrooms, baths, and sitting areas—the estate had once operated as a luxury resort. But the members of the Steen family liked their privacy. They each had their own business interests, their own friends, and their own lovers. Most important of all, they each had their own secrets and their own ambitions. He had raised them that way and encouraged the rivalries and conflicts that always simmered just beneath the surface.

Celina, Benedict, and Adriana were his longest-running experiments. They all shared his DNA—he had had them tested at birth—but each had a different mother, who had been carefully selected for her latent psychic ability. Each woman had suffered an unfortunate accident shortly after the birth of her child.

He had himself back under control now. He was able to contain the rage and near-panic that had threatened to overwhelm him. It was time to accept the reality of the very expensive failure in Carnelian and move on. Celina had disappointed him but she nevertheless had certain talents. Neither Benedict nor Adriana could prowl the dark net as well as their sister, and in today's world that skill set was as valuable as privacy.

The corporate jet landed on time. Celina was whisked up the hillside to the estate in one of the armored SUVs. She walked into the great room a short time later. He knew from the look in her eyes that she was dreading this meeting. Everything about her was brittle.

He crossed the tiled floor to give her the obligatory kiss on the cheek. "Welcome home, my dear."

"I'm sorry that Carnelian was a disaster," she said. "There were unforeseen complications."

"I understand. You can tell me all about it later. You've had a long flight. You need to unwind and relax. Why don't you change into something more comfortable and join me and Benedict and Adriana out on the terrace for drinks?"

Celina gripped the small bag that held her phone very tightly. Her eyes were stark. "Of course."

"I trust you brought me a souvenir of your time in Carnelian. A lovely little crystal ornament, or perhaps a scented candle?"

"I didn't think you'd want any reminders of a failed project."

"Perhaps not," he agreed. "But tell me, was it fun to play the roles of Serenity and Iona Bryant? I've always enjoyed acting. One gets such a sense of power when one assumes another identity."

"No, I did not enjoy the experience of assuming other identities for all those months," Celina said, her voice tighter than ever. "It was a very lonely life."

For a few seconds he allowed his irritation to break through. "Was that why you wasted so much time with those damn video games?"

Celina surprised him with a flash of anger. "You're the one who told me that the games were a good way to practice and perfect my talent for game theory and strategy."

"How many times have you been warned that the source of your power is always the source of your greatest vulnerability?"

Celina got her anger back under control but he could sense it burning just under the surface.

"Everything was going as planned until the podcast team arrived," she said.

"Ah, yes, *The Lost Night Files*. I will admit I did not think those three women would become a problem. In their case, the enhancing protocol was interrupted by the fire and the earthquake. I assumed that the effects of the drug, if any, would be minimal at best. There has been no indication that they developed strong talents. The opposite, in fact. They appear to be deteriorating."

"Has it occurred to you that you may be wrong?" Celina asked.

Without warning the rage crashed through the barrier of his control. He seized the teapot off his desk and hurled it against the wall. Celina watched in silence, speculation heating her eyes. He pulled himself to-gether.

"All three subjects are failures," he said. "So is Ambrose Drake. It's obvious they have become unstable. Their lives are in chaos. Their careers have foundered. Their personal relationships are in turmoil. In the case of the three females, they are obsessed with that ridiculous podcast. If they have developed any serious talent it's clear they are too weak to handle it. I'm telling you, they are failing. They will soon be living on the streets, locked up in a psych ward, or, quite probably, dead."

"You are overlooking one important factor," Celina said. "There is a bond between the women, and now Drake has become part of their world. They are close friends, bound together by their secrets. In case you haven't noticed, they are in the process of forming a fam-ily of choice. You are the one who insists that family is everything."

She turned and walked away.

Steen went back out onto the veranda and gripped the railing. Celina's project was in ruins, but there was no denying she possessed a strong talent for strategy and game theory. She was the one who had been on the ground in Carnelian. She had watched the carefully planned operation fall apart thanks to a podcaster and a no-name writer. Her observations could not be ignored.

Maybe he should pay more attention to his failures.

CHAPTER FIFTY-ONE

THEY GOT TOGETHER on a video chat after breakfast the following morning. Pallas was in her hotel room, packing to leave Carnelian. Ambrose was with her. His duffel was already in the trunk of his car. Talia beamed in from Seattle and Amelia joined from a motel room somewhere off the interstate in Southern California.

"It's a shame about Serenity or Iona Bryant or whatever she called herself," Talia said wistfully. "Her ability to manipulate social media and the dark net is extremely impressive. We could have used someone with her skill set. She would have been the perfect virtual assistant for *The Lost Night Files*."

Pallas tossed her nightgown into the suitcase and glared at Talia. "She was running an operation designed to conduct dangerous and highly illegal experiments with unknown drugs on unwitting research subjects. Also, she murdered at least one person that we know of. Granted, Dr. Fenner was not one of the good guys, but still."

"Yes, well, no virtual assistant is perfect," Talia said.

Pallas peered closely at her but, as usual, it wasn't easy to tell if Talia was trying to make a joke or if she was serious.

"I'm not clear on how Emery Geddings died," Amelia said.

"With the video from room A and the photo of that logbook page he figured he had some blackmail material," Pallas said.

"For all we know he may have had other incriminating evidence as well," Ambrose added. "Maybe some of the transdermal patches. Whatever, he wanted to cash out. He set up two appointments at the asylum. The first one was with Guthrie and Moore. He probably promised to hand over all the evidence in exchange for one big payoff. But they had their own plans."

"They murdered him using a lethal sedative that Fenner provided, stuffed the body into a body bag, and dumped it in the asylum crypt," Pallas said.

Ambrose drank some more coffee. "By the time I showed up, it was all over."

"As far as Guthrie, Moore, and Fenner were concerned, that should have been the end of their problems," Pallas said. "Instead it was just the beginning, because Ambrose called in *The Lost Night Files* to help him figure out what was going on at the Institute."

"And none of them had any way of knowing that Serenity-Iona was also in a panic," Ambrose said. "She tried to get a handle on things by volunteering to talk to us about the Carnelian ghosts, but the situation was already out of control. We mentioned Geddings's disappearance, but she didn't give herself away with a lie because she honestly didn't know what had happened to him. She assumed the same thing everyone else in town did—that he was a drug dealer who had probably been murdered by some of his competitors."

"When she heard about the explosion at Geddings's house she must have figured she had caught a lucky break," Talia said. "She hoped you two were the two bodies found in the wreckage. Then you showed up alive. When it became obvious you were not going to give up and go away she started making plans to shut down the project."

"She murdered Fenner because he knew too much about the mystery drug and what it could do," Pallas said. "He also must have known that she was the anonymous donor's intermediary. Afterward she went to the Institute and made sure there were no incriminating records. Then she got into her car and vanished."

"Calvin is trying to track her," Ambrose said, "but no luck."

"It's as if she simply disappeared," Talia said.

Amelia got a thoughtful expression. "You know, Pallas, it's a wonder that she didn't try to kill both you and Ambrose."

"I'm sure she considered it," Ambrose said, "but there were a few problems with that approach. The first, of course, is that there was no way to make us conveniently disappear. There were too many people who would come around asking questions."

Talia got a fierce expression. "Amelia and me, for starters."

"Damn right," Amelia said, equally fierce.

"And then there is my ever-loving family," Ambrose said. He smiled, wincing a little. "They would have torn the town apart."

Pallas grimaced. "My family would have had a few questions, too. They might not approve of my career choices, but that would not have stopped them from demanding answers. So the only practical thing to do was pull the plug on the Institute project. But I can tell you Serenity-Iona was not happy about it."

"Looks like we are now searching for a very wealthy individual who is funding research into the paranormal," Talia said.

"Don't be too sure it's one person who is behind this," Amelia warned. "It could be a clandestine government agency, for all we know."

There was a moment of silence while they all absorbed that possibility. Then Pallas shook her head.

"I keep coming back to the feeling that the project in Carnelian had a personal angle for Serenity-Iona," she said. "She wasn't just closing down a drug trial that had run into trouble. She was very upset by the failure. It was personal. I can't imagine a trained government agent getting so emotionally involved in what was essentially a dangerous science experiment."

"I agree," Amelia said.

Talia pushed her glasses higher on her nose. "So do I. When you think about it, that might give us a bit of an edge. It's bound to be easier to track down a crazy mad scientist or a criminal mastermind than to fight our way through the government bureaucracy."

"Way to go, Talia," Amelia said. "Look for the silver lining."

Ambrose tapped the side of his coffee mug. "I'll tell you what I'd like to find."

They all looked at him.

"What?" Pallas asked.

"The list," Ambrose said.

They stared at him.

"What list?" Amelia asked.

It was Talia who lit up like a lightbulb. "He's right. There must be a list."

"A list of?" Pallas prompted.

"The four of us didn't know each other before we were drawn into this situation," Ambrose said. "But we all have a few things in common. We're all about the same age, and prior to our amnesia episodes, we were each aware that we had a bit of a psychic vibe."

"You're right," Pallas said. "We knew it even if we didn't want to admit it to ourselves or anyone else."

"After our lost nights, that vibe was enhanced," Amelia said. "It's as if whoever is behind this was able to identify us as candidates for a research experiment designed to enhance paranormal talents."

"We were selected because we already possessed some psychic

ability," Talia said. "Ambrose is right; there must be a list. The question is, how did we get on it?"

"We have another problem," Amelia said, her eyes very grim. "I just found out that the Lucent Springs Hotel is scheduled for demolition. The new owners have given up the idea of renovating it. They say the earthquake and the fire did too much damage. They are going to use explosives to take down what's left."

Pallas stilled. "Explosives will destroy whatever evidence is in those ruins."

"I know there is something there," Amelia said. "Something important. I'm sure I sensed it the morning we escaped. I need to find it before the hotel is destroyed. Time is running out."

CHAPTER FIFTY-TWO

THANK GOODNESS FOR delivery," Pallas said.

She set the pizza on the coffee table and dropped onto the sofa. Five days had passed since they left Carnelian. They were in her tiny one-bedroom apartment in Keeley Point because after one brief visit she had concluded that rebalancing Ambrose's wine country house would require a lot of energy. She did not feel like tackling the project just yet. They both needed time to unwind and process the events in Carnelian. Her place was decidedly smaller, but the energy was more harmonious.

Ambrose emerged from the kitchen with the bottle of red wine he had just opened. "Smells good."

She gave him her best innocently inquiring look. "Did Iona Bryant handle the pizza ordering when she was working for you?"

Ambrose shot her a suspicious glare and set the bottle of red on the coffee table. "Why do you feel it necessary to remind me yet again that Iona Bryant was not the perfect virtual assistant?"

Pallas smiled her sunniest smile and patted the sofa. "It's for your own good. We don't want you to make any more mistakes when it comes to hiring a personal assistant."

"Thank you," Ambrose said. He poured two glasses of wine. "I understand and appreciate your concern. I feel the same way about you."

"Me?" she asked, wary now.

"Nice little talent for interior design you've got there." Ambrose gave her a beatific smile. "Be a real shame if you risked a potentially brilliant career by going into partnership with Collier again. Sadly, we both know you're a little naive when it comes to business."

"No worries," she shot back. "I've learned a lot lately. I know how partnerships work. If I decide to accept Theo's offer I'll insist on being a consultant this time, with the final say on which commissions I want to handle."

"That won't matter. The clients won't read your contract. They'll read the one they sign with Theodore Collier. It will be his name on that contract. As far as everyone involved is concerned, you'll be a member of his firm."

"At least I'll make a lot of money," she said.

"Maybe, but you won't be your own boss. You'll be working on the projects that Collier wants you to work on. Shopping malls. Fast-food restaurants. I can see your future now, and it includes a lot of laughing chickens and happy cows and cute pigs, all looking delighted by the prospect of being slaughtered and made into a deep-fried sandwich."

"Don't you dare lecture me on how to build my design business," Pallas yelped. "You're the one who hasn't been able to write a third book. Talk about pissing away a career."

"I thought I told you I'm over my case of writer's block."

"This argument is ridiculous," she said through clenched teeth.

She shot to her feet with so much fierce energy that her knee collided with the coffee table. The glass of red wine that Ambrose had just poured for her wobbled precariously. So did the bottle. She got a nightmarish visual of red wine spilling across the table and dripping onto the abstract carpet. What had she been thinking? She never drank red wine in the living room. Talk about inviting disaster.

But Ambrose was already in motion. Somehow he was able to set his own glass aside and deftly pluck her glass and the bottle off the table and out of harm's way without even bothering to get up off the sofa.

It was just so unfair. She wanted to scream but she managed, barely, to regain some composure.

"Thank you," she said, her voice shaking a little with the effort required not to burst into tears. "You can put the bottle and the glass back on the table."

He set them down and looked around the space. "Is there some bad energy in the vicinity?"

"No, that was on me." She sank down onto the sofa and took a fortifying swallow of wine. "I've been under a lot of stress lately. Got a little emotional. Overreacted. Don't worry, I'm fine, blah, blah, blah."

He watched her, his eyes burning. There was a lot of energy heating the atmosphere. She could feel herself responding to it, so she gulped down some more wine as an antidote.

"You're right," Ambrose said.

She blinked. "About what?"

"I am in serious danger of pissing away a career," he said. "For the past few months I've had good reasons for not being able to write. Insomnia. Nightmares. Sleepwalking. The fear that I might be going mad."

"I know. I understand." She sighed. "On top of everything else you were being manipulated by the virtual assistant from hell. Don't worry, I'm sure you'll be able to write now that you've got some answers and a plan for the future. You've been sleeping much better lately, and you haven't had any sleepwalking incidents since that last one in Carnelian."

"I'm not as worried about the insomnia and the sleepwalking now," he said. "But I'm still in danger of pissing away my career."

Pallas stared at him, alarmed. "I'm sure you'll be okay. You just need to give yourself a little more time to adjust to your new normal."

"Who needs normal?" Ambrose said. "You and I are never going to be what other people would call normal. What I *need* is the answer to a different question."

"Right. The question about who funded the Sleep Institute. I understand, believe me, but just remember you are no longer looking for the anonymous donor on your own. You're part of the *Lost Night Files* crew now."

"That's not the question that's going to keep me awake tonight," Ambrose said. "What I want to know is, do you think you could learn to love me? Because I fell in love with you the day I met you in the Carnelian Psychiatric Hospital for the Insane." He groaned. "And doesn't that rank up there with the worst romantic lines ever uttered?"

She stared at him, stunned speechless. Unlike all those times when he had known she was off-balance and had reached out to catch her, he made no effort to steady her now. He just watched her, not touching her, waiting for her to find her equilibrium. Waiting for her to make the decision.

She put her fingertips on the side of his face and opened her senses. A soft, gentle sense of balance and harmony whispered through her.

"Do you really have to ask?" she said. "Can't you see the answer in my aura?"

"I can see a lot of things in your aura, and I am enthralled with all of them," Ambrose said. He caught her wrist and kissed her palm. "But I can't see the answer to my question. I need the words."

She moved her hand to his shoulder. The heat of his body radiated through his shirt, warming her to her core.

"I love you," she said. She leaned into him and brushed her lips across his. "I'm not sure when I first knew it, but I do know it. I have never been more certain of anything in my life."

"That's all that matters to me."

He wrapped his arms around her and pulled her close and tight against him. He did not say anything else. Instead he covered her mouth with his own.

She went into the embrace with all the delight and passion and satisfaction she experienced when she knew what was needed to bring harmony and balance to a space.

Right energy. Right man.

CHAPTER FIFTY-THREE

THE LOST NIGHT FILES PODCAST
Episode 6: "The Disappearance of Brooke Kendrick"
Podcast transcript:

PALLAS: Her name was Brooke Kendrick. She was a software engineer who lived alone and worked from home. She must have had difficulty sleeping. Perhaps she suffered from nightmares. What we know is that a few weeks ago she checked into the Carnelian Sleep Institute in Carnelian, California, to undergo an overnight sleep study. She was attached to several electrodes that recorded everything from her heart rate and oxygen levels to her eye movements. There was a camera on her at all times while she was asleep in room B at the Institute. But at approximately two o'clock in the morning, she disappeared.

AMELIA: No one reported her disappearance. No one seemed to notice that she was gone. There was no body. No police investigation. Later it was discovered that someone attempted to destroy all of the records of Brooke Kendrick's appointment at the Institute. We know now that she was murdered in room B. The question is, why?

TALIA: This is the story of a cold case that involves murder, illicit drugs, and dangerous research into the paranormal. Welcome to *The Lost Night Files*. We're in this together until we get answers.